THE
FOURTH
BIBLE

A James Acton Thriller

Also by J. Robert Kennedy

James Acton Thrillers

The Protocol	*Amazon Burning*	*The Templar's Revenge*
Brass Monkey	*The Riddle*	*The Nazi's Engineer*
Broken Dove	*Blood Relics*	*Atlantis Lost*
The Templar's Relic	*Sins of the Titanic*	*The Cylon Curse*
Flags of Sin	*Saint Peter's Soldiers*	*The Viking Deception*
The Arab Fall	*The Thirteenth Legion*	*Keepers of the Lost Ark*
The Circle of Eight	*Raging Sun*	*The Tomb of Genghis Khan*
The Venice Code	*Wages of Sin*	*The Manila Deception*
Pompeii's Ghosts	*Wrath of the Gods*	*The Fourth Bible*

Special Agent Dylan Kane Thrillers

Rogue Operator	*Death to America*	*Retribution*
Containment Failure	*Black Widow*	*State Sanctioned*
Cold Warriors	*The Agenda*	*Extraordinary Rendition*

Templar Detective Thrillers

The Templar Detective	*The Sergeant's Secret*	*The Code Breaker*
The Parisian Adulteress	*The Unholy Exorcist*	

Kriminalinspektor Wolfgang Vogel Mysteries

The Colonel's Wife

Delta Force Unleashed Thrillers

Payback	*The Lazarus Moment*	*Forgotten*
Infidels	*Kill Chain*	

Detective Shakespeare Mysteries

Depraved Difference	*Tick Tock*	*The Redeemer*

Zander Varga, Vampire Detective

The Turned

THE
FOURTH
BIBLE

A James Acton Thriller

J. ROBERT KENNEDY

For my mother, my friend, my advisor, my confidante.

Your loss crushes my soul every day.

THE FOURTH BIBLE

A James Acton Thriller

"Life is life—whether in a cat, or dog or man. There is no difference there between a cat or a man. The idea of difference is a human conception for man's own advantage."

Sri Aurobindo

"The life of an ant and the life of my child should be accorded equal respect."

Michael W. Fox, Humane Society of the United States
Jan. 15, 1989

PREFACE

In 692 AD, Abbot Ceolfrid of the Wearmouth-Jarrow Abbey in the Anglo-Saxon Kingdom of Northumbria, commissioned the creation of three Bibles. An estimated 500 calves were raised and slaughtered to produce the vellum each volume would require, and after an unimaginable amount of work from farmers, parchment makers, and skilled scribes, the three massive tomes, each weighing over 75 pounds and numbering a thousand pages, were complete.

Two were placed in the twin churches of Wearmouth and Jarrow. One of those has been lost to history, the other is now in tatters, a mere remnant of its former self.

The third was taken by Ceolfrid to Rome in 716 as a gift for Pope Gregory II.

He never made it.

It was lost to history for centuries, before turning up in Tuscany. After a storied past, it now rests in Florence, Italy, nearly perfectly preserved.

This is all documented fact.

What isn't known is why, if it took 500 calves to produce each Bible, were documents later found in Ceolfrid's personal papers that showed 2000 had been slaughtered instead of the expected 1500?

Guggenheim Bilbao

Bilbao, Spain

Present Day

"Ready?"

Archaeology Professor Laura Palmer's heart raced as she stared at the shroud-covered table in front of them. Their host, Professor Yves Marchand, stood beside it, one corner of the shroud gripped in his hand as her husband, James Acton, shook with anticipation. "Does a bear—"

She squeezed his arm hard, ending what was to be yet another unfortunate one-liner.

"Yes," he said wisely.

Marchand removed the shroud with a flourish, and they both gasped in awe at the sight. The Bible lay split into two halves under protective glass, highlighted from above as if from the heavens, the massive tome.

"Unbelievable!" whispered James as he slowly circled the incredible historical find. She had seen one of the other Bibles several years ago,

3

and had planned on watching her husband's reaction, but those thoughts were lost as she was taken in by the pristine condition.

"It's remarkably preserved," she observed. "I knew from the pictures it would be, but in person…" She sighed, shaking her head. "Simply stunning. This is in better condition than the Codex Amiatinus, I can assure you."

"After the discovery, I was fortunate enough to be able to see the Codex Amiatinus for comparison purposes, and I have to agree."

James pointed at a thin hole that appeared to go through one half of the Bible, perhaps a couple of inches in length. "What do you think made—" A faint alarm sounded and they all froze. "What's that?"

Marchand dismissed any concern with a wave of his hand. "It's nothing. Just the alarm from a fire door. I accidentally set one off this morning when I went for a cigarette."

"There's no sign?"

"There is." He shrugged. "I thought it was just for show!"

Laura leaned in to examine the cut sliced through the center of one half of the Bible, curious as to what could have made such a distinct hole, when the unmistakable sound of gunfire shattered their calm.

Signaling what was certain to be another harrowing day in their tumultuous lives.

Wearmouth-Jarrow Abbey

Kingdom of Northumbria

716 AD

Arledge leaned back in his hard wooden chair and stretched as he unsuccessfully stifled a yawn. His entire body ached, as it had for months, each day a little worse than the last. His only reprieve were Sundays, when Abbot Ceolfrid permitted him to participate in the services with his fellow brothers. That one day of rest was precious to him, allowing him to reconnect with his Lord Jesus Christ—all he needed to renew any waning vigor in his duty.

The recreation of the most beautiful things he had ever seen.

The Bible.

Abbot Ceolfrid had commissioned three copies years ago. It had been a herculean effort, involving man and beast. All three volumes were written on vellum, over 1500 calves had been raised and slaughtered for their skin, the thousands of pages necessary to produce the three copies painstakingly manufactured by the hands of the believers in the surrounding villages.

It had been a monumental undertaking.

Yet what he was doing would receive none of the accolades the glorious work undertaken by his fellow monks had. For he toiled in secrecy, locked in a room on the second floor of the abbey, a room he hadn't known existed until Ceolfrid had shown him where he would work. It was sparsely furnished with a table at which he worked, a chair in which he sat, several candles for light, a lone window that gave him some sunlight, though most days seemed dreary, and a simple bed on which to rest should he need it, though he rarely did. The abbot brought him his midday meal, his breakfast and supper enjoyed with his brothers.

And it was his brothers that made things the most difficult.

He had known them all for years, some for as long as he could remember. Many had grown up together in the monastery, like him, and they were his friends. His good friends. Yet he couldn't talk to them.

Literally.

On the same day he had agreed to do the work, Ceolfrid had announced at the morning meal what turned out to be the most challenging aspect of what was to come. "Brother Arledge has taken a vow of silence to bring himself closer to God. I ask that you refrain from posing him any questions, or speaking to him in any manner. Respect his wishes, and know that I have given him my blessing in this most pious of endeavors." He had been congratulated, then left alone. His brothers always greeted him with genuine smiles, always welcomed him to their table, yet obeyed the abbot's wishes.

And despite being surrounded by his friends, he felt more alone than he ever had.

That was why he relished the thrice-daily visits from Ceolfrid. In the morning, he would bring him his day's work, at noon his meal enjoyed over a brief conversation about his progress, then the end of the day to collect what had been completed, and to take the work still remaining into safekeeping.

For no one could know what he was doing, though he wasn't certain why.

The three copies of the Bible had been created quite publicly. One didn't raise 1500 calves without people taking notice, one didn't create thousands of pages of vellum without stories spreading far and wide about what was being undertaken.

Yet his work was secret. He was to create an exact copy of the Bible. An exact copy known only to him and the abbot. For what purpose, he had no idea—Ceolfrid hadn't shared his reasons, though he was certain they were just and pure. The abbot was the kindest man he knew, and was like a father to him, his own parents having died ravaged by disease when he was a child. The monks had taken him in, fed him, clothed him, and when Ceolfrid had discovered he had an aptitude for letters, had taught him how to read and write. It was later that his artistic side had been revealed.

Making him the perfect man for the job.

He understood the text he was reading, could recreate the drawings and decorations that adorned its holy pages, and apparently had another necessary skill.

The ability to hold one's tongue, his slip-ups in his vow of silence few over the months he had been working, though speaking with the abbot did make things easier, giving him several brief reprieves.

He rubbed his sore eyes, the sun low on the horizon, signaling an impending visit from the abbot. He smiled at the footsteps on the stairs beyond the door to his locked chamber, then rose as the key hit the lock. He bowed as Ceolfrid entered. He waited for the door to close before speaking.

"Father Abbot."

"My brother, how does your work progress?"

"Very well. If my memory of the Bible is correct, all I have left are the final verses of Revelation. I should be done tomorrow, assuming you have the vellum I requested?"

"The final shipment arrived earlier today from a faithful benefactor." He sighed. "These thousand pages were far harder to procure than the first three thousand."

"Because of the secrecy of what we are doing?"

"Exactly. I have had to source it for years, a few pages here and there so as not to arouse suspicions. It was a difficult task I am happy to put behind me."

Arledge stared at the floor. "Umm, may I, umm, ask why all the secrecy?"

Ceolfrid stared at him for a moment, then pursed his lips, nodding. "You deserve the truth. As you know, I intend to personally deliver a copy of the Bible to the Pope himself."

"Yes, Father. You informed us all last night."

"Exactly. And because the existence of our Bibles is so well known, it will be impossible to keep our journey a secret."

Arledge's eyes widened. "You expect trouble!"

"Yes, I do. I fully expect someone will attempt to steal the Bible during our travels."

"Then why take the risk?"

"Because something as beautiful as what we have created, at such great sacrifice, must be kept at the holiest of all sites."

"But if you're certain it will be stolen, then what's the point?"

Ceolfrid smiled. "Because while we travel, with the world watching, the Bible you created will be journeying in secret, unbeknownst to those who would do us harm."

A smile spread on Arledge's face at the genius of the abbot's plan. "Because one cannot steal what one does not know exists!"

Rolampont, France

Present Day

Three months earlier

Emanuel Fillon stood at the edge of the construction site, carefully watching as the excavator worked at digging out the foundation for the future home of the town's most significant industrial development to date. It had been controversial, with tree-huggers literally hugging trees they had chained themselves to, trees that looked no different than the thousand others he saw each day on his drive here.

These fools are going too far.

What was the point of saving the planet if nobody had any jobs? But then that seemed to rarely be the concern of these types. They had no jobs. He saw the same faces here, day in and day out. If they were gainfully employed, contributing to society, then they would have had to miss at least five days a week of chanting their ridiculous slogans.

It made him sick. He was all for saving the planet, but not at the cost of destroying Western civilization. It wasn't Western civilization that was the problem, it was China, Russia, India, the developing world. The plastics in the ocean? Almost 99% of it came from Asia and Africa. If these people wanted to save the world, they should go to Asia and help implement waste management programs, rather than leaving them dumping everything into the rivers to be carried away and out of sight. Want to cut down on greenhouse gas emissions? Go to China and tell them to cancel their plans for 500 more coal-fired power plants in the next ten years.

But stop the building of an industrial zone that would create jobs, jobs in a heavily environmentally regulated country, jobs that would pay some of the highest taxes in the world, some of which would help fund programs that cleaned up the environment?

It was idiocy.

And thankfully, the courts had seen it the same way, the issued injunction enforced immediately.

Now they were digging, and digging fast. The moment the protesters had been cleared, he had moved in with equipment to remove the trees in a matter of hours, ensuring there was nothing left for anyone to chain themselves to, should the lawbreakers return.

And now it was fenced off with a massive hole being dug that, once completed, should mark the end of any more possible delays.

Only one thing could delay them now, something that too often happened in France.

"Emanuel!"

He sighed, closing his eyes.

What now?

The excavator operator waved as he climbed out of the cab, stepping down into the dirt then to the front of his vehicle. He beckoned him. "You need to see this."

Fillon frowned then stepped from the stable ground and slid down the side of the embankment and into the pit, curious others following suit. He stumbled his way toward the freshly dug hole and cursed at the stone structure just revealed, fresh claw marks from the excavator visible, blemishes that could have them in serious trouble if whatever was buried here was of significance.

"What do you think it is?"

He shrugged at the operator. "No clue, but the law says we stop." He waved a hand in front of his throat. "Shut it down!" Engines all around were cut, the entire operation at a halt, all over what might be nothing, or everything, to those who cared about the past.

He wasn't one of them.

He believed in the future. Of progress. Europe was filled with the past, and it was ridiculous that they were constantly forced to stop work whenever something might be found. It was almost impossible not to find something. About the only thing he believed merited halting of work was an unexploded bomb.

That, he would respectfully shut down a site for.

He fished out his phone and dialed the City, and an hour later, a bookish looking man with an audacious Belgian mustache showed up with a tablet computer in hand. He climbed down a ladder set up earlier in preparation for his arrival, then approached with a broad smile.

"Hello! I'm Professor Yves Marchand, from the University of Paris. I happened to be in the area, so they sent me rather than the usual fellow. Saves you a few hours, I suppose." He grinned. "Unless you've actually stumbled upon something."

Fillon shook the man's hand, finding it as limp as he'd expect from an academic like this. "I'm the foreman, Emanuel Fillon." He pointed at the scraped stone "something" they had discovered. "This is it."

Marchand stepped over to the hole and peered inside. "Well, you definitely have something here. Manmade, and judging from the depth, likely middle ages." He smiled at Fillon. "Don't worry yet. Could be nothing of importance. We can't be stopping everything from moving forward just because somebody found a fifteenth-century outhouse." He roared at his own joke and Fillon forced a smile, indicating with his fingers behind his back that the others should join in.

It was a bad call, the laughter so obviously forced, the little professor noticed. "Sorry, they can't all be gems." He handed Fillon his tablet then scrambled down into the hole. He held out a hand. "Can someone give me a shovel?"

Fillon indicated for one of his men to fetch one, and moments later Marchand was digging around the stone, revealing what appeared to be a large slab, discolored in several spots. "What is it?"

"Gentlemen, I think you have found an old forge."

Fillon glanced at him. "A forge? As in a blacksmith's shop?"

"Yes. Blacksmith. Ironmonger. Somebody who worked with metal."

Fillon tensed. "Is that important?"

"Yes." Marchand extended a hand and Fillon hauled him out of the hole then handed him his tablet. "To him. To you and me, not so much. If we were to find an entire community under here, then perhaps, but this discovery in itself is nothing." He circled the hole, taking video then photos of the discovery, then stepped back. "Go ahead and remove those stones. As gently as possible. If this turns out to be something more, we'll need to be able to put them back as we found them."

Fillon turned to the operator, suppressing the urge to roll his eyes. "You heard the man."

The operator climbed back in the excavator and the engine roared to life, a burst of diesel exhaust spoiling the air. The bucket lowered into the hole and curled inward, the teeth hooking under the far edge of the stone slab, lifting the corner.

And snapping it in two.

The far edge hopped overtop the near edge, slipping forward, the teeth losing their hold, releasing the broken piece, the resulting thud likely heard for miles.

"Stop!" cried Marchand, tossing his tablet at Fillon as he leaped into the hole, the cloud of dust still settling, whatever the professor had seen still not visible from Fillon's vantage point. "Give me a hand!"

Fillon bent over and picked up the tablet, the professor's athletic prowess as expected, then handed it to one of his men before climbing into the hole to join the best Paris had to offer. "What is it?"

"There's something under the slab. Look."

Fillon took a knee beside the professor, squinting at the sight. It was another piece of stone, though much smaller, perhaps two-feet by three-feet. But Marchand's bare hands, digging furiously around it, had already revealed other stones, laid vertically, clearly suggesting this was a box of some sort. "What do you think it is?"

"I don't know, but it must be of some significance."

Fillon's heart sank. "What makes you think that?"

Marchand stopped, pointing at the cracked stone. "This was on top of it."

"So what? That just means whatever this is was already there when our blacksmith set up his forge."

Marchand shook his head. "No, it was *directly* on top of it. Perhaps a few centimeters of dirt between the two. That means they are both from the same time period."

"Again, so what?"

"It means that most likely this forge was intentionally built overtop this."

Fillon sighed. "To hide something that is inside it?"

"Exactly!" He pointed to the piece of stone covering the carefully crafted hideaway. The two of them lifted off the top and placed it to the side. The entire crew now ringed the hole they were in, and everyone murmured in excitement at what was revealed.

Something wrapped in animal skins.

"My tablet!"

It was handed down to Marchand and he took more video and photos. He passed it to Fillon. "Now, I must be very careful here. We don't know what this is protecting. It could be very fragile after all these years." He bent over and gently tugged at a corner of the animal hide, gingerly pulling it aside. He repeated the process twice more, something inside, what, Fillon had no idea, slowly being revealed. Marchand lifted the final corner out of the way, and gasped.

"Oh, my Lord!"

Wearmouth-Jarrow Abbey

Kingdom of Northumbria

716 AD

Arledge leaned back and closed his tired eyes, the burn palpable, though the discomfort was easily overwhelmed by the agony his shoulders and back inflicted on him. It had been months of excruciating work, yet it was finally finished, the closing verse of Revelation now copied, the illustrations and decorations on the page lovingly and meticulously recreated.

It was as identical a copy as one could expect from the hand of a mere mortal, and he was ashamed at the sense of pride he felt.

It was God's work he had done, and He had given him the strength to persevere through the pain and isolation, He had guided his hand as each letter, each word, each embellishment was replicated from the original, an original also created by the divinely guided hands of other scribes like him, though they were blessed with the luxury of sharing their work with their brothers.

He folded his hands in silent prayer and awaited Ceolfrid's visit, a visit that, judging by the sun's position on the horizon, visible through his lone window to the outside world from his secret second-floor workspace, should come at any moment.

He smiled at the plodding footsteps on the stairs and rose, bowing his head as his abbot entered, closing the door behind him.

"Do you have the news I have been anticipating all day?"

"I do, Father." Arledge smiled. "I have completed my work."

Ceolfrid stepped forward, examining the pages, careful not to touch the still drying ink. "Remarkable. Your hand is truly guided by the Good Lord Himself."

A surge of pride rushed through Arledge, and he apologized silently to his Lord. "You humble me, Father."

Ceolfrid returned the pages to the table then put both of his hands on Arledge's shoulders. "I'm afraid your task is not yet done."

Arledge's heart thumped as the strength washed from his body at the thought of even more of the grueling work he had suffered through all these months. The only thing that had sustained him was the knowledge that there was an end, an end he could see coming from the very first page.

The Book of Revelation. Chapter 22.

He dreaded the answer to the question he must now pose. "What…what more do you require of me?"

Ceolfrid smiled. "Don't worry, my brother, your work in this room is done, your vow of silence is finished. You will never see the inside of this prison again."

Arledge's shoulders sagged in relief as his strength slowly returned. "How may I serve?"

"As you know, I and the others are leaving for Rome tomorrow with the copy meant for Pope Gregory the Second."

"Yes, Father, of course."

Ceolfrid pointed at the pages on his table. "I will bind this fourth copy tonight, then place it in this room." He smiled. "I suppose I spoke too hastily. You *will* see this room, one last time."

Arledge's eyes narrowed, puzzled. "I don't understand."

"After we leave tomorrow, you will take a donkey, provisioned for several days. I will leave the fourth Bible in this room, with a map. You are to follow this map exactly to your final destination."

"Which is?"

"Rome."

Arledge gasped. "Father, I don't understand! Why would you ask such a thing of me? Aren't you already going to Rome?" He stopped, his jaw dropping, recalling yesterday's conversation. "You expect trouble."

Ceolfrid nodded. "I expect trouble."

"You expect your copy to be stolen."

"I do."

"And you want me to follow you, with the copy no one knows about, in case your fears prove true."

"Exactly." Ceolfrid stepped over to the window, peering outside as if to be certain no one was somehow listening despite being so far from the ground. "Only you and I know this fourth Bible exists. No one else. That means it must be you who transports it. You will trail us by a day. As you make each stop, you will confirm if we arrived the night before through casual conversation. If we did, then you will know our journey continues unencumbered. But if we don't, then you will know something has happened to us, making your mission all the more vital. Should we both arrive in Rome, we will reunite, and discuss with the Pope whom he feels should receive the gift of our creation."

Arledge bowed his head, honored a task so important was being entrusted to him, but at the same time overwhelmed at the daunting task ahead, for a journey from here to Rome would take months, and the road would be treacherous if traveling alone.

"You seem troubled."

Arledge raised his head and stared at his abbot. "I am, Father. It is a long journey, again leaving me alone with my thoughts, with the added pressures of the dangers that lie ahead on the roads from here to Rome. It is a cruel world in which we live, filled with heathens and ne'er-do-wells. I fear I might not be strong enough to accomplish the task."

Ceolfrid smiled, gently squeezing Arledge's shoulder. "My brother, I can think of no man more capable." He gave him a gentle shake, pointing again at the drying pages. "And as the Good Lord guided your hand these past months, He shall guide your feet as well, and deliver you safely to Rome, where you shall rejoice in the power and glory of God, among the most faithful of His believers."

Arledge closed his eyes, drawing in a deep breath, the words comforting, though not enough to completely allay his fears. He said his own silent prayer, beseeching the Lord to deliver upon Ceolfrid's words. "Amen."

Antwerp, Belgium
Present Day

Hugo Peeters growled at the video playing on his laptop, then punched the headboard of his twin-sized bed eliciting an angry shout from his father upstairs. He ignored it. This was simply too much. It was outrageous.

And it made him hate humanity even more than he already did.

The world was screwed, and as far as he was concerned, he was fine with that. He hoped civilization collapsed, that the cities crumbled, that his decadent parents upstairs would be the last generation to thrive, and that his would preside over the transition as this wretched planet was handed back to Mother Earth, to whom it belonged.

His only concern was the creatures that were meant to survive.

The animals were being harmed by humanity's wickedness, by its cruelness, by its inconsiderate slaughter. To call the way animals were treated as inhumane was fundamentally flawed, for there was no humanity in humans. Humans were cruel by necessity. They always had been, and if it weren't for opposable thumbs and a larger brain, would be either extinct by now, or no more important in the grand scheme of things than chimpanzees were today.

Yet humanity had thrived and created a society based on cruelty. Animals were farmed for food, oceans were emptied of their resources, forests were raped for building materials and to make room for farms, the creatures that had once made these cleared landscapes their homes, left to die.

The world disgusted him.

And now it disgusted him even more, the rich and famous gathering in two weeks to celebrate the discovery of a Bible made over a thousand years ago, one so decadent and cruel, that it required the slaughter of over 500 baby cows just to make the thousand pages upon which it was written.

The number was staggering.

500.

And apparently, there had been three others, this one unknown to history. That meant 2000 calves were slaughtered, and he had no doubt that anyone so cruel as to think this was a good idea, left to rot what remained after their flesh was torn from their bodies.

Argh! I hate people!

He attacked his keyboard, diving down the rabbit hole he so often did, researching what was about to become his next cause. He would gather the Animal Protection Brigade for a meeting, everything else they had planned now on hold. The gala, planned for two weeks from now, couldn't be allowed to proceed, not without a statement being made, not without the rich and powerful of this world knowing that what they were celebrating was an abomination.

His heart nearly stopped at what he saw in front of him.

A post on Facebook from a name he recognized, a name he trusted.

I just heard from a very reliable source that they're going to announce a plan to create another one of these monstrosities, using the original methods! That means another 500 innocent creatures will be massacred!

His blood boiled, his pulse pounded in his ears, and his stomach contracted with rage at the very notion. The gall of these one-percenters, the entitlement of these monsters, had him seeing red, the world losing focus as his rage turned to irrepressible fury.

This madness has to be stopped!

He drew a deep breath, calming slightly, his mind turning to what could be done, what must be done, and how it might be accomplished. He smiled slightly as he realized there was someone among them who had the knowledge the Animal Protection Brigade would need to do what was necessary.

But one wouldn't be enough. He would have to ask the other few he had found that believed as he did, to commit the ultimate sacrifice with him, for this was too great a task.

And too great an opportunity to leave the world a message it would never forget.

Wearmouth-Jarrow Abbey

Kingdom of Northumbria

716 AD

Arledge unlocked the door to the room he had toiled within for so long, the key left hidden in a gap in the stone wall, exactly as Abbot Ceolfrid had promised. He stepped inside, closing the door, and found the map sitting on the table, along with the massive tome that was the fourth Bible, created over so many months by his steady hand.

It's enormous!

He had never seen it bound together. It had been delivered to him a few pages at a time, and the sheer number of pages, on something as thick as vellum, he had known would clearly be large. He had seen the other three from a distance, but never this close.

How am I supposed to hide that?

He had thought of the journey, and little else, from the moment Ceolfrid had informed him of his next task. At first, he had thought of keeping it on his person lest he be separated from his donkey, but now that he was standing in front of it, he couldn't see how it would be possible. It was wider and thicker than his spread hand, and taller than the distance from his elbow to his fingertips. He lifted it and grunted. It weighed as much as a very heavy stone, if not a boy of fifteen.

How can I possibly transport this?

Doubts entered his mind at the very feasibility of one man transporting the document securely to Rome with a mere donkey. Ceolfrid and the others at least had a cart, and were content to transport it in a box constructed specifically for the journey, a box that would be carried in the cart drawn by two stout horses.

There would be no way the donkey could carry him, his supplies, and the Bible.

That meant he would be walking.

All the while trying to keep pace with six men with a horse-drawn cart.

He stared at the heavens, closing his eyes.

Lord, give me guidance.

He placed the satchel he had brought on the table then frowned. It simply wasn't big enough to fit the massive volume. He scratched his chin as his head shook. No, this wouldn't work. And even if it did fit, having all the weight on one side would be too much for the poor beast tasked to transport it.

If only I had a horse!

Though a monk on a horse would attract attention.

A donkey?

Not so much.

He chewed his cheek as he stared at the problem. He opened the Bible near the center, spreading it out into its true enormity, though halving the height.

I wonder…

He leaned over the Bible, examining the binding, something he hadn't seen before, the pages delivered and replicated one at a time. He smiled as he realized how it had been done.

Then his ears pounded at the very notion of what he was about to do.

What choice do you have?

He flipped to the front and began, all the while muttering for the Lord's forgiveness at what he feared might be blasphemy.

Acton/Palmer Residence

St. Paul, Maryland

Present Day

"I'd give my left nut to see that thing."

Archaeology Professor James Acton's wife, Laura Palmer, eyed him. "I'm not sure that's a look you could pull off."

He laughed. "I think I could pull off any look, though passing out testicles for invitations to fancy galas might not be making the best use of my anatomy."

She grabbed a boob in each hand, lifting them up. "Maybe I could donate one of the girls?"

He shook his head vehemently. "Never! I lay claim to those puppies!"

She let go and he enjoyed the bounce. She wagged a finger. "Don't you go getting all randy on me now. We have to be at Greg and Sandra's in an hour."

"An hour, hell, I could get 'er done four times and still be able to shower."

"I'm not sure that's something to brag about, nor do I think you are physically capable of that anymore, old man."

He threw a pillow at her and she caught it, whipping it back at him. "Who you callin' old?"

She pushed him back and straddled him, running her fingers through his hair then stopping. "There's a gray, there's a gray, there's a—"

He rolled her off him. "Hey, that's not fair. You realize how stressful it is keeping all those young hunks from hitting on my gorgeous wife? It's a full-time job."

"Oh, sure, I don't know how I get anything done with all the men that are after me." She climbed off the bed and continued dressing.

"So, this isn't happening?"

"No."

"After we get home?"

"Perhaps."

He jumped off the bed. "Good enough for me." He stood in the mirror, staring at his junk. "You don't think I could pull it off, huh?"

She smacked his bare ass. "Get in the shower and make it cold. Somebody is at half-mast with a mind of his own."

He gave a toothy grin. "Umm, any body parts of yours that have minds of their own?"

She put her bra on, killing half the show, then pointed to the bathroom. "Go. Now."

"You're no fun. Even your fun parts."

He climbed in the shower and turned on the water, still hot from Laura's turn minutes ago. He reduced the temperature a little too much and shivered. A few minutes later, he was done and toweling off, Laura now fully dressed, perched in a chair in the corner, tablet in hand.

"It would be a treat for you to see it."

Hope returned, something twinged, and a smile spread. "It would be!"

"Not that, you pervert. I mean the Bible."

Acton sighed, no nookie in his immediate future. He grabbed some underwear instead. "It would be."

"Then why not make it happen?"

"What do you mean?"

"Well, didn't you say you knew Professor Marchand? Why not call him?"

Acton shook his head as he slipped his socks on. "He's probably getting hundreds of calls. Besides, I haven't seen him in years, and we only exchange maybe half a dozen emails a year."

She shrugged. "That's probably more than most of those contacting him for free tickets." She wagged her tablet at him. "Why don't you send him an email congratulating him? Don't ask to see it, just congratulate him. If he wants you there, he'll suggest it. He knows we can afford the tickets, but he also knows they're sold out."

Acton tugged his shirt down then ran his fingers through his hair as he stared in the mirror, not spotting any of the grays his wife had teased him about earlier. She was right. They could afford the tickets, and Marchand was aware of her—and now their—wealth, a wealth he wasn't certain he'd ever get used to. If her suggestion worked, and they were invited, he would offer to pay for the tickets, or at least make a generous donation to a charity of the man's choice.

Though it still didn't sit well with him.

Yet he desperately wanted to see what was a most incredible find. A near-perfectly preserved Bible, a previously unknown copy made by the monks at Wearmouth-Jarrow Abbey over 1300 years ago, found under a blacksmith's forge in France, marred only by the fact it was in two halves, the stitching separated for some unknown reason, a narrow hole through the center of one half, and what had been determined to be blood saturating several of the pages.

It was a find that rivaled one of the original three created by those same monks, the Codex Amiatinus. One had been destroyed over the years, one was in tatters, and the third, the Codex Amiatinus, was mostly intact.

He had to see this fourth Bible.

"I suppose there's no harm in congratulating him, even if he sees right through me."

Laura tossed the tablet onto the bed and he grabbed it, quickly firing off an email to a man he considered a casual friend at best.

His stomach churned with guilt as he handed the tablet back.

"Maybe I can call Mary and see if she can get some tickets for us. She's not just a travel agent. She has incredible connections. It might be a nice getaway. We could invite Hugh to join us." The tablet beeped and she looked at it. "Well, it seems like you're better friends than you thought."

"Huh?" She handed him the tablet and he opened the email from Marchand. He grinned. "He thanks me for the email, and would love it if the two of us would be his personal guests for a *private* viewing at the gala!"

Laura beamed. "That sounds fantastic!" She paused. "Oh, what about Hugh?"

He tilted his head. "Do you really want me to push our luck?"

"I supposed not. But he'll be so disappointed."

He eyed her. "He doesn't even know about it. Besides, you know how he feels about these types of things."

"I suppose you're right."

He could hear the disappointment in her voice. "How about we drop by to visit him on the way back?"

"Let's! It's been too long."

"You're right. What has it been? Two weeks?"

She wagged a finger at him. "Don't get smart with me, mister. You know I love that man."

"If I didn't know it was like a father, then I'd be jealous." He fired back a reply to Marchand, accepting the invitation, then handed the tablet back to Laura.

"When is it again?"

"Next Saturday." He hopped up and down on his toes, unable to contain his excitement. "I can't wait!"

She gave him a withering look. "Don't let any of your friends see you doing that. Especially those Delta boys. They'll insist you return your Man Card."

He stopped, suddenly self-conscious. "Can't a guy just be excited about something without being judged? You *do* know what year it is, right?"

She shrugged. "Yes, it's the year when everybody gets judged for everything they do, even if they did it forty years ago."

Animal Protection Brigade Headquarters

Antwerp, Belgium

"We have to do something! It's time to take action!" Hugo Peeters slammed his clenched fist on the arm of his threadbare chair. "We can no longer stand by while the rich slaughter the defenseless creatures of Mother Earth for their own entertainment. What is this? The Dark Ages? What I've been reading on the Internet has me so angry, I can taste the blood that must be spilled to quench it."

Heads bobbed as the others in the room, the six he trusted the most, listened to his proposal. Only one, the key to the plan, already knew what he had in mind, for he was the only one who could make it possible.

He had the military experience necessary to pull it off.

And the contacts.

He drew a steadying breath, lowering his voice slightly as his father would no doubt start screaming for him to keep the noise down. "The only cause these people care about is climate change. Why? Because big business recognized they could make money off it. That's the only reason these people care about it. But what about the animals? Nobody cares anymore unless they can link it to climate change. I don't give a shit about climate change, and neither should you. Our goal isn't to save the planet so humans can continue to rape it. Our goal is to save the animals so that when man is a distant memory, these innocent, noble creatures, from the whales and kelp in the oceans, to the elephants and ants on the land, to the eagles and mosquitos in the air, all will be able to live in harmony without worrying about being enslaved or slaughtered by some supposedly more evolved primate."

He rose to his feet, slowly circling the room as he spoke, staring each of his trusted Brigade members in the eyes. "We need to send a message, we need to let the world know that slaughtering five-hundred calves just to recreate a book that preaches animal sacrifice, shouldn't be allowed, and won't go unpunished. If we act now, we can stop this atrocity before it begins, and send a message to the world that no more will we sit idly by and allow the carnage to continue, no more will we let the rich indulge while the creatures who were here long before us suffer, no more will mankind be the only species that matters on this planet. Agreed?"

Everyone leaped to their feet, cheering him, his father's pounding upstairs going unheard through the ruckus. He held up his hands, calming everyone, then returned to his seat. "There's only one way to send a message that can be heard by the rich and powerful of this world. Our protests to date have fallen on deaf ears. Yes, we have thousands of supporters on social media, but they are the poor, trodden souls we see every day on the streets we walk. They have no say, they have no power, they have no sway. Even *we* have no power. What has changed in all the years we've been together? Nothing! We've sworn off the flesh of animals, the products made through their suffering, and vowed to live a simple, thoughtful life, while trying to spread the word through social media and protest. And it's gotten us nowhere. But now, thanks to Karl, we have a chance to change everything."

Smiles and fist bumps were exchanged with their newest member, a former German Army explosives specialist who had served in Afghanistan, and a recent convert to the cause after viewing one of their videos online about the inhumane conditions chickens were forced to exist in—for it wasn't living—so humans could enjoy nuggets and buffalo wings. It had disgusted Karl as it had him when he first saw it.

And he had joined the few determined to fight back.

"Thanks to Karl, we've crafted a plan that will change everything, but we need every one of you for it to succeed. We need the people who truly love the animals, who truly love the natural world, who truly believe that man is no more important than any other animal on this planet. It's up to us to take action." He paused, his audience captive. "Who are the ones killing the animals? Who are the trophy hunters, the ones who go to Africa and slaughter innocent, endangered animals? Who are the ones who have heads stuffed and mounted on their walls, who have rare elephant tusks adorning their homes, who fly in helicopters and shoot defenseless animals with automatic weapons? The rich.

"Only a rich person could afford to do anything like that. The rich go out and actively slaughter. They wear the furs and the leathers, they eat the foie gras. They're the ones who are destroying our natural beauty, who think that they are above all other creatures on this planet, including the poor. They're the ones who should be made to pay. We must teach them a lesson! And then, and only then, will there be change. Kill a few dozen of them, and every rich person on this planet will take notice, because a friend, or a friend of a friend, will have died."

He rose again. "It's up to us to make a statement by punishing the rich for their decadence! Are you with me? Will you sacrifice your own lives to finally save the animals?"

And his heart filled with joy as every single man and woman in the room leaped to their feet, their solidarity with the cause unwaveringly displayed.

It's time to change the world!

Wearmouth-Jarrow Abbey

Kingdom of Northumbria

716 AD

"My word, I thought you were dead!"

Arledge paused, staring at his friend Olin, dumbfounded. "Why would you think such a thing? You've seen me at mealtime."

"Where you've said nothing for months, which means you might as well have been dead to us, your brothers." Olin eyed him up and down. "Well, I see you've found your tongue again. Your vow of silence is over?"

Arledge nodded. "It is."

"Difficult?"

"As one would imagine."

"And why did you undertake such a thing?"

Arledge's stomach flipped as yet another lie was about to be uttered. "Penance."

Olin's eyebrows shot up. "Penance? For what? It must have been something horrible for it to have lasted so long."

He searched for words, words that might save him from lying to his friend. He suppressed a smile. "I'm too ashamed to say."

Olin frowned. "Then it must have been something truly terrible." He patted the donkey at Arledge's side. "Where are you off to now?"

"The abbey in Sunderland." This, at least, wasn't a lie. It was his first stop marked on the map.

"What for?"

He stared at the ground, more to hide his shame, though it did fit his act. "Additional penance."

"My word! Did you murder someone? What could you have possibly done to merit such punishment?"

"I-I cannot say." He led his donkey toward the gate. "I'm afraid I've already said too much. The abbot said I don't deserve conversation with my brothers after what I've done."

Olin stared at him in horror, his eyes wide, his mouth agape. "I-I'm truly sorry, Arledge. I will pray for your soul and the Lord's forgiveness for whatever it is you've done."

Arledge flashed him a weak smile, not feeling very worthy of any prayers after lying to so close a friend. He passed through the gates, following the very path the abbot and the others had passed a day ago, his heart heavy as he stared at the only home he had known for so long, leaving behind the only friends he had ever had.

The only family he remembered.

The story of his disgrace had been concocted by Abbot Ceolfrid before he left, and Arledge had been assured he would be forgiven for any sins he might commit in furthering the belief he had committed some atrocity worthy of banishment from the abbey for a period of time. The damage to his reputation was heartbreaking. Ceolfrid had also assured him that all would be set right when he returned successfully, and his brothers would rejoice in the truth of what he had done.

Yet if Ceolfrid's fears were correct, and the abbot didn't return from his journey to Rome, then there would be no one to set the record straight, leaving his good name tarnished among his brothers forevermore.

He stared at the lonely window as he turned the corner, his sole bit of freedom from his workplace prison, and closed his eyes, burning it into his mind, for he feared this would be the last time he would see his home, and his brothers, who now thought him a sinner beyond pale.

Please, Lord, should I fail, at least clear my name of all the ills heaped upon it this day, so that my memory never bears this false shame that now burdens me.

Marchand Residence

Paris, France

Present Day

"I can't believe there might be protests at the gala. What is this world coming to when people protest such a stunning discovery?"

Professor Yves Marchand shrugged at his wife, Sophie. "The world has gone mad. I can't believe people give any credence to anything they read on social media. The fools are claiming that we're going to announce a project to attempt to create another copy of the Bible we found, using the same materials and methods the monks did."

"What's the big deal about that?"

"It would require a thousand pages of vellum."

"Vellum?"

"It's made from the skin of young animals, in this case, calves."

"Baby cows! No!"

He gave her a look. "Oh, don't you start. It's a nonsense story that doesn't need any credence given to it by you getting upset over animals killed thirteen-hundred years ago."

She frowned. "You're right, but you could see how people would get upset if they believed the story was true."

"Agreed, but they seem to be completely willing to believe the nonsense stories that are obviously fake news, but are also completely unwilling to believe our denials. It's ridiculous. Nobody is going to slaughter five-hundred calves to recreate a Bible. It's complete bullshit spread by that damned Internet. They should shut that thing down. The world would be a better place."

His wife gave him a look, a wry grin emerging. "Well, that might be a little extreme. The world does kind of rely on it."

"Then shut down social media."

She jabbed a finger at him. "Now *that* I could get behind, though I don't know how you'd do it."

He sighed. "Neither do I, but there needs to be serious consequences for libel and slander, especially if committed on the Internet. This anonymity we have today is ridiculous. You used to have to say something to someone's face, then get the knuckles taken to you if needed. And when we were young, nutbars didn't have a platform to spread their vitriol or idiocy like these anti-vaxxers and their ilk."

A knock at the bedroom door ended their conversation. "Can I come in?"

He rolled his eyes at his wife at the sound of their sixteen-year-old daughter. "Speaking of people obsessed with social media," he muttered. "Come in!"

Petra opened the door, staring at the messed bed. "Eww, were you two doing it?"

"Like animals!"

"Yves!" His wife admonished him with the stink-eye, then turned to their daughter. "Not that it's any of your business, but your father took a nap after work. He had a busy day."

"And a long one, what with the gala next week."

Petra frowned. "About that, can I go to Zoe's birthday party instead?"

His wife saved him from being the bad guy as he bristled with anger and hurt. "You know very well that you can't. The gala at the Guggenheim is important to your father."

"I don't want to go. It'll be boring."

"It's only boring if you make it boring. There will be plenty of famous people there for you to post to your Facebook or whatever it is you're using, and great food."

"But I don't want to go! I'm sixteen! I don't have to go! I have rights!" Her hands were on her hips now, her face red with wasted indignation.

"As long as you live under this roof, you don't. You're going whether you want to or not."

Tears poured down Petra's cheeks. "But I want to go to Zoe's birthday party! Everyone is going to be there!"

His wife shook her head. "You barely know her!"

"I hate you!"

He sensed his wife was about to lose it, and had been the bad cop long enough. He stepped in front of his daughter, putting his hands on her shoulders, keeping his voice calm, a gentle smile on his face. "Sweetheart, this is an important night for me, okay? I need my family with me to help me get through it." Her expression softened slightly and her shoulders slumped in his hands. "Listen, do this for me, and I'll pay for you and your friends to go to that restaurant you're always talking about."

Her face brightened. "L'Espadon?"

"If that's the one you can't stop talking about, then yes."

His wife cleared her throat. "Umm, dear, that's awfully expensive."

He paused, glancing at her. "Is it?"

She nodded. "It's two Michelin stars."

His eyebrows popped. "What? I thought you kids went there all the time!"

"We do, but Marie's father pays. He's rich."

He pursed his lips. "Umm, well, I'm not. How about McDonald's?"

"Dad!"

He laughed. "Fine, fine. Burger King."

Animal Protection Brigade Headquarters
Antwerp, Belgium

Peeters sucked in a slow breath, steeling for the conversation ahead. He hated rich people. Detested them. But sometimes they served their purpose.

Like today.

He had reached out to their benefactor in the hopes he might give them one last chance, and the man had agreed to talk.

Talk.

It would be the first time they had ever done so, all previous communications via the Internet, and it had him nervous.

The phone rang and he answered it before his parents could. "Hello?"

"You wanted to discuss Bilbao?"

"Yes, sir. I believe a statement must be made."

"I agree, but are you the people to make it? You're not very effective. You're too small. After all this time, nobody has heard of you."

"But that's what makes us perfect. The bigger organizations are too concerned about their reputations, and losing their funding. We don't care. We'll do whatever it takes, because our motivations are pure. We care about the animals, not the money."

"You have a point. What do you need from me? Money?"

"No, money isn't the key this time, though we'll need some. I need something that only you can get because of who you are."

There was a pause. "You have no idea who I am."

"I know that. What I mean is that you're one of them. The one-percenters. The ones with the real money and connections."

"Go on."

"I need an invitation."

"An invitation? What are you talking about?"

"I need an invitation to the gala at the Guggenheim. It's the only way we'll be able to get in."

"You can have mine."

Peeters' eyebrows rose. "You received one?"

"Of course I did. They send invitations to the Forbes list for all these things." There was a burst of static. "You're not planning anything crazy, are you? I don't want my name associated with anything violent."

"You don't need to worry, and besides, perhaps you never received your invitation."

"What do you mean?"

"Well, who knows you received it?"

"Only myself and my butler."

Butler! How ridiculous!

"Good. Then just make sure he understands you never received it, then get it to me, and no one will be the wiser."

A heavy sigh caused another burst of static. "You realize that if I do this, it changes the dynamic of our relationship."

Peeters' eyes narrowed. "What do you mean?"

"My name is on that invitation. Once you have it, you'll know who I am."

Peeters scratched his chin, tilting his head. "I hadn't thought of that. Does it really matter? There's no way to connect you and me, is there? I mean, the way you've sent us money, there's never been any type of trail, paper or electronic. All the world would ever know is that I somehow stole your invitation. If it traced back to you, you can just deny ever receiving it. Who are they going to believe? Me, a so-called animal rights activist, or you, a mega-rich gazillionaire?"

His benefactor said nothing for a few moments, then finally sighed. "Nothing too crazy?"

"Just a publicity stunt. But I can guarantee you that after we pull this off, not a person on the planet won't know the name Animal Protection Brigade."

Frankish Burgundy

716 AD

Arledge's body ached, though he was tolerating it better now that he was weeks into his long journey. Having spent months cramped up in the room, bent over a table while he worked, he had become weak. Walking to the coast, taking a boat to Calais, then the weeks on end of walking since had cured him of that affliction, and he was now as trim and fit as he had ever been.

And as hungry.

He devoured his meal provided by the brothers of the abbey in which he now found himself. He had forgotten the name, this place a mere X on the map left by Abbot Ceolfrid. Yet he had been welcomed with open arms by the abbot and the brothers that made this place their home.

"I still say they're fools."

"You mean the ones from last night?"

"Of course, who else could I possibly mean?"

"I don't know. I've seen all manner of fool pass by here. You are aware that the average person is an idiot."

"Present company included."

"That's not very nice."

The monk that had initiated this new line of conversation, Creatus, eyed his friend. "Let me get this straight. If I insult you, you take offense, yet you only moments ago insulted the entire Godfearing world."

His friend grinned. "That's right."

Creatus rolled his eyes. "Let's ask our guest." He leaned forward to get a better look at Arledge. "What do you think?"

Arledge swallowed. "About what?"

"Yesterday, six monks arrived, one of whom was an abbot, no less, and showed off a fancy Bible they had made. They said they were taking it to Rome to give to the Pope."

He suppressed his relief at hearing that, yet again, his friends had survived another day of the journey. "That sounds nice."

"Nice? Nice, he says!" cried Creatus, looking at the others. "It's foolish! Do you have any idea how valuable a Bible like that is?"

He shrugged. "I would think very. I imagine a lot of work went into it."

"Forget the months of work the poor fools put in to create it. He said it was a thousand pages of vellum, and that there were two others! A thousand pages! How many cattle had to die to make three thousand pages of vellum! I've never heard of such a thing."

He shrugged again, his ire piqued slightly at the insulting words. "I'm sure the cattle didn't go to waste. The skin was used for the Lord's work, and the food, I have no doubt, went to feed the poor."

"How can you be so sure?"

Arledge waved a hand at the tables filled with brothers. "If you had slaughtered hundreds or even thousands of cattle, what would you have done with the meat?"

"Well, we would have given it to the poor, of course."

"Then why would you think they did anything different?"

"Because they're fools!"

Arledge motioned toward the man's friend. "Yet he just said we're all fools, so if we're to assume he's right, then I think we can safely assume even those fools would not have let anything go to waste if you fools wouldn't."

Creatus stared at him for a moment then roared with laughter, stabbing a finger at him. "I like you, brother!"

The rest of the table joined in, several of the closest slapping him on the back and shaking him by the shoulder, some extra food pushed onto his plate, not a morsel of which he let go to waste. After the meal, prayers were said, chores were attended to, then it was to bed, a not-uncomfortable one provided him among the communal room in which the monks slept.

Yet sleep eluded him.

His mind was preoccupied with what had been said earlier by the brothers. And it wasn't something new, though it was the first time he had heard it called foolish in such blunt terms.

And it *was* foolish.

Why was Abbot Ceolfrid showing everyone the Bible? At each abbey or church he had been to along the way, he had heard tell of the monks from Northumbria and their incredible Bible and their ultimate destination. Why was Ceolfrid telling every soul they encountered about their precious possession? Why wasn't Ceolfrid, a man he had considered of extreme intelligence and prudence, not keeping it a secret? Wouldn't there be far less risk?

His stomach flipped with a horrifying thought.

Did Ceolfrid want attention drawn to them so that they would become the targets of anyone who might desire the Bible, thereby leaving him free to safely reach Rome?

The very thought was chilling. Inhumane. How could Ceolfrid be willing to sacrifice himself, and the innocent brothers that accompanied him, all who had served the Lord so faithfully, had served Ceolfrid so faithfully, for so many years? He had questioned the fanfare when they had left, yet Ceolfrid had explained it to him in terms that made perfect sense at the time.

"Everyone already knows, my brother. One cannot raise and slaughter over fifteen-hundred cattle without the entire countryside knowing the purpose. We made no secret of our undertaking all those years ago. There would be no keeping this secret, no matter how hard we tried."

It *had* made sense.

But this didn't. Nobody in these parts knew what had happened.

Though perhaps on the path behind them, word would have spread already, despite any secrecy that hadn't been undertaken. And if the wrong person found out, the wrong people, anything was possible. Bibles were rare. Bibles such as the one he now had hidden under his robes were rarer still. The amount of work, the amount of resources expended, made them priceless.

Yet that was just a word.

Everything had a price.

Someone, somewhere, would put a number on it, and gold or currency of some sort would be exchanged should it fall into the wrong hands.

But these were his friends. These were his brothers, so foolishly putting their lives at risk so that his might not be.

He couldn't let this continue.

Yet what could he do?

He couldn't warn them without revealing himself. Only Ceolfrid knew he was following them, and who was he to go against the desires of his abbot?

Lord, please send me guidance so that I might help my friends.

Acton/Palmer Residence

St. Paul, Maryland

Present Day

"I'm excited to see it."

Archaeology Professor Laura Palmer gave her husband a look. "You think? You've been giddy for a week. Frankly, I'll be happy when this trip is over and I can have my husband back."

James Acton stuck out his lower lip at her, feigning a pout. "You're so mean."

She threw a pillow at her man-child. "Don't make me spank you."

He grinned. "Ooh, kinky."

She laughed, wagging a finger at him. "Don't you get randy on me. I don't want to be late for our flight. Just because it's a private jet doesn't mean there aren't consequences to being late."

James frowned at her. "Yeah, yeah, I know."

They both resumed packing, and as she thought of what they would see tomorrow, she became more excited, though mostly for him. "If it's anything like the Codex Amiatinus, you're going to be gobsmacked. I saw it when it was in the UK a few years back. Thanks to my position at the British Museum, I was able to get a good look at it. It's an incredible, awe-inspiring creation. When you think of what went into it, and the fact something from so long ago could be in such good condition thirteen-hundred years later…" She sighed. "You're right to be excited."

He gave a schoolboy bounce then winked at her. "I just can't believe there's a fourth copy that no one knew about."

"I guess it explains that document they found referencing two-thousand cattle being raised. I had always dismissed it as the poor recollection of an aging man, or that the document was fake. Most thought it was a fake and unfortunately dismissed the entire set of documents as questionable in provenance."

"Well, I guess there'll be a little egg on some faces. Hopefully, those documents will now be accorded the attention they deserve."

"I'm sure they will."

"Yves said it was in near perfect condition."

"That's the beauty of vellum. It can last for millennia." She zipped up her carry-on. "It was generous of your friend to give us a private viewing."

James nodded. "It was." He frowned, sitting on the edge of the bed, his shoulders slumping. "I'm a little worried about leaving, though. Mom's not feeling well. She's in a lot of pain."

She rounded the bed, concern on her face as she knew how worried he was. "She'll be fine. Didn't your dad say they thought it was just side effects from her new medicine?"

A tear rolled down his cheek as he gasped. "Yeah, but…it's heartbreaking to hear it." He squeezed his eyes shut as another tear escaped. "I just wish there was something I could do."

She sat beside him and wrapped an arm around him. "There's nothing you can do. You just have to trust that the doctors will do the right thing."

He sniffed, drawing a deep breath. "I know, but…it's my mother."

She checked her watch. "If we're going to catch our flight, we have to leave now, but if you want to cancel this, I'll understand."

He squared his shoulders, shaking his head. "No. She wouldn't want me to put my life on hold because of her. You're right. This is just side effects from the meds. Once she's off them, she'll be fine." He stood. "Let's go. It'll help take my mind off things."

She smiled and hugged him, wiping the tears from his face with her thumbs.

And prayed for her husband's sake that the doctors were right.

Frankish Burgundy

716 AD

Arledge stared with envy at the saddlebags draped across the back of his donkey, each containing half of the precious cargo in his charge. He had carefully unstitched the binding back home, splitting it into two equal halves, thus spreading the load the poor beast would carry.

He only wished it could carry him as well.

It might, at least for short distances, yet he couldn't risk the poor creature's health. If it should falter, he would be forced to lug all the supplies it now carried, and his mission would be doomed.

If only I didn't have to keep pace.

His instructions from Ceolfrid had been clear. He must keep up. Yet it was an impossible task. Surely Ceolfrid had been aware of this. Though despite his doubts, each day he arrived at his destination, exactly one day behind his friends, each day met with tales of the monks and their precious Bible destined for Rome.

It had taken him quite a while to realize it was Ceolfrid spending time showing off the Bible that had allowed him to keep pace. Barely. Despite his abbot's deliberate delays, at the end of each day, he would arrive aching from head to toe, his feet, toughened after weeks of travel, still taking a beating. His brothers along the way had been generous, providing him with fresh clothes and new footwear when needed, and he was tempted to ask if a sturdier beast might be possible at his next stop. Though the animal had served him well, and still did, he could tell the journey was taking its toll on her.

She was slowing, albeit slightly, but every moment lost made his journey that much more difficult, especially considering his friends had horses and a cart.

He would have to switch the ass out for another if possible.

Too bad I can't switch out my own.

He chuckled, rubbing his sore buttocks, when the pounding of hooves behind him sent his heart racing. He turned to see six men on horseback galloping down the road toward him, their dress suggesting either men of means, or the servants of those with. They slowed and he stopped, guiding his donkey to the side of the narrow road to make way.

"Is he whom we seek?" asked one of the men.

"It can't be. We were told to look for six monks, not one." The lead man rode past him then turned around, blocking Arledge's path. "Do you travel alone?"

Arledge's spoken Frankish wasn't perfect, though it was better than most of his countrymen. He had been taught to read and write when he was young, his aptitude recognized early, languages such as Latin and

Frankish voraciously consumed. All languages that would help him on his journey. He patted his donkey. "This poor beast is my only traveling companion."

The man cursed. "Have you seen a group of your brothers, a party of perhaps six, on this road?"

Arledge's pulse pounded in his ears. "I'm afraid I have not."

"Let's go!" The man turned his horse and the party pounded off into the distance, soon out of sight, leaving Arledge frozen in place as he struggled to control his breathing. Who these men were was of little importance. Their intentions, however, were. Were they eager to see the Bible for themselves? Or were they motivated by something else, something more nefarious? As much as he'd wish he could have faith in the general good of his fellow man, he had seen little evidence in his lifetime to think such desires were likely. He had no doubt these men meant to steal the Bible his friends were transporting, and to do so, that likely meant killing them.

He climbed on his donkey, urging it forward, praying for the Lord to give them both the strength to do some good before it was too late.

Guggenheim Bilbao

Bilbao, Spain

Present Day

Petra Marchand scrolled through her Instagram feed, as bored as she had ever been. Every post of her friend Zoe's birthday party restoked the fire in her belly, and she glared at her parents as they mingled with the crowds, her father getting all the attention, enough so, that he apparently lost track of her mother's cocktail habit.

She frowned.

That wasn't fair. Her mother was likely still nursing her first, though at this moment, she preferred to think the worst of both of them.

I wish you were here! Party of the decade!

She growled.

"What?"

She glanced down at her little brother. "Go away."

He stared up at her. "Mommy said to stay with you."

She growled again.

What did I do to ever deserve this?

She swiped up on her phone, a list of apps displayed, and she stared at Uber's large U, beckoning her to join it on the dark side. She could call an Uber and be out of here in minutes.

But what purpose would that serve? The party was in Paris. She was in Spain. She growled again, her frustration making her stupid. And besides, even if she were in Paris, the punishment of leaving would far outweigh any momentary satisfaction the act of rebellion might give her.

"Wipe that scowl off your face."

She flinched at her mother's voice, her focus on her own misery having her losing track of the stealthy woman. She gave her an exaggerated, toothy smile.

Her brother giggled.

"Don't ruin this night for your father." Her mother pointed toward an exit behind them. "Go out in the hall, cool off, then come back in when you're ready to be a part of this family."

She thrust her arms down her sides, audibly glaring at her mother, then stormed toward the hallway, past several gaping guests. She disappeared around the corner and spotted a set of stairs. She sat on one of the steps and groaned when her brother sat beside her.

"Go away."

"But Mommy said to stay with you."

She sighed. "Fine, but stop speaking."

"I wasn't until you told me to go away."

"Argh! I can't wait until I'm eighteen and free of all of you!"

"I think I'm underdressed."

Acton gave his wife an exaggerated elevator assessment, taking in her slim form. "I think you're breathtaking."

She beamed. "You're not so bad yourself. It's been a while since I've seen you in a tux."

He glanced down at his fine self. "Sometimes it's nice to get dressed up. We should do it more often."

"Jim!"

He turned to see Yves Marchand waving at them, beckoning them over. Laura took his arm and they joined their host. "Yves, so good to see you. It's been too long."

Marchand grasped him by the arms, giving him the traditional French greeting, something of which Acton was never a fan. "So good to see you, my friend. May I present my wife, Sophie."

This time he was treated to a gentle handshake. He turned to Laura. "And may I present my wife, Professor Laura Palmer."

"A pleasure, madame." A hand was kissed, then shook, and the greetings were finished, leaving Acton and Marchand competing on who was giddier.

"Congratulations on your discovery, Professor. An impressive find."

Marchand waved a hand at Laura. "Please, call me Yves. I feel like I'm in class when I hear 'professor.'" He bowed slightly. "But, thank you for your kind words, though I fear they are undeserved. I was merely the lucky soul who was assigned to investigate what was supposed to be nothing." He shrugged, displaying his palms. "But, alas, it was much more than a blacksmith's forge that was found that day in northern France."

"Any theories as to how it got there?"

"Many!" Marchand laughed, the man, whom Acton had only met a couple of times, both of those years ago, the happiest he had ever seen him, and for good reason. "You've seen the pictures of how we found it?"

"Yes."

"Then you know it was obviously very deliberately, and carefully, buried. Why it was, one can only speculate, and unfortunately, I can see no way for us to ever know for certain. The fact it was directly under a large stone that once served as the base of a blacksmith's forge suggests some effort went into hiding it, and I must assume it was hidden by the blacksmith himself, for I can see no possible way his own forge would be moved without his knowledge. In those times, he would have lived where he worked."

Acton's head bobbed in agreement. "It's fascinating to speculate, but…"

Marchand grinned. "But you want to see it, don't you?"

Acton laughed. "Is the Pope Triarii?"

Marchand's eyes widened slightly. "Huh?"

Laura's hand gripped his arm a little tighter. "Nothing, an inside joke. Too long to explain."

Marchand shrugged. "Please, follow me."

"I'll stay here," said his wife. "I've seen it before, and if I don't get some of those hors d'oeuvres, this cocktail is going to hit me about the same time Yves starts his speech." She gave her husband a peck then smiled at their guests before pursuing a server with gusto.

Marchand watched her for a moment, clearly a proud husband much in love, then led them out of the atrium where the guests were gathered, and down a series of hallways before reaching a room with a coded panel. He entered a code, covered by his hand, then pushed open the door. He held it aside and Acton allowed Laura to enter first before following, his eyes widening in anticipation at the shroud-covered wheeled trolley that could only contain what they were all there to see.

"Ready?"

Acton's heart hammered. "Does a bear—" His arm was viciously squeezed. "Yes."

Marchand removed the shroud with a flourish, leaving Acton and Laura to both gasp in awe at the sight. The Bible lay under protective glass, the light from above highlighting it as if from Heaven, the massive tome split into two halves.

"Unbelievable!" hissed Acton as goosebumps raced across his entire body, a shiver rushing up and down his spine. He slowly walked around the impressive work, carefully taking it in from every angle, before finally stopping in front of it and bending over the glass.

"It's remarkably preserved," observed Laura. "I knew from the pictures it would be, but in person…" She sighed, shaking her head. "Simply stunning. This is in better condition than the Codex Amiatinus, I can assure you."

"After the discovery, I was fortunate enough to be able to see the Codex Amiatinus for comparison purposes, and I have to agree."

Acton pointed at a thin hole that appeared to go through one half of the Bible, perhaps a couple of inches in length. "What do you think made—" A faint alarm sounded and they all froze, Acton tensing. "What's that?"

Marchand dismissed any concern with a wave of his hand. "It's nothing. Just the alarm from a fire door. I accidentally set one off this morning when I went for a cigarette."

"There's no sign?"

"There is." He shrugged. "I thought it was just for show!"

Peeters watched the argument between mother and daughter, then turned his attention to the man of the hour, the vile intellectual who had made the discovery, from all accounts accidentally, yet was still fêted by the elite of the antiquities world.

It disgusted him to no end, yet this gathering could do more to further the cause than a thousand marches.

Gaining entry had been easy. The invitation had been in his parents' mailbox two days after his conversation with a man who turned out to be Oskar Richter.

He had never heard of him.

He had Googled him and confirmed he was nouveau riche, his wealth from the telecommunications industry, his company based in Berlin.

The man meant nothing to him.

Though his money—and connections—meant everything.

Apparently, he was a bit of an eccentric, hated being in public, and was rarely seen, few, if any, recent photographs to be found on the Internet.

A rarity these days.

Though it had served Peeters well.

No one knew what the real Richter looked like, so when he showed his invitation, he was waved through with smiles and wide eyes.

He felt as if Howard Hughes had just made an appearance after a decade of isolation.

Fortunately, no one was announced as they entered, and the paparazzi were left outside beyond the gates, the elite of society here tonight with no desire to be on camera, though the Hollywood types he had no doubt were disappointed with the overruling by the rich that funded them. Yet phones abounded, selfies quickly filling the newsfeeds of a society that relished lifestyles they could never attain, video taken by those who had wrangled an invitation without being among the upper crust of society, many, he assumed, arm-candy purchased for the night by old men desperate to be perceived as virile.

Mankind should be wiped from the earth.

He headed toward the bathrooms as he sent a text message.

Ready?

His phone vibrated with a response.

30 seconds.

He pulled a cigarette case from his rented tuxedo, Richter having come through with a few thousand Euros, eager to see this event disrupted.

If only he knew.

He popped a cigarette in his mouth, returning the case to an inner pocket, then fished out a lighter as he walked with confidence past the stairs leading to the upper level, past the bathrooms, and toward a fire door at the far end of the hall.

He continued the thirty-count in his head, staring at the sign warning an alarm would sound the moment he pushed on the handle.

Thirty.

He pushed.

And an alarm sounded.

The door was hauled open and the rest of the Brigade chosen for the mission rushed inside. He yanked the door shut and the alarm cut off as Karl handed him a weapon, one of many procured by contacts he had made during his days in the German Army, his exit rather ignominious.

"Everyone ready?"

Nods all around.

"Then let's do this!" He rushed toward the opulence he had just left. "For the animals!"

Petra glanced over her shoulder from her perch on the stairs, the alarm startling her. She spotted a man holding open a door to let in some party crashers. She activated her camera and started recording, clasping a precautionary hand over her brother's mouth.

But the gasp came from her own as she spotted the guns.

Oh my God!

"For the animals!"

She quickly tapped at her phone and began live streaming as the seven men and women rushed toward the atrium, the atrium where not only the guests were celebrating, but where her parents were.

Gunfire erupted and Jean Luc cried out as she flinched. She rose, pointing at him. "Stay here! No matter what!" She rushed toward the atrium, coming to a halt at the edge of the wall, then peered around the corner, her phone leading the way, as the gunmen continued to fire, shouting in several languages for everyone to get down. To her horror, many were complying, but more weren't, too shocked to obey.

Three security personnel were mowed down as they entered the atrium, and that was when she noticed half a dozen were dead or dying only feet away from her, perhaps sent to investigate the alarm, likely expecting a smoker like her father this morning.

Then she heard the screams and sobs, and as she recorded the terrorists surging through the room, shooting anyone with a gun, the unsuspecting security quickly overwhelmed, she searched for her mother and father, but couldn't find them.

Someone grabbed her hand and she almost screamed.

It was her brother.

"What's going on?"

She picked him up and rushed him back toward the stairs, searching for someplace to put him where he might not be spotted. She put him down, pointing at the dark shadow under the bottom few steps. "Get under there, as far as you can, and stay quiet, okay?"

He nodded, scurrying into the darkness, and if she didn't know he was there, she wouldn't have noticed.

She crawled under with him then nearly peed when her phone vibrated with a call.

It was her friend Anne.

She swiped her thumb.

"Oh my God, what's going on? I'm watching your feed!"

And suddenly it became real. It wasn't some figment of her imagination, it wasn't some misinterpretation of innocent events.

It was real.

And she was in the middle of it.

Her family was in the middle of it.

"I-I think terrorists have taken over the museum. Wh-what do I do?"

"What do you do? You keep recording! I'm sharing this with everyone. Keep shooting. This is going to make you famous!"

And her terror was forgotten, the tremble of fear replaced with that of excitement. Anne was right. This was her moment. This was the moment everyone hoped for, that one moment that could change a life, that one chance to turn everything around and become famous.

It was the moment that could mean her freedom.

If she played her cards right, she would be the next Khloé, the next Kim.

The next Kylie.

Someone screamed and a gunshot rang out, silencing it.

And she shook anew with fear and horror, as she realized the price being paid for her future fame.

"What the hell was that?" asked Acton, spinning toward the closed door to the secure room, his question redundant for there was no doubt what he had heard.

Laura cocked an ear. "That's gunfire!" She turned to Marchand. "You don't have something planned, do you? A movie, some fireworks?"

Marchand shook his head, visibly pale, evidently not as used to the sound of gunfire as they were. "No, nothing of the sort." He headed for the door. "I'll go check."

Acton blocked him with an arm. "No! Call the police."

Marchand shook out a hasty nod, retreating into the far corner with his phone. Acton pointed at Laura. "Pull up a map of this place. We need to figure out how to get out of here." He stepped over to the door as she started tapping on her phone. He placed an ear against the door, listening for anything. There was security here, and he had heard several different weapons types. A single shot rang out, then nothing beyond muffled cries.

Is it over?

He opened the door a sliver so he could hear better, and it was shoved into him, the barrel of a gun pressed against his forehead.

"Thank you. I wasn't sure if we'd be getting in here quite so easily."

Peeters pushed the fool who had opened the door into the corner with his friends, one he recognized as the bastard who had discovered the abomination, an abomination that sat in all its hideous glory at the center of the room, lit from overhead and behind protective glass.

It enraged him, bile filling his mouth as he took in its massive bulk, every square inch representing the skin of an innocent creature raised from birth and slaughtered before its time for the sole purpose of creating the pages that this monstrosity required so long ago.

"Disgusting."

The man from the door took one step forward, his arms spread, protecting the two behind him. "What is it you want? What can we do to help resolve this, so no one else gets hurt?"

Peeters turned slowly, glaring at the man, his finger twitching on the trigger of his submachine gun. He stabbed a finger toward the Bible. "Do you really think there is anything that *you* can do to atone for *that*? That abomination! That testament to all that is wrong with mankind! Can you bring those poor creatures back to life? Can you in your infinite self-absorption not see that its very existence is an affront to all that we should hold dear? Can you—"

Karl rushed into the room. "The police are here!"

Peeters spun. "What? Already?"

"Yeah, a car just pulled up. I think more are coming."

Peeters cursed. "Fine, secure the doors and get everything we'll need from the van now. We're going to have to speed things up."

"What are you people planning?" asked the doorman.

Peeters glanced at him over his shoulder, his eyes boring into the beast who would dare partake in this sinful creation. A sneer crawled up Peeters' mouth. "Something you won't like, I can assure you."

Frankish Burgundy

716 AD

Only his faith carried him forward now. He had stopped as scheduled, but had only taken advantage of a meal, fresh provisions, and a fresh horse, a significant upgrade agreed to by the abbot when he informed him of his fear for the previous night's guests hosted within his walls.

Yet a horse in the dark wasn't nearly as swift as one during the day, at least not one with an inexperienced rider. While the horse could see, if his skittish master continually panicked rather than trusting the animal to find its way, the two could be injured. This had led to a far slower pace than he would have liked, but by the time the sun broke the horizon to the east, he had covered far more distance than he would have lying in a bed.

As he passed through a small town marked on his map, he knew the abbey his friends should be at was only a few hours ride from here. He made for a blacksmith with a stable and several horses visible.

He bowed to the proprietor. "Do you mind if I water my horse?"

The man regarded him for a moment. "Not at all, Monk. It would be my honor to feed him as well."

Arledge smiled. "That would be very kind of you. I shall mention you in my prayers."

The man chuckled. "Mention my wife, and I'll feed you too."

Arledge laughed, making the sign of the cross. "You shall both be mentioned tonight. You have my word, though I am in a hurry."

A woman appeared, round with child, startled to see him in his robes. "You're not one of the ones those unpleasant creatures are looking for, are you?"

He averted his eyes. "I should hope not, though I don't know upon whom you refer."

She pointed toward the road he had been traveling, in the direction he was heading. "About an hour ago, a group of men on horseback came through. Very rude, very rough. Began asking about a group of monks that might have traveled through here."

Arledge's heart thumped. "What did you say?"

"We said nothing, but others weren't so tight with their tongues."

The blacksmith eyed him. "You seem to know who she's talking about."

Arledge shook his head, scrambling for an explanation to his poor reaction. "No, I don't, though I do know *of* them. They stayed at the same abbey as I did last night. I guess they're about a day ahead of me. Probably on a pilgrimage to Rome as I am."

"A long journey."

"Yes, it is, though to see the Vatican firsthand, to attend mass with the Pope and the thousands of faithful who have Jesus in their hearts…" He sighed. "It is something I have always dreamed of, and am lucky enough to have been permitted to undertake."

The man chewed his cheek. "It seems odd, a simple monk being sent on a journey such as what you describe."

Arledge controlled his panic at the challenge. "Yet you don't question a group?"

The man grunted. "Those men were on a mission to deliver a fancy Bible. They were showing it to everyone. Fools."

Arledge was happy to hear he wasn't alone in his misgivings. "It does sound foolish." He decided it was best to change the subject. He clasped his hands together and bowed slightly. "There was mention of a meal?"

The man laughed. "I'll let my wife fill your empty belly while I tend to your horse." He patted the beast's neck. "A fine horse for a humble monk."

Arledge nodded, escaping an explanation by following the wife inside. He would have to make quick work of his meal before too many more questions were asked. The stop had turned out to be riskier than he had expected, though nonetheless fruitful. His horse was being taken care of, he was being fed, but more importantly, he was only an hour behind his friends' pursuers.

Unknown Location

Present Day

Oskar Richter flinched at the sound of the buzzer. Only one dared disturb him at this time. He tapped his phone, silencing the whale songs he had been meditating to, then tapped another button unlocking the door with an audible click.

His butler, Gerhard, entered, appearing as flustered as he had ever seen him.

"What is it?"

"Sir, we might have a problem."

Richter sat up, the concern in his longtime servant's voice palpable. "What's going on?"

"Remember you asked me to get your invitation to the Guggenheim gala to Hugo Peeters so that he could disrupt the party and make a political statement?"

Richter hated stupid questions. "Of course. It was only last week."

"Well, there's been a terrorist attack at the Guggenheim. It's happening right now."

Richter bolted upright in his chair. "What? Are you serious? Has anybody been hurt?"

"I'm not sure yet. There's been reports of gunfire, though."

Richter tapped a few keys and half a dozen news feeds replaced an underwater vista on his far wall. He scanned each one, shaking his head. "Are you sure? I'm not seeing anything."

Gerhard held up his phone. "I saw it on Twitter."

Richter's shoulders relaxed and he leaned back, dismissing his man's concerns with a flick of the wrist. "Twitter? You know ninety-percent of what's on there is bullshit."

"No, no, it's true! Footage is starting to come out. Some girl is even live streaming it. It's actually starting to trend. The news will probably catch up in an hour or so." Gerhard thrust his phone in front of him and Richter gasped at what he saw.

"What does that idiot think he's doing?"

Gerhard shrugged. "Ransom?"

"He said he was making a political statement." He pulled out his burner phone and called who he thought until only moments ago was a man who was all talk.

Guggenheim Bilbao

Bilbao, Spain

Peeters tugged on the chains now securing one of the doors. The museum was a large complex, and whether the police had access to the rest of it wasn't his concern. He only had to keep a small section secure for a short period of time, and thanks to fire regulations, he had doors where architects would have preferred there weren't.

He spotted several police cars out front, their lights flashing, and had no doubt the place would be swarming with them any minute. Again, not his concern. He wanted the press. He wanted the world to see what was happening here tonight, and it would be his only demand when asked.

He returned to the atrium where his fellow soldiers of the Animal Protection Brigade had collected all the hostages into the center of the impressive room, then made a circuit around them, inspecting Karl's homemade explosive devices retrieved from the van outside once they had secured the scene. He paused beside Karl.

"Everything set?"

"Yup."

"Detonator?"

Karl handed him the device. "Just flip the cover off the switch, then flick it. Kaboom."

Peeters smiled, patting Karl on the back. "Good work." He turned and headed for the front of the atrium, standing behind a podium set up for the planned festivities. He turned on the microphone. "May I have everyone's attention, please?" A hush fell over the terrified crowd as they turned to face him. "Now, I will be making a statement to the press when they arrive, however I felt you all deserved to know why we decided to join you tonight. We are the Animal Protection Brigade. Who is that, you might ask? We fight for those who can't help themselves—the animals of our planet. We fight for the equality of all Mother Earth's creatures, from the smallest plankton to the massive whale, and all creatures in between, cute and cuddly, or vicious and ugly. And yes, that would normally include even yourselves.

"But sometimes to save the whole, you must sacrifice the part. Just as a diseased foot must sometimes be amputated to save someone from dying, sometimes a group of creatures must be sacrificed to save the rest." He paused, then jabbed a finger at his hostages. "*You* are the disease. *You* are the infection. It is the rich of society who have the power to save the creatures of this planet, yet most of you sit idly by and do nothing. You wear furs, leathers, perfumes and makeups made from animals or tested on them. You hunt them for sport, you mount them on your walls, you tear at their flesh with your teeth as you seek out the most exotic meals as you jet across the globe. You disgust me.

"And today, you gather here to celebrate the discovery of a manmade creation that is an abomination. This Bible you are all here to see, written on one thousand pages of vellum, was only made possible because over five-hundred calves were raised and slaughtered, before their time, all for their skin, skin that would be turned into the pages you are all gathered here to gawk at!

"But that wasn't enough for you, was it? It wasn't enough for you to celebrate this atrocity. Someone here was set to announce to the world a plan to recreate the feat. To raise another five-hundred cows, slaughter them before they reached their prime, rip the skin off their flesh, stretch it out and dry it to create another thousand pages so modern scribes could reproduce a fifth copy, all to demonstrate the techniques that went into creating these…these…things! Someone here was planning to put their extreme decadence on display to recreate for their own entertainment and vanity something that should never have been created in the first place, for the price paid was too high. Two-thousand cattle, innocently slaughtered for the pleasure of man."

He sneered at the crowd. "But after tonight, whoever you are, you won't be able to fulfill your twisted desire. I intend to find out who you are, and put an end to your murderous ways once and for all." He pointed at the bombs surrounding them. "Every one of these devices is a bomb powerful enough to kill everyone in this room." Gasps and cries erupted anew at what they already must have surmised. "If anybody tries to leave, if the police try to get in, if anyone tries to stop us, then we'll detonate the bombs and everyone will die." He smiled. "So, you're all reliant on each other. If you see someone trying to do something, it's up to you to stop them, because if you don't, you will die for their actions."

His phone rang in his pocket and he fished it out, cursing at the poor timing.

It was Richter.

He strode out of the atrium as he took the call. "Not a good time, sir."

"What the hell are you up to?"

He was taken aback at the venom in his benefactor's voice. And the fact he was calling at all. "I didn't expect to hear from you. How did you find out?"

"It's all over the Internet. Is it true you've taken hostages?"

"Yes."

"From what I can see, you've already got police outside."

"Yes."

"How are you planning on getting out of there?"

"We're not."

There was a pause. "What do you mean you're not?"

"I mean, we never were. Our plan all along was to play this out as long as we could in front of the cameras, and then when the police move in—boom—it's all done. That way, the world will know why we did it and how resolved we were."

"And you think that will make a difference? That a bunch of eco-nutbars killing themselves will make a difference?"

He tensed at the vitriol. "We're not nutbars."

"I'm not saying you are. I'm saying that's what the world will think."

"Well, the world won't be concerned with our deaths. They'll be concerned with all the millionaires and billionaires and the Hollywood types that are standing in that room right now, and the fact that they're dead. Maybe then their friends and families and the one-percenters who rule us all will think twice about harming an animal in the future."

Richter's voice softened. "Perhaps. What about the Bible?"

"We have it."

"What do you plan on doing with it?"

"Blow it up with us. Nobody should be allowed to celebrate a disgusting creation like this, a testament to the death of five-hundred innocent creatures. Nobody will dare think of trying to recreate a copy using the traditional methods."

"You know that's fake news, don't you?"

Peeters' eyes narrowed. "I know what I read, and I believe those reports."

"You fool! That's my people who put those reports out there. You know that's how we operate. We put out disinformation to confuse the issue, to gain support for our cause."

Peeters' mouth watered as his stomach churned. "What are you telling me?"

"I'm telling you that if you kill yourself today, there never was going to be another Bible created. If that's the only reason you're killing yourself, then don't do it."

The blood drained from his face as the speech he had made replayed in his head, as the speeches he had made to rally his people echoed. He drew a breath of resolve. "It's too late now. Besides, killing all these people that secretly rule the world will still serve a purpose."

"I highly suggest you rewrite whatever speech you're giving so it doesn't make any reference to a fifth Bible, otherwise you'll go down in history sounding like a fool."

He didn't bother telling the man it was too late. "I'll take it under advisement."

"Do you want me to figure out a way to get you out of this?"

Peeters grew suspicious. "Why? You seem quite concerned about my welfare suddenly. Just a month ago, you refused our regular protest fee."

"Hey, I'm not going to give a hundred Euros a day to people who can't get more than a dozen out for a rally. If you can't fill a bus, then you're not worth my time or effort."

Peeters sneered. "Well, when we're done today, we'll be able to fill a cruise ship."

"After today, there will be none of you left. You'll be killing your cause at the same time you're saving it."

"Are you suggesting an alternative?"

"I am. Before you go killing yourself, wait for my call. Oh, and by the way, you've got some kid in there live streaming everything you guys are doing."

The call ended and Peeters' heart hammered. He stepped back into the atrium and looked about the room, but saw nothing untoward. He beckoned Karl who jogged over.

"What's up?"

"Apparently, somebody's kid is live streaming everything to the Internet."

Karl's eyebrows shot up as he cursed. "We'll start searching the place."

"No, forget that. Just go on the Internet and find out who it is. Chances are their parents are here tonight. We'll just call them out then use them as bait."

Karl smiled. "Yes, sir."

Frankish Burgundy

716 AD

Arledge had galloped the entire way to the next abbey on his map, and where he hoped his friends had spent the night. The horse was a gamechanger. It was sturdy enough to carry his slight frame plus the heavy Bible, as well as his supplies.

Though his poor body wasn't used to the abuse, as riding a horse was a rare occurrence for him at the abbey.

He was paying the price, though he had no choice. He had to warn his friends of the men that were pursuing them, regardless of what Ceolfrid's instructions had been.

"They left perhaps two hours ago at a leisurely pace," informed the abbot that had hosted his friends. "With your horse, you'll easily catch them by midday."

He had thanked the man then continued his pursuit, the sun high in the sky. He was certain he would be upon them any moment now, and the thought had him slowing. He glanced at the saddlebags carrying the Bible, then the horse that carried them. If these men were thieves, they might steal his horse, and that meant they would have the Bible. That couldn't be allowed.

Yet what could he do?

He continued forward, his mind puzzling out the problem.

Then he smiled.

He brought his horse to a halt then dismounted, making sure he was alone. He hauled his robe over his head, then took the saddlebags off the horse, draping them instead around his neck. He tossed the robe over his head then drew it down his body and over the saddlebags. He appeared ridiculous, though at a distance or in the heat of an exchange, he might simply pass as overweight.

He struggled back on the horse, the creature not pleased with the new weight distribution, then finally urged it forward, soon at a gallop, the heavy Bible slapping against his stomach, something he would be paying the price for tonight.

Shouts ahead, including cries for help, had him slowing rather than charging forward as his fantasies had suggested he would. He cautiously rounded a bend in the road and gasped in horror at the sight that lay before him. The half-dozen men on horseback, swords drawn, had Ceolfrid on his knees, the tip of a blade pressed to his throat, the others, his dear brothers, all dead or dying on the blood-soaked road.

Ceolfrid bowed his head, making the sign of the cross, then pointed to the back of the cart. Two men jumped in and the box containing the

Bible was opened, one of the men holding it up in triumph. The man holding Ceolfrid ran him through.

Rage surged through Arledge's stomach at the unnecessary act, when a horse whinnied behind him.

"And who might you be?"

He turned to find one of the men from yesterday, his sword drawn, obviously a lookout he had missed, his count of those attacking his friends one too many.

The man looked at him, askance. "I recognize you. You're the monk from yesterday. I thought you said you didn't know of your friends there."

The blood drained from Arledge's face as all strength left his body. "I—I don't know—"

The man's blade thrust forward, into Arledge's stomach, the pain instant and overwhelming.

"There can be no witnesses."

Guggenheim Bilbao

Bilbao, Spain

Present Day

Acton stood with Laura and Marchand in the far corner of the room. The door was closed, and they hadn't seen any of the terrorists since the initial encounter when all their electronic devices were confiscated. Though they had heard them. A speech, if it could be called that, had been piped through the speakers before it was interrupted by the ringing of a phone.

Very unprofessional.

He prayed the amateurish display meant this would soon be over without any further violence. Yet could he take that risk? Sometimes amateurs panicked. He stared at the door. He could try it again, though there was a good chance that someone was on the other side of it.

Like the last time when he had foolishly opened it, letting the hostiles inside.

Sometimes you should just leave well enough alone.

Though that had never been him, and from what he had seen, it had never been Laura either.

But Marchand?

He was trembling in the corner, a bundle of nerves that could be set off with the slightest provocation.

The door opened and Marchand yelped in fear, as he had when the code had been demanded of him.

A man entered saying nothing, the circular saw he carried delivering his message. He fired it up and made quick work of the acrylic encasing the Bible, every spark, every shard that touched the priceless artifact causing Acton to wince.

The man finished rounding the enclosure then powered down the circular saw, the unbearable din finally over. He tossed aside the cover, leaving the Bible exposed.

Acton could hold his tongue no longer. "What are you going to do with it?"

"None of your concern."

"It's a piece of history and I'm an archaeologist. Of course it's my concern."

The man jabbed a finger at him then slapped the weapon slung over his shoulder. "Your concern could get you killed."

Acton frowned. "From what I've seen here tonight, it looks like I'm going to die anyway."

"I'd be more worried about *how* I'm going to die."

The man left, closing the door behind him. They all rushed the Bible, gently picking off the debris, carefully blowing away anything too small to grip.

"I fear none of this matters," said Marchand.

Acton regarded him. "You think they intend to destroy it?"

Marchand nodded.

Acton clasped his hands behind his head. "So do I."

Unknown Location

Richter's head slowly shook in stunned silence at the reply he had received. He leaned back from his computer, his brilliant mind racing as he ran through all the possible scenarios that lay ahead should he proceed with his rapidly developing plan.

"Look." He gestured at the screen and Gerhard rounded his desk, his eyes popping at the number.

"Unbelievable."

"That's why I asked twice. This could fund the cause for years."

Gerhard returned to his customary position in front of the desk. "But it's profiting off the death of hundreds of innocent animals."

"Yes, but by doing this, at least some good might come of their deaths." He scratched his chin, regarding Gerhard. "Honest assessment?"

Gerhard chose his words carefully, as he always did. "I think it's a risky move, but not for you. If something goes wrong, then Hugo Peeters and his group are the ones that will take the blame. If it succeeds, then you and the cause will benefit, and no one will be the wiser."

Richter chewed his cheek at the assessment. "True. But I'm not sure the world would believe that a moron like Hugo Peeters would be capable of pulling off something like this. There needs to be brains behind the operation."

"But he did pull it off, sir. They have the museum. That wasn't at all what we were expecting of him."

Richter sighed. "You're right, I wasn't expecting that. I thought he was going to go in there and disrupt it by throwing fake blood on something—his usual heavy-handed thing. Instead, he somehow managed to not only procure weapons, but apparently explosives if what I'm seeing on the Internet is true."

"Are we sure it's true? You know how we do things. Maybe someone else is doing the same."

Richter shook his head. "No, the girl who is broadcasting, I don't think she's in on it, I think she's just an idiot teenager trying to get her fifteen minutes of fame. No, if we're going to keep this thing from blowing up in our faces, we need brains behind this. *I* need brains behind this. It was one thing for him to go and scream and shout in the middle of a gala to then be hauled off by security who would later find out he used my invitation to get in there. But if he goes and kills people, hell, just with what he's already done, there will be a thorough investigation, and there's no way anyone is going to believe he intercepted an invitation meant for me. Because he's taken it to the extreme, it could implicate me."

"What are you going to do?"

"Get me that review we did of the guest list last week."

"Right away, sir."

Guggenheim Bilbao

Bilbao, Spain

Karl watched highlights of the live stream posted earlier, the denizens of the Internet already grabbing their favorite parts and posting it.

She's giving away everything! We have to find her!

He pulled her username from Instagram and Googled it, finding the same name linked to a Facebook page with barely anything on it, likely created for her parents' benefit.

Though it gave him what he suspected was a real first name.

Petra.

He stuffed his phone in his pocket then scanned the guest list, finding the lone person here with that name.

Petra Marchand.

And smiled when he saw three others with the same last name.

I've got you now.

Acton pressed his ear to the door, hearing nothing. He stepped back, his voice low. "We could try to take them down."

Laura gave him a look. "But we have no idea how many there are."

"True, but I've never seen more than two of them come in this room, and that was only when this thing began. Since then, there has never been more than one among us."

Marchand pointed a trembling hand at the door. "We don't even know if someone is on the other side."

Acton glanced about. "There's no other way out of this room, is there?"

"No."

"Air ducts?"

Marchand shook his head vigorously, leaving Acton uncertain if the man would tell him the truth if he knew it. "No, this place has special security for that. Nobody is climbing through the air ducts here."

Acton frowned. The man was probably right. "Okay, well, the next time that door opens, we could take care of that person easily, then escape."

Laura shook her head. "We can't do that. You heard what he said. He said if anyone tried anything, he'd kill everybody."

He sighed. "You're right. Then what do we do?"

"I think we just play along and let the authorities figure it out. If they decide to take them down, and there's some way we can help, then we do it, otherwise we just stay here and keep our mouths shut and try to survive."

"Sounds like as shitty a plan as any."

She smiled. "Sometimes shitty is all you've got."

Unknown Location

Gerhard handed the guest list to Richter, along with a bundle of pages with quick bios on each of them prepared when he found out Peeters was planning something. "Highlights?"

"If you're planning on what I think you're planning, then I might have found who you're looking for." He pointed at a name. "Professor Yves Marchand. He's the man of the hour, the one who discovered the Bible. He's there with his wife and two children, but he also had two special guests with him that were added last minute."

"Who?"

"Professors James Acton and Laura Palmer. Husband and wife archaeologists."

Richter bit his lip. "Why do those names sound familiar?"

"They've made it into the press a few times over the years. They seem to have a knack for meddling."

"Interesting. Solid reputations?"

"Impeccable, sir. He's a well-respected professor, and she was head of archaeology at the British Museum until she took a position at the Smithsonian to be closer to him." Gerhard paused. "And she's rich."

Richter's eyebrows shot up. "Oh? How rich?"

"She's almost one of you, sir."

His eyebrows rose even higher. "Oh really? An archaeologist with that kind of money?"

"Her brother owned an Internet company and sold it before the bubble burst years ago. When he died, he left all the money to her."

"Very interesting. So, they have means to pretty much do whatever they want in life."

"Yes, sir, just like you." Gerhard smiled slightly. "Nefarious or otherwise."

Richter chuckled. "That's exactly what I was thinking."

Guggenheim Bilbao
Bilbao, Spain

"I need Yves and Sophie Marchand to step forward, please." Peeters scanned the crowd from behind the podium, but nobody moved. He pointed his weapon at the nearest woman. "Come forward at the count of three, or she dies. One...two..."

"Wait!" A woman held up her hand and stepped forward. "I'm Sophie Marchand."

He smiled. "Very good. And where is your husband?"

"I-I'm not sure. He was giving a private viewing of the Bible to some friends."

His smile broadened. "Ahh, I see." He pointed at Karl. "Go get him."

Karl left, returning a couple of minutes later, dragging the rather unimpressive man by the arm, his mustache however anything but. Karl shoved him toward the wife, the two of them holding on to each other for emotional support.

He ignored them, instead leaning into the microphone. "Oh, Petra! Show yourself! I have your parents here!" He paused, hearing nothing beyond the whimpers of the parents who now realized why they had been summoned. "If you don't show yourself, I'm going to shoot your mother in the head! You have sixty seconds to show yourself, otherwise you'll never see your mother alive again."

Petra trembled with fear, tears flowing as panic threatened to render her useless. She suddenly took a breath, oxygen flowing once again, her mind piercing the thundering in her ears.

She stood, and Jean Luc grabbed her by the arm.

"Don't go, please."

She stared down at her brother, the boy only a blur through her tears. "If I don't go, they'll kill Mom and Dad."

"No, don't go." His eyes widened. "Take me with you!"

She shook her head, wiping the tears away. "No, they only asked for me. They might not even know about you." She pointed at their hiding spot under the stairs. "Stay here. Only come out if you hear my voice, okay?"

He nodded, then scrambled deep under the stairs and out of sight. "You'll come back for me?"

She stared into the dark consuming her brother. "I promise."

She turned toward the atrium then stopped, pulling out her phone and restarting the live streaming, hoping that whatever she was about to see might help save her and her family, the eagerness of gaining a following on the Internet forgotten. This wasn't her chance to be famous, this was her chance to show the police outside what they were facing, so they might rescue them all.

She rounded the corner and stepped into the atrium. Her mother spotted her first, crying out her name, tears erupting as an arm extended toward her.

"Mom! Dad!" She rushed past the terrorists and into her parents' arms, feeling safe for the first time since this ordeal had begun, an ordeal barely fifteen minutes in.

"How sweet."

She turned to see the man she had spotted earlier, letting his friends inside. He held out his hand.

"Give me your phone."

She frowned, her phone an appendage. He flicked his fingers and she handed it over. To her horror, he dropped it on the floor then drove his heel into it several times, smashing it beyond recognition. She resisted the urge to claw his eyes out, and was about to say something unwise when he jabbed a finger at her.

"You caused me a lot of trouble, little girl. What did I say when I took this place?"

Her mind raced. She knew exactly what he had said, her vantage point allowing her to hear everything. But he couldn't know that, could he? "I don't know. I couldn't hear what you were saying from where I was hiding."

He eyed her and she trembled. "I'm not sure whether I believe that or not, but I'm not going to kill all these people over what a stupid little teenage girl did." He glanced around. "Where's your brother?"

She almost lost control of her bladder. "He's not here. He wasn't feeling well so he stayed at home with the nanny."

The terrorist turned to her parents. "Where's your son?"

"Like she said, at home," replied her father.

The man pursed his lips. "Now, why don't I believe you?" He pointed at the guests. "Back to the group." Her father grabbed her by the arm and led her and her mother back to join the hostages in the center of the room.

"Where's your brother?" Her father's voice was barely a whisper.

"He's hiding under the stairs."

"Is he okay?" asked her mother.

"He's scared but he's okay."

Another terrorist approached and held out a tablet computer to her, Instagram's login page showing. "Log in."

"What?"

"Log in."

She was indignant at the thought. "Why?"

"So I can delete the damage you've done."

Her father implored her with his eyes to obey. She sighed and logged in, handing the tablet back to the man who walked away, muttering obscenities.

Peeters' phone vibrated and he answered it, heading out of the atrium. "Hello?"

"How are things going there?"

"We found the source of the leak."

"Who was it?"

"The daughter of the professor who found the Bible. We got her. I destroyed her phone so no more information will be coming from inside here that we don't control."

"Good. I have a plan. I'm putting it into place now. Whatever you do, don't do anything to harm that Bible."

Peeters tensed, suspicious. "Why?"

"Just do what I say, and you'll have enough money to fund your organization until the end of time."

Unknown Location

Richter glanced up from his computer as Gerhard entered. "Is it done?"

"Yes, sir. Our people have cloned all their social media accounts using two of our Social Justice Warrior profiles built up over the past few years."

He hated using two of the carefully crafted dummy social media profiles they had cultivated, but this opportunity was worth burning dozens if necessary. The dummy accounts were filled with myriads of posts about various social issues, but with nothing naming the poster, so they could be assigned to anyone.

They were expensive to create, time-consuming, but immensely valuable to the cause. "They're already up?"

"Yes, sir. They're completely public, and if anyone searches, they'll find these profiles and think they're rabid activists. It will be believable, at least for the short term."

He pulled up one of the accounts on Facebook. "Short-term doubt is all we need. We just need a little delay."

"Are you sure you want to do this? I still think this is risky."

"It's nothing that I'm worried about. As long as there's no way for it to trace back to me, then I think it's worth pursuing."

"You'll be destroying the reputations of two innocent people."

He grunted. "For the greater good. Besides, with money like hers, they might be able to actually get it cleaned up. But they're not my concern. I want that Bible. It will fund our operation for years. We'll be able to save millions of animals, with none of the money traceable back to me."

Guggenheim Bilbao

Bilbao, Spain

Marchand stood with the others, one arm around his wife, the other around his daughter, his eyes searching the opening to the hallway she had emerged from only minutes before.

Please, God, take care of Jean Luc for me.

The terrorists had done a quick search, finding nothing, which had him confident the hiding place his little boy was in was a good one.

"Dad, are those bombs real?"

"I don't think so, dear," replied his wife, her voice unconvincing. "Why would they kill themselves and everybody?"

"Maybe they're not planning on killing themselves. They might leave then kill us."

Marchand spotted the leader of this enterprise walk past, something that appeared homemade gripped in his left hand. It had to be the detonator, and the white of his knuckles told Marchand that these explosives were indeed real, as was the stress the man was under. The terrorist's phone rang and he answered it, handing the detonator over to the one who had asked Petra to log into her social media.

He surveyed the area, wishing he were as calm and collected as Acton was. How he had taken command in those first few seconds, directing everyone on what to do, had been impressive. It made him believe some of the rumors he had heard about those two.

What would Jim do?

He'd look for a way out, he was certain. Yet there was none. All of the exits from the atrium were guarded by machine-gun-toting crazies, and he was forced to accept the fact they weren't getting out of here. He eyed the bombs surrounding the cluster of the rich and famous huddled together amidst them, and knew their only hope was to use the others as human shields.

His stomach churned with the thought, but he had his daughter to think of, not only himself and Sophie. There were no other children here tonight, only adults. If they could somehow survive the initial blast, Petra might survive, and perhaps even Sophie. They and Jean Luc were his only concern. His life was forfeit. He would sacrifice himself to save them.

He examined the placement of the bombs and searched for anything that might block the blast waves. He found none. Human flesh was all that was available. He gently guided his family toward the center of the mass, avoiding eye contact with those he hoped would shield his daughter, then stopped near the center of the living barrier.

He placed his mouth to his wife's ear. "I don't think we're getting out of this. If things go bad, get on the floor and cover Petra. I'll cover you both." He pulled away and stared into her tear-filled eyes. "I love you."

A tear rolled down her cheek and she quickly wiped it away before Petra noticed. "I love you too."

"Do you understand the plan?"

Peeters' heart pounded and his stomach churned with understanding. "Yes. I don't understand the purpose, however."

Richter sighed. "The purpose is quite simple. We're going to make some good come out of the evil that went into the creation of this abomination."

He gripped the phone tighter. "You're going to sell it, aren't you?"

"Yes. I already have a buyer who's willing to pay an obscene amount of money."

"How much?"

"Does it matter?"

"I think it does."

"Let's just say we're talking nine figures."

His jaw dropped slightly. "Nine? As in hundreds of millions?"

"Yes."

His pulse raced with the possibilities. "And if we pull this off, you'll fund my group?"

"In perpetuity."

"How do my people get out of this?"

There was a pause. "Your people were willing to sacrifice themselves, weren't they?"

"Yes."

"Are they still willing to?"

His eyes narrowed. "What do you mean?"

"Well, for this to work, we need the world to think you're all dead and the Bible destroyed along with them."

A fire burned in his stomach. "So, what you're saying is that my people are expendable."

"For the greater good, yes. You can save yourself, however."

"And just how am I supposed to do that?"

"By acting fast."

"How am I supposed to get out of here?"

"Act. Fast. The police haven't secured the perimeter yet. If you act in the next five minutes, you can still get out the way you got in."

"How do you know how I got in?"

"Because it's on the damned Internet! Stop talking. The longer you talk, the less chance there is of this working. Go, do it now."

"Okay, okay!" He ended the call, his emotions a blend of excitement, guilt, and confusion.

This isn't what was supposed to happen.

He cursed, then strode swiftly toward the room containing the Bible.

And the two most important pawns in the game about to be played.

Acton spun toward the door as it opened, the man he presumed was the leader entering and closing the door behind him.

Bold.

He could take the man apart before help could be called for, his National Guard training greatly augmented by Laura's security team led by a former Special Air Service colonel.

Laura's hand gently gripping his arm ended his debate.

They couldn't risk the lives of the others.

"Listen to me carefully if you want to live."

Acton's eyebrows shot up, the man's words unexpected. "What the hell are you talking about?"

"This has gotten out of hand. I don't have control of the others anymore." The man pointed at the Bible. "I don't want this destroyed, or any of those people to die. I need you to take it out of here." He held out a set of car keys. "I'll show you to the door. There's a van parked outside." He handed over his cellphone. "Take this. You'll be called with instructions on where to go. Follow the instructions, or I'll detonate the bomb myself."

Acton eyed him suspiciously. "Why are you doing this?"

"Because I'm not insane."

"Then why not just let us go with the Bible?"

"Because I also have an agenda. It just doesn't include murder." He grabbed the Bible and shoved it into Acton's hands.

"What about our friends?"

"There's nothing I can do for them now. They're in the atrium with everyone else. If I figure out a way to calm my people down, they'll be okay."

"Then you're staying?"

108

"Yes. Now, come quickly." He opened the door and peered in both directions before beckoning them to follow. He directed them down a hallway and several turns, his weapon trained on them the entire time, before reaching a fire door. "The van is on the other side of the door. Get in and turn to your left and follow the lane out to the main road. The police are still securing the area. If you don't draw any attention, you'll get away." He pushed open the door, the alarm sounding. "Good luck."

Acton stepped out into the cool evening air, spotting the van less than ten feet away. "You drive."

Laura nodded, taking the keys from him, then climbing in as he did the same on the passenger side, placing the Bible in his lap. She started the engine and pulled away from the rear of the museum, no police in sight, their response so far apparently focused on the front.

And that was when he realized how little time had passed since this had all begun.

They pulled onto the road and merged into traffic, a police car ahead blocking the opposite lane causing his heart rate to pick up slightly, then settling at the realization the officer was merely blocking anyone from entering the area, and waving through those leaving.

The phone the terrorist had given him rang, causing them both to flinch. He answered it, putting it on speaker. "Hello?"

"Good evening, Professor Acton. It's a pleasure to be speaking to you."

"Who's this?"

"The man who controls your life for the next twenty-four hours."

Frankish Burgundy

716 AD

Arledge woke to a groan, several moments passing before he realized it was his own. He forced his eyes open, the effort tasking, his body weak, his energy spent. A jolt surged through him as panic overwhelmed him. He grabbed at his stomach, not concerned for the wound from where he had been run through, but for the Bible.

And sighed in relief at feeling it still there.

He lifted his robes, finding them blood-soaked, along with a thin hole marring the once perfect Bible where he had been run through. Blood oozed through it, enough to know he was done for, though if it weren't for the Bible, he would be dead, the thick tome having saved his life.

He peered down the road, confirming what he already knew. His friends were dead, as was Ceolfrid, their precious gift for the Pope stolen, their assailants long gone, having left him for dead, his horse apparently not worth their time.

He wouldn't make Rome.

Yet he still had a duty to perform, no matter how near death he might be.

He had to deliver the Bible into the hands of those he could trust.

But who might that be?

He couldn't go forward, for his map told him a town lay between him and the next abbey. His only choice was to return from whence he came, and pray to the Good Lord that he made it to the abbey he had left only hours ago, before he was taken to wherever He felt him worthy of spending eternity.

He turned the horse around and urged it forward. His heart fluttered, his vision blurred, and his body grew weaker as he collapsed onto his steed, the spark of life fading to near nothing.

Guggenheim Bilbao

Bilbao, Spain

Present Day

Jean Luc scurried back to his hiding place as the alarm cut off, the same alarm he had heard earlier when the bad people had arrived. But this time he had been prepared. He watched the video he had taken and smiled.

Now I'll be famous too!

He posted it to his Instagram account, an account with barely any followers as he wasn't allowed to have it. The only people who would see it would be a few of his friends with their own secret accounts, and they were probably getting ready for bed.

It wasn't fair. Why should only his sister get all the followers when he had great video too?

He smiled.

She could share it with her followers!

He quickly sent her a direct message with the link, asking her to do just that. If she was able to, then he might get a ton of followers as well, and that would give him the start he needed in life at only eight years old. By eighteen, it could snowball into something huge where he could be famous just for being famous, and not work a day in his life.

He heard something and pressed his phone against his chest, squeezing deeper back into the darkness.

Chief Inspector Liliana Sanchez of the Spanish National Police Corps stepped from the back of the mobile command center, surveying the area as she prepared to take command. An inspector, in charge until now, ran over.

"Chief Inspector! Thank God you're here. I heard traffic is backed up for kilometers."

"It is. Status?"

"We've evacuated all other areas of the museum, and we're sweeping it for stragglers, but we're keeping away from the atrium and the immediately adjoining areas."

"Have you established a perimeter yet?"

"We have the front covered, but not the rear yet. We're still waiting for additional units."

"They'll be here shortly. They're stuck in the same traffic we were. Have they made any demands yet?"

"No, we haven't been able to establish any communications with them."

"Do we know who they are?"

"No, we know nothing about them or anything that's going inside beyond that there were gunshots. We received a 1-1-2 call about the attack, then when we arrived, we saw someone at the door with a gun, then people chaining the doors shut. It looks like they intend to be here for a while."

"Let's hope they just want to make a statement then surrender." She leaned back inside the mobile command center. "Start checking social media for any type of posts from inside. Everybody has a phone now and is looking for any chance to gain followers."

"Yes, ma'am."

"And get me a megaphone." She was promptly handed one from inside. She walked over to the front entrance of the museum and placed the megaphone to her mouth. "This is Chief Inspector Sanchez of the National Police Corps. I would like to speak to you to discuss your demands." She saw a shadow near the door move then disappear. She looked at the others. "Let's hope he's fetching his boss and not taking a piss." Her tension-breaking joke was greeted with chuckles from her stressed team.

And she had a feeling it might be the last bit of levity of the night.

Peeters stood next to the door, counting to sixty, preparing to "escape" from the terrorists inside, when one of his men called for him. He cursed, putting his hand on the door, preparing to push it open.

"Hey, what's going on?"

He pretended to have been closing the door and walked toward Rudy. "I thought I heard something, so I was just checking to make sure the police weren't up to anything."

"Oh, so that's why we heard the alarm again." Rudy jerked a thumb over his shoulder, back toward the atrium. "Well, speaking of police, you better get out front. There's a cop out there who wants to discuss our terms."

"I don't care about police. Is the press here yet?"

Rudy shook his head. "I haven't seen anything, but maybe they're being held farther back. Maybe you can tell her to bring them up so you can make a statement."

"Good thinking." Peeters reluctantly followed Rudy back into the atrium, cursing to himself as he wondered how he was making his escape now.

"What the hell is this?"

Peeters flinched at the rage in Karl's voice as he rushed toward him, the detonator in one hand, his phone in the other. Karl shoved the screen in his face.

"Explain this!"

Peeters' mouth dried at the video playing on the phone showing him letting the professors go with the Bible. "How did you get that?"

"I've been monitoring the kid's account. It just showed up in a message sent to her."

Peeters glanced back toward where he had just been. "Obviously, there's someone else loose out there recording what we're doing. Go find—"

"I don't give a shit about that! I want to know what the hell is going on! You just let two of our hostages go with the Bible. Destroying that and killing these people was the whole point of this, wasn't it?"

He tensed, realizing he had no choice now but to come clean with what had happened over the last five minutes. "Yes it was, but things have changed."

"What the hell are you talking about?"

He held up a calming hand. "I can't tell you now, but if everything works out, the Brigade will be funded for the rest of our lives."

Karl's face was red. "You're telling me you're going to sell that thing? Is that what's going on? What about our cause? Are you saying we're going to profit off the death of all those animals? That's not what we stand for. Even if it could help us as individuals, we would never want to profit from the slaughter of innocent animals!"

The others had gathered now, abandoning their positions, and none appeared happy. He had only moments to salvage this situation, let alone escape. "Not me, someone else. A benefactor of ours."

"That rich guy that gives us money? You know I never wanted a one-percenter helping us out."

"You know as well as I do that it's one-percenters in the background that help most organizations like ours. The people who support our cause can't afford to fund us, but there are some one-percenters who do."

"Yeah, for their own twisted reasons. Even you said they only oppose the pipelines because they own the trains that will transport the oil instead."

"Yes, there are hypocrites like that, but this particular man I trust to have the best interests of our animals at heart."

"You might trust him, but I don't trust him as far as I can throw him, and I want no part of this!"

"Then walk away now."

Karl glared at him. "How the hell am I supposed to do that? All our faces are on camera. This was a one-way mission. We were supposed to make our statement then kill everyone here including ourselves, then we'd go down as martyrs to the cause. But instead, when all is said and done, they're going to find out that the Bible is gone, and that this was all done for profit." He drew a quick breath then his eyes narrowed. "Were those professors in on it?"

"Of course not. They're patsies."

Karl spat. "Well, it sounds like we are too."

Peeters had had enough. There was no more time. "I'm leaving before it's too late. Any of you who want to live, come with me now, otherwise, stay here and stick to the original plan. You'll still make your statement by killing all these people."

His friends, his comrades, exchanged looks with each other, and he could see the fear and confusion on their faces, their disappointment. They had all been chosen for a reason. They were all true believers, they were all willing to sacrifice themselves to send a message to the world that their lives were no more important than any animal's.

Yet he had no time to wait for them to make up their minds.

"I'm leaving. Join me if you want." He turned and headed for the fire exit, praying there was still time to get away.

"Hugo!"

He turned and paled as Karl raised the detonator above his head.

"Burn in hell with the rest of us!"

Marchand cursed as he shoved his wife and daughter to the ground. He threw himself over them, protecting the two most precious women in his life, though it would be no use. It felt like an eternity, though it was likely less than a second, before a screeching terror ripped through the atrium, enveloping them as those still standing were shredded by the shrapnel released by the bomb.

Agonizing daggers of pain tore through him as he was hit repeatedly. His wife and daughter screamed as a burst of flame rushed over them. He gasped, holding his breath as the heat washed past, searing his back, the agony too much, forcing him to scream as the oxygen was consumed around him.

And as the death and destruction continued, his pain proved too much, and mercifully, his world faded, the last sounds he heard those of the screams from his terrified family, the only solace of his final moments the knowledge they still lived.

Goodbye, my loves.

Chief Inspector Sanchez peered through the glass door of the museum then saw the flash. "Everybody down!" But it was too late. The front windows of the main level exploded outward, shards of glass and debris tearing through the evening as a fireball clawed at anything in its path. The blast punched her in the chest, knocking her backward as she gasped for breath, her eyes squeezed shut as a wave of heat enveloped her. She hit the ground hard, skidding until she slammed into something, abruptly bringing her to a halt. She sat in a daze for a few moments then felt hands on her.

"Chief Inspector! Are you okay?"

The voice sounded as if it were from far away, and it took her a moment to realize it was the ringing in her ears making it difficult to hear. She took several breaths, self-assessing her condition. "I-I think so." She extended her arms. "Help me up."

"Wait, let me check you for wounds."

She didn't bother protesting the intrusion as hands roamed her body.

"Tell me if you feel any pain."

She did, but none of the jolts were worth talking about. If she screamed, then it was something to pay attention to. The examination was soon over.

"I think you got lucky, ma'am."

She extended her arms again and was hauled to her feet. She examined herself, then gingerly moved all her muscles and joints, making certain she was indeed fine.

"You should get checked out. You've been cut up."

She leaned into a still intact window of one of the police units and frowned at the reflection revealing little abrasions all over her face. "I'm fine. What about everyone else?"

"Nobody else got hurt. Just you, ma'am."

"That's what I get for being curious." She sighed, surveying the area. The flames were almost out, and the only damage appeared to be the large glass outer wall of the atrium. The blast had been powerful only because she had been so close, and with what it had done to her, she could only imagine the horrors that awaited them inside. She pointed at the mess of vehicles. "Clear a path. I want fire and ambulance to be able to get in and out of here. And keep the press back." She looked about. "Is the bomb squad here yet?"

Somebody pointed. "That's them arriving now."

She frowned. "Okay, no point in waiting. Send them in to check for secondary devices. Have fire douse those flames when they get here, but everybody stays outside until the bomb squad says we're good to go. Understood?"

"Yes, ma'am!" Her gathered team broke off to execute her orders while she leaned back against the vehicle that had stopped her skid, rubbing the back of her aching head.

You're going to have to get yourself checked out.

She spotted an ambulance rushing toward them. As it stopped, it turned off its siren, exposing one of those rare moments of silence bookended by chaos.

Revealing the cries of agony and terror from inside.

Something flashed behind them and Acton spun in his seat, poking his head out the window to see a fireball erupt from the main level of the Guggenheim, then just as quickly disappear. "Oh my God, what have you done!" he shouted into the phone.

"What are you talking about, Professor?"

"There's been a massive explosion at the museum!"

For several moments they heard nothing but muffled sounds, as if the mouthpiece of the phone was being covered. Finally, the man behind this horror returned. "A…little ahead of schedule, but so be it. Those people were always going to die. Better to end their suffering sooner rather than later, wouldn't you say?"

Laura's eyes were wide, her mouth agape as she stared at the phone. "You're insane!"

"No, Professor Palmer, I'm a businessman, though I am one who believes that killing animals is as cruel as killing humans. I believe everyone, all creatures, are equal."

Acton growled. "It sounds to me like you're just another greedy criminal." He ran his fingers over the cover of the Bible in his lap. "This Bible is priceless. It should be shared with all mankind, but you intend to sell it to some private collector so you can profit, and killed all those people to do it!"

"What my motivations are, Professor, are none of your concern. Your only concern is that you are now under my control. And you must do what I say."

"Why? What leverage could you possibly have over us now? All those people are dead!"

"Professor Acton, what you fail to realize is that right now, I have security footage of you and your wife leaving the facility with the Bible, as well as a set of keys that allowed you to escape in the getaway vehicle. Right now, after I post this footage to the Internet and send it to law enforcement, the world is going to think you two were the masterminds, not the simpletons who died."

Acton stared at Laura for a moment, horrified at the thought.

"Nobody will believe that," said Laura.

"Oh, they will. Your social media profiles have been faked, and are filled with posts going back for years, showing you're both card-carrying members of the cause. And after what you've done, with all those people now dead, they'll be shooting first before asking questions. So, if you want to live, you'll do everything I say otherwise you're dead."

Acton shook his head. "I still don't see the leverage. We'll just walk into the nearest police station and turn ourselves in. Let them sort it out."

"Professor Acton, how many people do you think just died?"

The very notion of what the number could be horrified him. "I don't know. Dozens, at least."

"If the bombs did their job, then over one hundred of the wealthiest and most powerful people in the world just died. If I'm not afraid to kill them, do you think I'll hesitate to kill others? You will be sent a set of instructions. If you fail to follow any one of them, I will detonate a bomb targeting those who would kill animals for pleasure. Perhaps a farm, a butcher's shop, a store that sells leather jackets. The targets are endless in today's decadent, cruel society. Do as I say, or the blood of hundreds more will be on your hands."

Frankish Burgundy

716 AD

"Bertrada! Come quick!"

Arledge felt hands on him, then heard a gasp.

"My Lord, what has happened to you?"

The voice was familiar, yet he couldn't place it. He was lifted from his saddle, a jolt of pain causing him to groan, the shock giving him the strength to open his eyes a sliver. Through the blur, he recognized the blacksmith from earlier in the day, the man carrying him into his humble home. He was placed on a bed as the man's wife, Bertrada, rushed into the room, crying out.

"Oh my!"

"He's near death. Fetch the priest!"

"But he's gone! He said so on Sunday that he'd be gone for two weeks."

"Curse that man for never being around! He is as much a man of God as Pierre's mule. I swear he's the Devil's lips on God's Earth, that one!"

Arledge reached under his robes, struggling to retrieve the Bible, but his arms collapsed. "Look," he managed, and the blacksmith eyed him for a moment before realizing what he was asking. He reluctantly reached under the blood-soaked robes then his eyes widened in surprise.

"What's this now?" He retrieved the Bible from the saddlebags and he and his wife both cried out. "It's the Bible those fools showed everyone yesterday!"

Arledge shook his head, forcing out the words that must be said in his final moments. "No, those men, they killed my friends, they stole their Bible. This is another copy. No one knows of it. Only my abbot and me. It must be…"

His strength was gone, the one last vital sentence necessary to see the safe return of the Bible to his home unuttered. If only he had not passed out, if only his horse hadn't brought him to the last place they had experienced the kindness of strangers, rather than the abbey where brothers such as himself resided.

All he could do was trust that these simple, kind people, would figure it out for themselves. He had to trust that this was the work of God, and that some day, the Bible would find its way into the hands of the worthy.

His last breath sighed from his body, and a moment of fear struck him.

I'm sorry for failing you, My Lord. Please forgive me.

Unknown Location

Present Day

Richter ended the call and slammed the phone on his desk as Gerhard entered the room, his face grim. Richter held up a finger before his butler could speak, then leaned over and grabbed his garbage can, heaving his dinner.

What have I done?

Gerhard rushed to his side, a handkerchief in his hand. Richter took it and wiped his mouth as Gerhard removed the garbage can from the room, returning a few minutes later with a new one, this time lined with a plastic bag.

"Are you feeling better?"

Richter nodded. "Yeah, it was just the shock. Any word?"

"It's been confirmed. There was a detonation. It will be hitting the news any moment now."

Richter glanced at the displays lining the wall with every major news network, one of them now showing a fireball erupting from the front of the Guggenheim. "Any word on the number of dead?"

"It's too soon. It's only been a couple of minutes. What do you think happened? Accidental detonation?"

Richter shook his head then dialed Peeters. He cursed, tossing the phone back on his desk. "Straight to voicemail." Peeters was dead, he was certain of it. When Acton had confronted him on the explosion, he wasn't sure what to believe. But he had compartmentalized his emotions and took advantage. What Peeters had done was an atrocity, though it had presented an opportunity.

Leverage. New leverage.

His leverage had been the hostages. As long as the professors thought those lives were at risk, they would do as they were told. The moment that explosion occurred, that leverage was gone.

But now he had it back, thanks to his quick thinking.

"What are you going to do?"

Richter regarded his trusted man, the closest thing he had to a friend in the world. "What do *you* think we should do?"

"I think we should walk away from this, sir. If you become implicated, you'll be going to prison for the rest of your life."

"But I didn't do it."

"Forgive me, sir, but I heard what you said before I could close the door. You just implied to two well-respected professors that you did."

Richter frowned as he leaned back. "Yeah, in retrospect that might not have been the wisest thing to say. I was thinking on my feet. I just didn't expect that explosion to happen so soon. I was hoping to leverage the fear of the explosion, and with them isolated, they might not discover the truth."

"What are you going to do?"

"I can't abandon this now. All those people are dead because of this. Some good might come of it if I get my hands on that Bible. I can sell it to the buyer, and we'll be able to save so many innocent animals from the proceeds, some good might come from this tragedy."

"Then we're proceeding?"

Richter drew a breath, steeling himself. He exhaled. "Yes, we are. Arrange everything as we discussed. Please tell me our people got the footage."

"They did, sir. Hacking the Guggenheim's system was child's play."

"Then post it. Make sure everybody sees what our fanatic professors did."

Guggenheim Bilbao
Bilbao, Spain

Liliana Sanchez's head pounded as she carefully picked her way through the devastation inside one of the world's most famous museums. She probably had a concussion, and was definitely in need of medical attention, but there was a job to do.

Suck it up.

It was stupid, but judging from the moans and groans surrounding her, there were people in much more need than her. She sidestepped what she assumed was an arm, though might have been a leg. She hated that she couldn't tell. It was carnage everywhere, unlike anything she had witnessed in her entire career. From the look of things, it had been some sort of shrapnel bomb designed to inflict maximum damage to flesh, not infrastructure.

Something moved to her left and she turned to see the scorched corpse of a man lying in a pile of bodies. Somebody was moving underneath him. "Give me a hand over here!" She stepped over the remains of a woman and took a knee beside the entangled bodies. With the help of one of her fellow officers, they gently rolled the man off of whoever was underneath. He groaned, causing them both to jump back. "Medic!"

Sanchez turned her attention to the relatively unscathed teenage girl that had been trapped underneath. A woman, her arm and leg draped over the girl, shrapnel mottling her side, moaned as they helped the girl to her feet.

"Are you okay?"

"Yeah, I think so."

"What's your name?"

"Petra. Petra Marchand." She suddenly noticed the two who had been draped over her. "Mom! Dad!"

Sanchez held her back as the paramedics tended to her parents.

"Are they going to be okay?"

"If they survived this, they could probably survive anything."

The young girl watched as her parents were loaded onto stretchers and rushed from the scene. "Wait, did you find my brother?"

"I'm not sure, but I'll check for you. What's his name?"

"Jean Luc Marchand."

Sanchez paused. "Wait, did you say your name is Petra Marchand?"

She nodded.

"Were you the one who was live streaming this?"

"Yes."

Sanchez smiled. "Good girl. Now, go with your parents. We'll look for your brother. If you're up to it, I want to ask you some questions later."

She shrugged. "Yeah, sure."

"Chief Inspector, you have to see this!"

She turned to have a tablet shoved in her face, a video playing that appeared to be security footage showing a man and a woman leaving a building then climbing into a waiting vehicle. "What am I looking at?"

"We think it's footage from one of the rear fire doors."

"Do we know who they are?"

Petra leaned in. "They're friends of my father's."

Sanchez looked at her. "Do you know their names?"

"Yeah, they're both professors. I think they're from America. I can't remember. Acton, I think? I can't remember her name."

"Get me the guest list."

The tablet was tapped a few times and handed back. She scrolled down and found the name. "Professor James Acton."

Petra's eyes widened. "Yeah! I think that's it. I think my dad called him Jim."

"And Professor Laura Palmer?"

"Yes, that's it, that's her."

"And you're telling me that those two people are friends of your father?"

"Yes, though I don't know how well he knows them. Actually, I think he met her for the first time tonight. I think he knows him from years ago."

"But they're friends?"

"Yeah."

Sanchez eyed her with a slight smile. "My kind of friends, or your kind of friends?"

"What do you mean?"

"Well, my kind of friends I've actually met and see them regularly. Your kind of friends are quite often ones you've never met, and you only know them from the Internet."

"Umm, I think it might be a little bit of both. I think he hasn't seen him in years."

"Okay, so your father invites these two, and they leave only minutes before the bomb explodes. And what's that they're carrying?"

Petra leaned in and shrugged. "I think it's the Bible that they were here for. My father showed it to me when we first arrived."

"Okay, you go get yourself checked out, then I'm going to have questions for you, okay?"

"Okay."

A man nearby groaned. Petra flinched. "Oh, *he's* alive. Great."

Sanchez immediately picked up on the disdain. "Is that a bad thing?"

"He's the leader."

"What?"

"He's the leader. He's the one who did all this."

Sanchez motioned to some paramedics and pointed at the suspect. "Check him out. And make sure he doesn't die. I want to find out what the hell is going on here." She shook the tablet. "And issue a warrant for Professors James Acton and Laura Palmer. There's no way they're not involved. And freeze all their accounts. I don't want them to have access to any money that might help them get away."

Reading Residence

Whitehall, London, England

Interpol Agent Hugh Reading leaped to his feet along with his son Spencer as they cheered England scoring a goal, a tie that had lasted until the last ten minutes of the game finally broken. Football might not be high scoring, but when one's team did, it made the entire wait worthwhile.

They both pounded their beers then sat back down. His phone vibrated on the table in front of them, and he picked it up to see a news alert about a bombing at the Guggenheim Bilbao.

His stomach churned as bile filled his mouth.

He grabbed the remote and switched to BBC News.

"Hey, what about the game?"

"There was a terrorist attack at the Guggenheim in Spain."

Spencer grunted. "What else is new?"

"You don't understand. Jim and Laura were there."

His son's jaw dropped. "What? Call them!"

Reading cursed for not thinking to do it himself. He dialed Acton's number and it went straight to voicemail. He tried Laura and found the same. He fell back on the couch, his chest tight, his ears pounding. "Oh my God, I think I just lost my best friends."

His son reached over and squeezed his arm. "You don't know that yet. Look." He pointed at the television. "They're bringing out somebody on a stretcher. They don't have him covered over. That means he's alive. There are survivors."

Reading struggled to control his emotions. He dialed his partner, Michelle Humphrey.

"Hi Hugh, a little late, isn't it? Aren't you off the clock?"

"Did you hear about the bombing in Spain?"

"Yeah, it just came up on my phone a moment ago."

He took a deep breath. "Jim Acton and Laura Palmer were there."

"Oh no! Are they okay?"

"I don't know." His voice cracked as his eyes burned. "I need to get there. I need to find out what's going on."

"Just a second, I'm logging into the office right now." He heard her tapping on her laptop, then a gasp. "Oh my God, you're not going to believe this."

He tensed. "What?"

"International arrest warrants have just been issued for them."

"For whom?"

"For your friends. Right now, Professor James Acton and Professor Laura Palmer are at the top of the Red Notices list as those behind the bombing of the Guggenheim."

Trinh/Granger Residence

St. Paul, Maryland

"I think that deserves a reward."

Tommy Granger smiled at his girlfriend, Mai Trinh, as she hugged him. Her wandering hand went unnoticed with visions of the car he might buy due to his recent work with the CIA. "I should be getting paid soon. We might be able to get that new car we've been dreaming about. That's reward enough."

"That would be nice." Mai ran a finger down his chest. "But that wasn't the reward I was thinking of."

He grinned at her and moved in for some nookie when his phone vibrated, followed several more times in rapid succession.

Mai stopped. "What's going on?"

"I don't know." He brought up his messages then popped over to his podcast's comments section and gasped as they rapidly rolled in. "Oh my God!"

"What?"

"The professors are wanted for mass murder!"

Mai pulled back. "What? Why?"

Tommy grabbed his laptop and checked Twitter, one of the better places to get unfiltered news quickly. It meant much of what was there was bullshit, but something like this would be trending if it were true. He gasped at what he saw. "There was a bombing at the Guggenheim in Spain. You know, that museum they were going to."

"To see that Bible?"

"Yeah."

"But why are they wanted for murder?"

"It says here they were seen leaving moments before the blast with the Bible. It says they're known animal rights fanatics. They think they blew up the gala to make a political statement."

"That's insane! We have to tell them that's insane!"

Tommy agreed. "It has to be a mistake. I'm going to try calling them." He dialed both their numbers, both going direct to voicemail as he continued to work his laptop. He tossed his phone on the couch beside him. "Voicemail." He gasped. "Oh my God, look at this!" He pulled up security camera footage showing the professors leaving the building, with the Bible, and climbing into a vehicle, the comments attached indicating it was taken only a few minutes before the blast.

"It's them!" Mai stared at the footage then replayed it. "And he has the Bible." She turned to him. "Could...could this be true?"

Tommy firmly shook his head. "No, there's no way that they're responsible for this. Something else is going on. You know that."

She nodded. "You're right, of course. What should we do?"

"Well, that footage has to be fake somehow. We need help."

"Who should we call?" Her eyes widened. "Dean Milton!"

Tommy smiled. "Good idea. You call him. I'm going to call someone else who might be able to analyze this footage."

"Who?"

"My *friend* at the CIA." He dialed the number and cursed.

"What?"

"It says the number is disconnected."

Milton Residence

St. Paul, Maryland

Gregory Milton expertly sliced the carrots then tossed them into the bowl with the potatoes, onions, and sweet potatoes, then drizzled olive oil over them before seasoning the mixture and tossing it all together several times. His back spasmed and he gasped, reaching behind to massage his still tender muscles.

"Are you okay?" asked his wife Sandra as she dried her hands on a dishcloth and rounded the kitchen island.

"Yeah, just overdoing it."

"You go sit down. I'll finish up."

He nodded, in no shape to protest.

"Daddy, are you okay?"

He forced a smile for his young daughter's sake. "Yes, sweetie, I'm okay. Just tired."

Niskha took his hand and led him into the family room where he sat in his chair. She pushed the ottoman closer and he put his feet up.

"Thanks, sweetie."

"Can I get you anything?"

"How about a hug?"

She leaped into his lap, squeezing him tight, his back protesting, but the pain worth it.

Sandra shooed her away. "Okay, that's enough, let your father rest."

"Yes, Mommy."

Niskha returned to the kitchen and hopped up on a stool at the breakfast bar, returning to her coloring as Milton massaged his back, first injured a few years ago when he had been shot twice, then again when he was beaten mercilessly a few months ago for information he had resisted giving up.

His life had been filled with hellish things, almost all due to his best friend's penchant for getting into trouble. He closed his eyes and tried to find a position where he could get comfortable, finally succeeding when his phone vibrated on the kitchen counter.

He opened his eyes. "Who is it?"

Sandra leaned over and checked the call display, her eyebrows shooting up in surprise. "It's Mai Trinh."

"Mai?" He beckoned her to bring him the phone and she grabbed it, walking it over to him.

"Has she ever called you before?"

"I don't think so." He took the phone and answered the call. "Hello?"

"Hello, Dean Milton, this is Mai Trinh."

"Hello, Miss Trinh. How can I help you?"

"Umm, have you seen the news, sir?"

He tensed, knowing his best friend was out of the country, which meant ample opportunity for trouble. "No, why."

"I think you should turn it on, sir. There's been a bombing at the Guggenheim in Spain."

His eyes shot wide and he leaped for the remote control, his back screaming in agony. "Oh my God! Are they okay?"

"Yes, well, no, well, they weren't killed, but the police are saying that they did it."

"What?" He turned on the TV, switching to the news, a commercial playing.

"According to the news, an international manhunt is on for them."

"What?" He paused. "Wait, if this is some kind of joke, I swear you're in serious trouble, young lady."

"No! I swear, it's the truth! Just turn on the TV!"

The commercial ended and any doubts he had were quashed with what he saw. The entire main level of the Guggenheim appeared a smoking wreck, fire crews still dousing the flames as rescue workers ferried the survivors and the dead out. The ticker scrolling across the bottom of the screen said at least 50 confirmed dead.

Then pictures of his two best friends appeared on the screen.

Known animal rights extremists.

Sandra stood beside him now, dinner prep forgotten. "Animal rights extremists?"

141

"Yeah, that doesn't make sense. Sure, they like animals, but they don't even have any pets. And aren't most animal rights activists supposed to be vegetarians or vegans? There's nothing Jim loves more than a good steak. There's something wrong here. Something's not right."

Sandra pointed at the screen. "Look at that! That's Jim's Facebook feed. Look at all those posts!"

Milton grabbed his tablet and brought up Facebook, tapping on Jim's smiling face in his friends list. It had exactly three posts, all automated from Facebook, with six friends—certainly no mention of any animal rights zealotry. "What the hell are they talking about? This doesn't look at all like what they're showing."

"Search it."

He jumped, forgetting he had a phone pressed to his ear. "What?"

"Don't bring him up from your friends list. Search for his name," explained Mai.

He tapped in the search box and entered his friend's name. It showed his listing, but there was another just below with the same profile picture. He tapped it and gasped. It was filled with the nonsense the news report had mentioned. "What the hell is going on here?"

Leroux/White Residence

Fairfax Towers, Falls Church, Virginia

"It's so nice to see all four of us together again."

CIA Analyst Supervisor Chris Leroux smiled at his girlfriend, CIA Agent Sherrie White, patting her leg, still reluctant to touch her after her recent ordeal. "Yup. It was rare enough on a good day. After everything that happened...well, you know."

His best friend, CIA Special Agent Dylan Kane, wrapped an arm around his girlfriend, Lee Fang, gently squeezing her, the former Chinese Special Forces operative still recovering from her own recent experiences. "We all got lucky."

Lee Fang agreed. "Some of us more than others. I don't recall seeing any real injuries on you."

Kane eyed her. "Did you see my body the next day? I was a mess."

Leroux grinned. "I didn't have a scratch!"

Sherrie punched his shoulder. "I took enough for both of us."

Leroux's phone vibrated in his lap and he checked the message, his eyes squinting at the report one of his decoy numbers had just received a phone call from a known contact.

Tommy Granger.

"What?" asked Kane, the trained agent detecting his friend's change in demeanor.

"Tommy Granger just called one of my decoy numbers."

"Has he ever called you before?" asked Fang.

"No, not unless I called him first." He frowned. "This is a little strange."

Sherrie shifted to face him. "Well, you better find out what's going on. There might be some emergency."

He dialed Tommy. The call was immediately answered, a tinge of fear in the greeting. "Hi Tommy, this is Chris Leroux."

"Oh thank God! I called your number, but it said it was out of service, so I thought I wouldn't be hearing from you."

"It's set up that way. I get notified when there are any calls to it."

"That's cool! How do you do that?"

He suppressed a smile at the tech geek's curiosity. "Is that why you called me, or is there something more important that merits this conversation?"

"Oh yeah, sorry, have you seen the news?"

"No, I haven't. Why, what's going on?" He grabbed the remote and turned on the TV, flipping to the news.

"There was a terrorist attack at the Guggenheim in Spain."

The footage on the screen put the conversation in perspective. "Why are you calling me about this?"

"Because Professors Acton and Palmer are being accused of being behind the attack."

Leroux's eyebrows shot up. "What! Just a second. I'm putting you on speaker with Dylan, Sherrie, and Fang." He tapped his phone then placed it on the table. "Say that again."

"Professor Acton and Professor Palmer are wanted as suspects involved in the bombing. They're saying they did it."

Kane leaned forward. "That's bullshit."

"I know that, and you know that, but that's not what the police are saying. Apparently, there's a huge manhunt on for them now. Spanish police are setting up roadblocks throughout the region, and every car is being searched leaving Bilbao. As far as the world is concerned, they committed this terrorist attack because this Bible was made of calf's skin and they're animal rights radicals."

Kane leaned back, stunned. "What? Where are they getting this garbage from?"

"I'm looking at what appears to be Professor Acton's Facebook page, and it's loaded with all kinds of insane stuff. And Professor Palmer's is the same. But these aren't their accounts. They're fake accounts. The press is reporting on these clone accounts. They have a lot of followers. It makes no sense. You know how he feels about social media. He hates it."

Kane's head bobbed. "That's true. He even rejected my friend request."

Fang patted his hand. "You're not serious."

"Well, he didn't reject it, but he didn't accept it. I'm not sure if he knows how. I think he said he has like six friends."

"Is there anything you can do?" asked Tommy. "Maybe tell the authorities that they're wrong?"

Security footage appeared showing the professors leaving the back of the museum, Acton gripping the Bible, and both of them climbing into the back of a van.

"Holy shit!" exclaimed Sherrie. "Are we sure they're innocent?"

"What do you mean?" asked Tommy.

"We just saw footage of them stealing the Bible."

"Yeah, I saw that too. It has to be a fake. They can do that sort of thing now with a deep fake. Is there any way you guys can analyze it?"

Leroux nodded. "I'll get my team on it right away. If you hear anything else or hear from them, let me know. If they're not involved—"

"Which they're not."

"I know, I said *if*. Look, I know, you're right, I don't believe for a second that they are involved. If this footage is genuine, then either they were trying to escape and save the Bible, or they were coerced into leaving with it. We need to figure out which one. For now, if neither of those are true, and it is a fake, then we have to prepare ourselves for the fact they may be dead."

"Part of me wishes they were behind the bombing, if that's the alternative."

Kane grunted. "I understand that feeling. If they did take the Bible for whatever reason, innocent or otherwise, right now, the police believe they are responsible for over fifty murders. The safest thing for them to do is to turn themselves in. If you hear from them, tell them that, and if they're afraid, have them contact me and I'll arrange a safe pickup and handover."

"Can you go there? Can you help them?"

Kane looked at Fang, concern in his eyes. She patted his knee. "I'm fine. You go help your friends. I'll be okay. Besides, Sherrie can take care of me."

Sherrie laughed, raising a weak hand. "Don't worry, I've got this."

Kane leaned closer to the phone. "Okay, I'm heading to Europe now. Chris is going to go into the office and have his team examine that footage, and see what the source of the fake social media accounts might be. You sit tight and let us know if you find out anything."

"Yes, sir."

Leroux ended the call then pointed at the screen. "They just updated the death toll to sixty."

"Unbelievable!" gasped Fang. "I don't really know them that well. Do you think they could be behind this?"

Kane shook his head. "No way. Impossible. But there's no way the world is going to listen to us. We're going to have to figure out who's actually behind this. We have to prove their innocence, because right now the entire world thinks they're guilty."

Bilbao, Spain

Acton needed time to think. They had been told to drive north until they reached the coast. That hadn't taken long, and from all appearances, they were just ahead of the roadblocks. Laura guided them into a parking lot and between two large vehicles, turning off the engine and the lights, but leaving the satellite news channel they had been listening to on, reports still pouring in about the horrors they had narrowly escaped.

And the fact the world was after them.

"What should we do?" asked Laura.

He sighed. "I don't know. I wish we had our phones. We could call Hugh or Dylan."

"I could go make a call."

"What if he calls us when you're gone?"

"Why don't we just use his phone?"

Acton shook his head. "No, we can't do that, it could be cloned."

"What do you mean?"

"I read somewhere that they can actually clone your phone so that another phone will receive all the same phone calls and text messages as yours. If we did anything on this phone, they could know, and they might kill other people."

She growled in frustration. "We have to do something. We're innocent!"

"You and I know that, but right now the world thinks we're guilty. We have to trust that our friends will set things straight. As soon as they find out, they'll take action."

"And in the meantime?"

He blew air through his lips, causing them to vibrate. "In the meantime, we have to make sure we don't get anyone else killed and do exactly as we're told."

"What do you think he's going to have us do?"

"He's going to have us deliver that Bible into his hands, or the hands of someone that works for him. And we're going to have to make sure that happens without getting caught or shot, or getting anyone else killed."

Laura stared at him. "You realize what that means, don't you? It means that we're going to prove to the world that we're guilty of mass murder."

He frowned. "You're right, but I don't see that we have any other choice."

"Our lives could be destroyed."

"We're innocent."

"The Internet never forgets."

He threw his head back against the seat. "God, I hate that damned thing."

"You and me both." She sighed. "You're right. We have to do what they say, and hope our friends can save us before it's too late."

1st Special Forces Operational Detachment—Delta

Fort Bragg, North Carolina

A.k.a. "The Unit"

Command Sergeant Major Burt "Big Dog" Dawson started flipping the two-dozen burgers and equal number of hot dogs grilling over two oil drum barbecues, as Bravo Team and their families enjoyed a glorious spring day behind the Unit. He was the leader of the team, a group of elite Special Forces operators and part of 1st Special Forces Operational Detachment—Delta, commonly known as Delta Force.

A military family that had each other's backs, and would do anything for their Unit and country, including laying down their lives.

But today, they were traditional family men. Some with wives and children, others with girlfriends, others chronically single like Sergeant Carl "Niner" Sung, putting on a hitting clinic with the kids.

Maggie Harris, his fiancée, left the table of better halves and joined him. "Need a hand?"

"I got it. How are you feeling?"

"A little tired."

"Do you want to go home?"

"No, but next time we have a barbeque to go to, I'm cutting you off at one go around."

He grinned. "Sorry about that."

"No, you're not."

"No, I'm not."

"Listen, when we get home, maybe—"

He held up a finger, cutting her off as he cocked an ear, catching the tail-end of a breaking news report. He pointed at the radio sitting on a nearby bench. "Somebody turn that up!"

Niner jogged over and cranked the volume, everyone stopping what they were doing except the kids.

"—are wanted in connection to the terrorist attack at the Guggenheim in Bilbao, Spain that has killed at least sixty and injured scores more."

"Is the religion of peace behaving badly again?" asked Sergeant Leon "Atlas" James, his impossibly deep voice drowning out the radio.

Dawson shook his head. "No, I could have sworn they just said the Doc and his wife are responsible."

"What?" exclaimed half those there. His entire team hauled out their phones and started tapping away, Dawson not bothering as he kept his attention on the burgers and hot dogs he was responsible for.

"Holy shit!" cried Sergeant Will "Spock" Lightman. "It says it right here. Professor James Acton and his wife Professor Laura Palmer, well-known animal rights radicals, are wanted in connection with the bombing

152

of the Guggenheim Bilbao earlier today. Security footage shows the two escaping moments before the detonation that killed over sixty people gathered for the unveiling of a controversial Bible recently discovered in northern France. The Bible has been condemned by animal rights activists due to the fact it was hand-drawn on vellum, which is made from calfskin. Experts say the thousand-page Bible would have required the slaughter of at least five-hundred animals." He looked up. "It goes on from there."

Niner walked over. "I didn't know the Doc was an animal rights extremist."

Dawson shook his head. "He's not. I've read his file. We've all read his file. Both of their files. Something doesn't smell right." His phone vibrated and he answered it. "Speak."

"Hey, BD, it's Dylan. Have you heard the news?"

"Yeah, assuming you're talking about the Doc and his wife. It was just on the radio. What do you know?"

"Not much. Leroux is heading into the office to have his team check out that footage. We're hoping it's a deep fake, but then if it is, they might be dead."

"Yeah, but if it's not a fake, then it doesn't make them look too good. Any thoughts on why they might have taken it?"

"No, I'm operating under the assumption that they're completely innocent. All that we've been able to come up with is that they were either escaping to save themselves and they took the Bible to save it as well, or they were coerced into it."

"Look at this," said Niner, handing his phone to Dawson, the security footage in question playing.

"There's a problem with one of your theories."

"What's that?" asked Kane.

"Where did they get the keys?"

"What?"

"The keys. Where did they get them? He handed them to her before they drove away."

"Huh. I missed that. Well, that definitely kills one of our theories, doesn't it? If they weren't saving themselves and the Bible, then that means they have to have been coerced."

Dawson watched the footage again. "They haven't turned themselves in yet, have they?"

"No, not as far as I know."

"Well, that seems more in line with them being coerced by someone. We're going to have to figure out who."

"I'm heading to Spain now."

"Sanctioned?"

"Nope. Got any leave coming to you?"

Dawson laughed. "I think I might have a day or two in the bank. I'll talk to the colonel and see if I can get a few days off."

"Sounds good. Maybe bring a few of the others with you. I have a funny feeling we might need more than two guns."

"I'll see what I can do. Can you equip us when we get there?"

Kane laughed. "Can I equip you? Have we met?"

Dawson chuckled. "I know, I know, I should realize you have weapons caches all over the damned world."

"Well, I was a Boy Scout, and I do believe in being prepared."

"Okay, I'll give you a shout back once I get things arranged at this end."

"Copy that."

Dawson ended the call and faced his men, all gathered around him now.

"What's the word?" asked Niner.

"I need three volunteers."

Everybody raised a hand, including his young godson Bryson.

He smiled. "Why do you guys always make is so damned difficult. Okay, Niner, Atlas, Spock, and Bryson, you're with me, assuming the colonel approves everything."

Bryson grinned. "Does this mean I get a second hot dog?"

Reading Residence

Whitehall, London, England

"I wish I could go with you."

Hugh Reading shook his head at Spencer. "No, you've got your job. Besides, there's nothing you could do there. I don't need anybody watching my back. I just need to get down there and figure out why my two best friends in the world are animal rights activists who just massacred over sixty people."

His phone rang and he glanced at the call display. "It's Michelle." He answered. "Michelle, tell me the good news."

"I've got approval for us to represent Interpol."

His eyes narrowed. "Us?"

"Us. There's no way I'm letting you go down there on your own in your emotional state."

He grunted. "Yeah, I suppose you're right. When do we leave?"

"Not until morning. The last flight left hours ago."

He stared at the suitcase he'd been packing in a rush. "Bloody hell." He sat on the corner of the bed. "Anything new?"

"I've been monitoring all the reports. All we know so far is that it appears the terrorist leader survived the blast, but he's in surgery right now. They don't know if he's going to make it."

He rolled his eyes. "Normally, I'd be rooting for him to die, but he might be the only one who can prove that Jim and Laura had nothing to do with this. Anything else?"

"You wouldn't believe the list of billionaires and millionaires and Hollywood types that are dead. It's like a who's who from the society pages."

"Anybody I actually care about?"

"Knowing you, probably not, but so far Jim and Laura are not on that list of dead or survivors, so the chances of that footage being fake are next to none now. They seem to have a body count that is pretty close to the number that matches the invite list."

"What about the guy who invited them? Did he survive?"

"What was his name?"

He cursed. "I can't remember. Oh, just a second." He pulled up a text message from Acton. "It's Professor Yves Marchand."

"Give me a moment...oh, here he is. He's in surgery. Wife and daughter expected to survive. The wife was seriously injured, and his son is missing."

"We need to talk to him. See if you can arrange it for when we arrive."

"I'm on it. See you tomorrow."

He ended the call and turned to his son. "I'm sorry we missed the end of the game."

"No worries, Dad, I think you've got a pretty good excuse this time."

Reading sighed as he thought of his friends. "I guess I do."

The Unit

Fort Bragg, North Carolina

"Have a moment, Colonel?"

Colonel Thomas Clancy looked up from his computer and waved Command Sergeant Major Dawson in. "I thought you were at the barbecue?"

"I was, but something's come up."

Clancy motioned to the chair in front of his desk and tapped his radio. "I assume you're talking about our professor friends who are in it up to their necks again, and that you and your men want to go gallivanting off to save the day?"

Dawson grinned. "You know me so well, sir. Kane's already on his way—"

Clancy's eyebrows shot up. "He is? Sanctioned?"

"Nope."

"Figures. The day he left the Unit was a good day for my hairline."

"I'd like to take credit for a couple of inches, sir."

"Careful. I just might reassign you." Clancy leaned back in his chair. "Okay, give me the skinny."

"I want to take Niner, Atlas, and Spock with me to Spain. We'll rendezvous with Kane. He'll equip us. We'll all use vacation time, pay for our own tickets. Nothing to tie back to the Unit or the government."

"And your mission?"

"Our primary mission is to find the professors and safely bring them in to the authorities before they get themselves killed."

"Sounds reasonable. And the second?"

"Find out who's responsible, and either take them down, or let the authorities know where to find them."

"And that's where things get sketchy. I can't have you guys off in Europe shooting people."

Dawson put on his best whiny voice. "Aww, but they'd be bad guys." It didn't work.

Clancy rolled his eyes. "They always are. But if you encounter armed police, what are you going to do?"

"Surrender, of course."

"Exactly. Then you get identified and I lose what's left of my hair trying to deal with it. No. Find the professors, hand them over safely. If you succeed, contact me and we'll go from there. Understood?"

"Yes, sir!"

Operations Center 2, CIA Headquarters
Langley, Virginia

Chris Leroux entered the state of the art operations center, noting only a few of the team had made it in so far, including his top analyst, Sonya Tong.

"Thanks for coming in, everyone. I know it's your day off, but the professors have helped us in the past, and we're convinced they're getting railroaded."

"No problem," said Tong. "Weekends are for wusses."

Leroux smiled. "That's the spirit!" He dropped his bag at his station at the center of the room and became all business. "What have we got so far?"

Tong pointed at the displays wrapping around the front of the room. "I've got the computer running an analysis on the security camera footage. When Randy gets in, he'll pull it apart. That's his area of expertise, but so far, I'm not seeing any discrepancies or anything to suggest this is anything but genuine."

"What about on the scene? Have they found them? If it's fake, then they're still inside."

"No, there's still a lot of bodies they haven't identified yet. Somebody leaked a list that the police have been putting together. Now the press is going apeshit because it's a who's who of Forbes and Hollywood."

Leroux frowned. "So, they haven't identified them among the survivors or the dead."

"No. And this list is pretty complete. It looks like they used shrapnel bombs. Just IEDs on a remote trigger. We're not sure yet why it was detonated when it was. They're interviewing witnesses, but I haven't been able to access any of that information yet. State has someone on the way there since there were so many of our people involved, so hopefully we'll have more answers shortly."

Leroux sat. "We need to find out why they left only minutes before. We all know they're innocent. I want to know why their Facebook profiles look like they're eco-terrorists. Tommy Granger says that they're cloned. Take a look and see. I want to know when they were created, who created them. I want to know everything there is to know about those profiles. And I want every damned camera we have access to in that city looking for them. If they left that museum, they had to go somewhere. I want to know where they went before the Spaniards find them."

"We're on it."

Leroux rose. "I'm going to go brief the chief."

"He's in?"

"I'm not sure, but I saw his car. I think I heard his wife is visiting her sister, so you know when his house is empty, he lives here."

Unknown Location

"I've made the arrangements. The flight has been booked through our usual proxies with our usual crew. I'll make sure the locals know tomorrow that we have a special delivery. We'll be able to send them anywhere you want."

Richter paused. "You're not letting the locals know tonight?"

"I felt it was best to wait. Even though this is one of our regular routes, with this all over the news, I figured it was best not to give them any time to speculate, then get any inconvenient ideas."

Richter smiled. "Good thinking. I want you to make the exchange."

Gerhard's eyebrows shot up, a rare expression of surprise from his longtime companion. "Me?"

"You're the only one I trust."

"Very well. Where?"

Richter chewed his cheek. "I'm thinking Rome. It's a short flight for them and you, and we've used it for exchanges before. Arrange it, but don't leave until we know they're in the air. No point having you leave if something goes wrong between now and then."

"Very well, sir."

Richter grabbed his phone. "Now to give our professors their destination."

Bilbao, Spain

Acton listened to the newscast on the car radio, shaking his head along with Laura. The reports were disturbing, horrifying, and all he could think about was what had happened to Marchand and his family.

And the fact the world thought they were responsible.

The phone rang, signaling the next stage of this horror.

"Hello?"

"Hello, Professor Acton. I want you to get to La Rochelle."

Acton looked at Laura who shrugged. "Where the hell is that?"

"Southern France, on the coast."

"How are we supposed to do that? According to the radio, there are roadblocks everywhere, and the police are looking for us."

"I don't care how you do it, Professor Acton, but I would suggest you go by boat."

"Boat?"

"Boat."

The call ended.

Acton slammed his head against the back of his seat. "How the hell do we get a boat?"

"Rent one?"

"Do you really want to use a credit card? They're probably watching those." He paused. "We could call your travel agent."

Laura shook her head. "I don't want her getting in trouble. I've got a little cash, but not much."

He cursed. "There's no way we're renting a boat to take to France."

"Then what should we do?"

He shrugged. "Well, we're already wanted for terrorism and mass murder. What more can they do to us?"

"You're not suggesting what I think you're suggesting."

He winked. "Argh! Let's be pirates!"

Director Morrison's Office, CIA Headquarters

Langley, Virginia

"Dylan is already on his way to Spain, unsanctioned, of course. He's still on personal leave."

Director Leif Morrison, National Clandestine Service Chief for the CIA, sat behind his desk as Leroux briefed him. His frown contradicted his words. "I don't care what he does on his personal time, as long as he doesn't go shooting up the place in our name. You know him."

Leroux chuckled. "What about my team?"

"Go ahead and work it. We've got extremely important Americans dead, so we'd have somebody on this anyway. It might as well be your team."

"But we can't sanction Dylan?"

Morrison grunted. "It's one thing to be tapping security feeds and analyzing intel, it's another thing to have an armed agent running around the Spanish countryside."

"Understood."

"We'll activate him if we need to. I'm still hoping this is a terrorist attack by a known group, and our professors are just patsies."

"You don't believe they're guilty either?"

Morrison shook his head. "Not for a second. Anybody who knows those two knows this is bullshit."

"Maybe someone should tell the Europeans."

"I have no doubt they'll be informed, but right now, the Spanish are out for blood. They can't risk it looking like they're not taking action. Not when this footage showing two people leaving moments before with a priceless artifact is out there. We need to find them and bring them in safely, and find out what the hell is actually going on. If we don't, more innocent people are going to die."

Bilbao, Spain

Acton struggled to steady his pace, his adrenaline insisting he walk far faster than the others out for casual strolls near the marina. Laura was helping by holding his hand and gently tugging it backward to keep him on pace. How she was remaining so calm during all this he wasn't sure, but he admired her for it.

Perhaps it was because she wasn't holding a 75 pound Bible, in two halves, under her right arm, all the while attempting to make it appear inconspicuous.

She was probably thinking more clearly. His mind was preoccupied with Marchand and his family, but without the personal connection, he had no doubt she was keeping things a little more straight in her head.

Like pointing out the fact they could see a marina with scores of boats moored not 200 feet from where they had been parked.

"Look," hissed Laura, indicating with her chin where she wanted him to direct his attention. He spotted a man refueling a boat, his coveralls indicating he was a marina employee. They sat on a bench and observed for several minutes, a plan slowly formulating in his muddled brain. When the dockhand was finished, he started up the boat and returned it to a slip at the far end, walked back, and put the key in the boathouse, a rack visible from their vantage point. Another key was taken, and the man headed to the opposite end to fetch the next boat.

He glanced at Laura. "Are you thinking what I'm thinking?"

"Grand theft boat? Yes. Are you sure?"

He rose. "Yes. Let's do this fast, though."

They walked through the gate and toward the boathouse as if they owned the place. Laura opened the door while he stood watch, the honor system apparently employed as the dockhand hadn't bothered locking the building housing dozens of keys to millions of dollars of boats. She emerged a moment later with a smile, gently closing the door behind her. They walked toward the boat at the far end of the dock, unnoticed, and climbed aboard.

And within minutes, they were not only wanted terrorists, but thieves as well, Acton guiding the boat out of the marina and toward the Atlantic Ocean only minutes away. As he familiarized himself with the boat's controls, he pointed at the navigation system. "See if you can figure that thing out. We need to get to La Rochelle."

Laura had it figured out within minutes and frowned. "If this is right, it says we won't arrive until mid-morning."

"Ugh. I'm exhausted as it is."

"Do you want me to do that?"

He shook his head. "No, but I think it's best if we get twelve miles offshore so we're in international waters. I think this thing can handle it."

She sat and pulled off her high heels, moaning in relief. "I forgot how much I hate these things."

Acton glanced at her feet as she rubbed them. "I can't remember the last time you wore heels."

"Not very practical at the dig site." She leaned over and grabbed something stowed on a shelf near her.

"What's that?"

"It's the manual for the nav system." She scanned the table of contents and smiled. "This thing has an autopilot."

Acton spun his hand at her. "Well, get a move on, babe. We need to find out where Otto is!"

She stared at him. "Huh?"

Acton rolled his eyes. "If we get out of this, we're watching Airplane! when we get home."

"Very well."

She didn't seem enthused.

He pointed at the manual in her lap. "Oh, and if this thing does have an Otto, you're blowing him up."

"What the devil are you talking about?"

He grinned as he stared out the window at the ocean ahead, saying nothing.

Trinh/Granger Residence

St. Paul, Maryland

Tommy Granger continued to work his laptop, digging deeper and deeper into the fake accounts created for the professors, continually shaking his head in awe of how far back the deception went. His custom designed algorithms were already scraping social media, grabbing the profiles of the followers of the fake accounts, and drilling deeper to find out any connections that might lead to who was behind this.

"Unbelievable," he muttered.

"What?"

"Well, I'm looking at these so-called friends they've got. They each have thousands of people that they like, all kinds of groups and pages that they follow and like, and there seems to be all kinds of common threads. When you go through them, there are hundreds that seem to like almost all the same things, and when you put them all together as a whole, there's no six degrees of separation here, it's two or three at most."

"What does that mean?"

"It means these are all fake accounts. We already know the professors' accounts are fake, but all their friends are fake as well. The pages and groups have so many fake accounts with links to the same posts and whatnot, that it looks like they were created by someone who wasn't too concerned about anyone diving too deeply into them."

Mai scrunched her nose. "What does that mean?"

"It means they probably never thought anyone would actually look. It's all meant for show. These pages and groups look like they have all kinds of support, but the reality is they don't. It's all fake."

"All?"

"Well, mostly. There are legit followers, but they're probably only doing that because they think what they're following is legit. If none of those fake accounts were linked, it would look like a one-man-band. Instead, it looks like an orchestra."

"Who would do that?"

He shrugged. "Well, not the government. It's not the Russians or Chinese. They'd be more careful, and I don't think they'd care about these causes enough to try and discredit them. I think this is some private group that's created this. It's all kinds of different social causes that they're all linked to. Quite often, what these groups do is they create fake accounts to make themselves appear more popular than they actually are. More important than they actually are. You don't have much legitimacy if you only have five followers on a page. Have a thousand or ten thousand, and suddenly you've got something that if people stumble upon it, they think, 'oh, this must be legit because look at how many people like it.' Last year, Facebook removed over three billion fake accounts in just six months. Can you imagine? This is why social media is so dangerous. Too many people think that what they're seeing is legit, when so much of it is bullshit created by bad actors or activists."

Mai cut off his diatribe before it could really get going. "So, what does this *mean?*"

"It means that somebody has spent a lot of time creating these profiles, and they're trying to frame the professors."

Mai's eyes narrowed. "But how would they know they'd be there? Didn't they just get the invitations a week ago? How long have they been setting up these profiles?"

"It looks like they've been setting them up for years. But all they need to do is change the profile photo and the name, and away you go."

"This *is* unbelievable. You need to send this information to your friend."

He pursed his lips, suddenly insecure. "Oh, the people on his team probably already know this."

Mai leaned over and squeezed his leg. "You're as good as any of them, if not better. Do you really want to risk them not knowing this right away?"

He flushed at the praise, and the love in her eyes. "You're right. I'll send it now."

Operations Center 2, CIA Headquarters

Langley, Virginia

Leroux skimmed the message from Tommy, shaking his head at how good the kid was. If it weren't for the young man's questionable teenage undertakings, he'd hire him tomorrow to work for him.

But today, he'd happily accept his pro bono work.

He hit a few keys, sending the message to Tong. "Sonya, I just sent you something from Tommy Granger. The kid's done on his laptop what we've barely begun."

Tong brought up the message and read through it, a smile spreading. "He's basically proven the accounts are fake, along with tens of thousands of other ones. Unbelievable."

Leroux agreed. "Double-check it, then bump it up the chain. Let's see if we can get these accounts traced by the social media companies, and get them blocked so they don't do any more damage. If we're lucky, some good might come of this."

"I'm on it."

Bilbao, Spain

Sanchez parked on the street then strode toward the bustle of activity. The van the professors had escaped in had been found, and her people were going over it now with a fine-toothed comb. If they were lucky, they might find some clue as to where the professors were heading.

For they were heading somewhere, and that route was obviously well-planned. They had escaped moments before the blast, had made it past the police blockades because they hadn't been properly set up yet, and had arrived here, undetected. Her guess was they had switched into another vehicle and were long gone, but the entire region was being cordoned off, and they wouldn't be getting through.

It was only a matter of time.

"What have we got?"

The scene commander pointed at the van. "This is the terrorists' vehicle. Security camera footage confirms it arrived at the museum only moments before the attack began. Six people exited, and it was left near the rear entrance. The man you've identified as the leader was already inside, and he let them in through a locked fire exit. Approximately fifteen minutes—"

"Yes, I know all that. The professors leave, with the keys, get in, then wind up here at some point. Any idea where they went from here? Were they met?"

"We're pulling camera footage, but I think we know where they went."

Her eyebrows popped. "Where?"

He pointed toward a marina. "One of my guys just reported that a boat was stolen less than an hour after the bombing."

She turned to where he was pointing. "That's too much of a coincidence."

"Agreed."

"Okay, let's find that boat."

Bay of Biscay

"I think that's it."

Laura stepped back from the navigation system and Acton let go of the wheel, everything remaining steady. They were in international waters, the course plotted suggested they'd remain that way, and would be in La Rochelle, France by morning.

Assuming everything continued to function, and they weren't intercepted on the high seas.

"Okay, let's take inventory to see what we have to work with. We're going to need to feed ourselves and get some rest if we're going to have any hope tomorrow morning."

"What if we get caught?" asked Laura as she double-checked the autopilot.

He shrugged. "Then it's out of our hands, isn't it?"

"But he said he'd kill people."

He frowned. "If it's not our fault, then I can't see him doing that. What are we supposed to do? Outrun the Coast Guard or whatever they call it here? If we're going to succeed in the morning, then we have to be prepared."

Laura sighed. "I can't believe this is happening. I hate to think what is being said about us."

Acton gave her a hug. "Let's just stay alive, follow his instructions, and hopefully Hugh and Dylan can figure a way out of this for us."

"If they even know."

"Trust me. You saw that explosion. There's no way they don't know. Not only were our names on the radio, Hugh knew we were going to that event. The moment he heard about the explosion, he would have tried calling us. They took our phones, so when he couldn't reach us, you know he started making calls. Trust me, he's on it, and that's all I need to know to keep going."

She squeezed him tight. "I hope you're right."

So do I.

Bilbao, Spain

"This is the dockhand. He's the one who reported the boat stolen."

Sanchez smiled at the young man, clearly terrified at the number of police swarming the marina for what he likely thought was a simple boat theft. "I'm Chief Inspector Sanchez. Why don't you tell me what you know?"

He shrugged. "Well, I was refueling the boats, and I came back to get the key for the next one when I noticed one of the keys was missing."

"How did you notice that? I imagine you have quite a few."

"I had just refueled it."

"Okay, then what?"

"Well, I checked, and sure enough, the boat was gone."

"And how do you know it wasn't just the owner taking it out?"

He shifted his weight to his other foot. "Well, the owner wouldn't have taken my key. The keys I have are so that I can service the boats. They have their own keys for when they want to take their boat out."

Sanchez's head bobbed as she learned something she hadn't known. "Okay, that makes sense. So, this boat, you noticed it missing, then what?"

"I called the police immediately, then I called the owner."

"And the owner's name?"

"Mateo Fernandez."

"Is he coming?"

"No, I wasn't able to reach him. I left a message on his voicemail. I seem to remember hearing that he was in the United States on business, so I'm not sure when he'll be able to get back."

"And this boat, what can you tell me about it?"

A smile spread. "It's incredible. A fifty-footer, fully equipped, fully stocked. You could live on that thing for weeks if you wanted to. They keep it prepped for long trips. He likes to go up and down the coast and park off of different cities. He does it for weeks at a time."

"So he's rich?"

He grunted. "Very. I think he's actually getting an even bigger boat. I know I heard him talking that when he retires, he just wants to sell everything and live on a boat with a crew."

"Must be nice."

"You're telling me." The young man sighed. "That's the most difficult thing about working here. I get paid a pittance by people who could buy me a million times over."

Sanchez sympathized. "That's the world we live in."

"Yeah, like it or not."

"So, you're sure this guy's in the US and wasn't at the Guggenheim?"

He shrugged. "I'm not sure about anything. I just think I heard mention of it. You'd have to talk to him to be sure." He eyed her. "Why? Did something happen? Did he do something?"

"You haven't heard?"

He threw a hand at the boats behind him. "I've been working my ass off all evening. The rich are out on their boats all day long, then they come back here and go to their luxury condos or their five-star hotels or their fancy dinners, and that's when I have time to service these things. I haven't heard anything."

"There was a terrorist attack at the museum. Over sixty people were killed."

His jaw dropped and his eyes shot wide. "Oh my God! That's horrible!" He looked about as he regained control. "And you think there's some connection to this stolen boat?"

"The vehicle the two terrorists escaped in was found near here, and the timing with the theft matches up. We need to find that boat."

"Well, it could be anywhere by now. It's a straight shot from here out to the Atlantic Ocean. The Bay of Biscay, you can see it from here."

"Do you have security cameras here?"

He nodded. "I've already called my boss. He should be here any minute now. I don't have access to that kind of thing. I'm just a dockhand."

"Fine." She pointed at one of the officers. "Give him a description of the boat. Everything you can tell us about it. Registry, color, everything."

"Yes, ma'am."

She walked away with the scene commander. "As soon as you get access to that footage, I want to see if our professors stole themselves a boat. I may not know where every single police station is in Spain, but I can guarantee you none of them are easier to access by boat. These people are on the run. They are not looking to turn themselves in. That means they're as guilty as sin."

Frankish Burgundy

716 AD

"These are the ones who found him."

Martinus looked up from his forge, forcing a smile as the village priest approached with another man, clothed as a simple monk. His chest tightened as he thought back on the young man who had died in this very home several months ago. He had done his duty, informed everyone of the man's demise, and helped bury him. Father Marellus had been given a full account upon his return, lest one thing.

No mention was made of the Bible.

In the two weeks before the vile man had returned, word had reached the town of the party of monks having been slaughtered mercilessly, and talk had turned to the Bible.

Then several uncomfortable questions had been posed of him.

Who was this monk that had died in his home? Why had he come there of all places? Was he a survivor, or someone else who had stumbled upon the attack?

Then the most disturbing of all, posed by a wretch who enjoyed stirring up trouble.

Where were you when they were attacked?

It wasn't the question that had disturbed him the most, it was the others that had gathered agreeing that the question should be asked.

His wife's grip on his arm had tightened, and he knew she was as terrified as he was at the turn of events. "He came the same morning he died, asking for his horse to be watered. I tended to his horse while my wife fed him, as any good Christian would, then he left. He must have been attacked along with the others, then the horse carried him back to where it had last been fed. There's no mystery here, you fool. You saw his wound. It was a miracle he lasted as long as he did. We all know who did this. It was those men that arrived that same morning, looking for them. To Hell with any of you who would think I had something to do with it!"

That had silenced them all, and he had returned home with his wife.

"What do we do?" she asked.

"What can we do? If we tell them of the Bible, it's only our word that it is another copy."

"But it isn't ours. We can't keep it."

"But if we reveal that we have it, they'll think I killed those monks and stole it. We'll be hanged for sure, if not worse."

"We should burn it!"

186

He gasped. "That would be blasphemy! The eternal damnation of Hell will be our reward in the end."

She sighed. "Then what do we do? We can't keep it here. What if someone finds it?"

"We must hide it."

"But where? If they get suspicious, they might search the house."

He thought for a moment, scratching his chin. Then smiled. "I know exactly where it will be safe, and no one will ever find it."

He shook the memories as Father Marellus and the monk approached him. His foot scraped against the base of his forge as his wife emerged from inside to greet their guests, their newborn daughter in her arms. The monk bowed to them.

"I am Brother Olin from Wearmouth-Jarrow Abbey in Northumbria. I understand a monk died here several months ago?"

Martinus nodded. "Aye, he did. It was a most troubling experience, I can assure you."

"I have no doubt. To die is one thing. But to die under such circumstances is an entirely different matter. I take some comfort in knowing he did not die alone, and that he died with strangers as kind as you, and apparently familiar to him."

"We did have the privilege of having him as our guest that morning. He was a very pleasant man. An excellent Christian, and a fine representative of your abbey."

Olin bowed deeply. "You humble me with your kind words." The man hesitated. "Did he mention anything that, well, in retrospect might have seemed curious?"

Martinus tensed. "Such as?"

"Well, I'll try to be delicate here. A letter was found on the person of our abbot, who was murdered with the others. It made it to us only a month ago. It made mention that Brother Arledge was carrying something of importance. If you had found it on his person, I have no doubt that as good Christians you would have informed the Father here. But since you didn't, then I must assume he did not have it with him."

Martinus tensed. "He had nothing but the clothes on his back when he died, I'm afraid. Everything else was on his horse, which I turned over to Father Marellus as soon as he returned from Paris."

Marellus took a step closer. "This is true. He was at my door almost the moment I returned. He had tended to the horse as if it were his own, and kept your brother's possessions in good order, as I showed you."

"Yes, and the item I'm looking for was not among those items, unfortunately."

Martinus cleared his throat, hesitant to say more than was necessary, yet a thought had occurred to him that might help divert any suspicion away from him and his wife. "If he were killed by the same men that murdered those other monks, perhaps they stole whatever it was you seek?"

Olin's head bobbed, a frown creasing his face. "Yes, that unfortunately is the conclusion I've come to as well. I was hoping against all logic that perhaps he had been able to hide it somewhere, and had made mention of its location to you in his dying moments."

"I'm afraid he was too weak by the time he reached us. He said nothing of anything hidden."

Olin eyed him. "But he *did* say something?"

Martinus cursed himself for the poor choice of words, and his wife stepped closer, wrapping an arm around his.

"I'm afraid the poor boy was delirious. My husband carried him from the horse and into our house. He lay him on the bed, and within moments he was dead. All he managed to say was something like, 'they killed my friends,' or some words to that effect. He was dead so quickly, there was nothing anyone could do. His robes were soaked in his own blood. I think the Good Lord wished him to be among familiar faces when he died, rather than alone on the road."

Olin smiled. "With him so far from home, the kindness you had shown him that morning would have made you the closest thing to friends he would have in these parts. I am pleased his final moments were spent among good Christians such as yourselves, as opposed to the end of the blade as wielded by the heathens that committed the atrocity that day." He bowed. "I wish you well. You will be in my prayers tonight."

They both returned the bow. "You are too kind," said Martinus. "You and your brothers will be in ours."

Olin and Father Marellus left, and Martinus began to shake. He eyed the base of the forge.

"Control yourself, you fool!" hissed his wife as she hauled him inside the house, a few of the nosier having gathered around the periphery during the exchange.

He sat in his chair, steadying his nerves. "I think we have to get rid of it. Leave it somewhere if we're not going to destroy it."

"Are you insane? We can't do any such thing. And besides, no one will ever find it where it is. That much is certain. Not with the effort we had to go through in order to hide it."

He sighed, closing his eyes, thinking back on that night. He had dug a deep hole in the dark, then lined it with stone, placed a wood box inside, then the Bible inside that, wrapped in sheep's skin. He had buried it, then used the horses to pull the heavy base of his forge enough to cover their secret. It would never be found as long as that forge stood, and that would be for as long as he could swing a hammer. Then what happened after that, after he and his wife were gone, and their children had moved on, was of no concern to him.

The Bible carried by young Arledge would rest in peace, hidden away, until the day the Good Lord wished it found.

Hotel Ercilla

Bilbao, Spain

Present Day

"Room service."

Dylan Kane grinned at Atlas attempting a girly voice. It came off rather disturbing. He walked over to the door, not bothering to check the peephole.

Nobody could fake that voice.

He opened the door and smiled at his former Delta Force comrades. "Right on time, gentlemen." He stepped aside, exchanging thumping hugs with each of them, only Atlas' slightly painful. "I was expecting a nice little French Maid's outfit."

Atlas dropped into a chair by the window. "We're not in France, otherwise I would have." He jerked a chunky thumb at Niner. "Besides, I'd have had him constantly trying to look under my skirt. Seeing what a real man is packing, he'd have been scarred for life."

Niner did a Michael Jackson junk-grab with one hand, and flipped the bird with the other. "I've never had any complaints."

"That's because you've only dated polite women."

Kane grinned, this the only thing he missed about the Unit.

The camaraderie.

The life of a spy was a lonely, solitary one. Even when with people, they were rarely your friend, and almost always had an agenda.

But with the Unit? Everyone had your back, everyone was your friend.

He missed it.

Though he'd never go back.

"If you two are done with your swordplay, I have some toys for you boys." He pointed to the bed where several large duffel bags were sitting. "Have at it." He patted one of them. "But this one is mine."

The boys attacked, the gear quickly unpacked, sorted, inspected, and doled out, while he hooked up the comms and jacked into Langley. "Control, this is Whiskers, do you copy, over?"

Dawson gave him a look. "Whiskers?"

He shrugged. "I was feeling frisky."

"Whiskers, Control Actual, we read you."

Kane smiled at his friend's voice, switching it to VOX so the entire room could participate. "Hey buddy, you're on speaker with some old friends."

A round of greetings was shouted deliberately incoherently at the radio.

Kane laughed. "What's new since yesterday?"

Leroux brought them up to date about the manhunt. "The bottom line is they haven't been spotted since last night. The police have found the van they used to leave the museum grounds, and it was parked near a marina just north of the city where a boat has been stolen. They think the professors might have taken it because the timing fits."

"Can they track the boat?" asked Dawson.

"We haven't heard anything on that yet. We're trying to find out."

"What about those social media profiles?" asked Kane. "I was looking at them and they're complete bullshit."

"We've been able to prove they're fake. We're still tracing back to see who created them. We've linked them back into all kinds of activist groups. Animal rights, climate change, save the whales. All kinds of things. It looks like whoever is behind this provides support to all these types of groups by supplying them with social media followers for their causes, so they look more legitimate. They generate posts and try to get things trending that shouldn't."

Niner inspected a Glock. "So, it's a big fake news type of scam."

"Yes, though this one doesn't seem to have anything to do with politics and everything to do with activism."

Kane chewed his cheek. "So, do we have any theories? Government? Private?"

"It's a little sloppily done in some ways, so we're thinking it isn't government. Besides, we can't find any motivation for a government to do something like this. Our working theory is that this is private. Some type of background agitators like Soros, Koch, Tides, that type of thing."

"So, some rich person with an agenda or well-funded group with few morals."

Niner grunted. "Well, that narrows it down."

Kane chuckled. "Okay, you guys keep working on it. Are you getting the word out that the accounts are fake?"

"We've already pushed this over to the FBI, and they're contacting the various social media platforms to have the profiles removed plus any others we've identified as fake. At the moment, we're hoping to have them down by the end of the day, but who knows. Sometimes they cooperate, sometimes they don't."

"Fingers crossed they get these things down soon before it does too much damage to their reputations."

"We've already got our own bots posting replies to pretty much every post involved, telling them that they're fake and to ignore anything they read."

"Will that work?"

"Of course not. It's the Internet. Too many people think that everything they see on there is true."

"Then why bother?" asked Atlas.

"Because intelligent people will realize it's fake and hopefully ignore it, but it also allows us to tag the ones who disagree with our opinion, so we can dive deeper into them to clean up anything they might post. Once we get these things down, we'll have our bots go through to find anything left that needs to be scrubbed. With the professors' deep pockets, they can sue to have anything that's left removed, but the quickest way to save their reputations and possibly their lives, is to find them and find out who is really behind this."

Kane agreed. "Yeah, we're here and ready to act on any intel you're able to get us, but we're going to need something to work with. I want to find them and get them into safe custody, but we also need to somehow get access to the witnesses to find out what actually happened inside that museum."

"State department should have somebody there by now. I don't know if I can put you in touch with them because you're unsanctioned."

"Do what you can, but I might have an idea of how to get around that."

"Don't do anything stupid."

Kane placed a hand on his chest. "Who? Me?"

Bilbao Airport

Loiu, Spain

Hugh Reading followed his Interpol partner Michelle Humphrey off the plane, already exhausted. He had barely slept all night, working the phones and reading the reports as they came in about his friends.

His friends who had not only escaped the bombing with the priceless Bible moments before the museum exploded, but who also might have stolen a boat.

What the hell are you two up to?

His phone vibrated in his pocket and he answered. "Hello?"

"Hi Hugh, it's Dylan. How are you?"

His eyes widened. "Dylan? I'm bloody awful. Have you heard what's happened?"

"Yeah, that's why I'm calling you. I've got a few of the guys here with me now. We're in Bilbao and ready to help, but we need somebody on the inside of the investigation to feed us intel. Can you get yourself to Spain?"

Reading smiled. With Kane here, along with whom he thought the CIA operative was obtusely referring to, there might be hope. "I'm already here. We just landed a few minutes ago."

"Fantastic! Okay, I'll let you get sorted out. Try to get us some intel and we'll use our resources to run it down. We need to find them and get them into police custody before they get shot by some overzealous cop, and we need to find out who's behind this and bring them in so that we can get their names cleared."

Reading grunted. "Agreed. As soon as I have something for you, I'll let you know."

"Excellent. Talk to you soon."

He ended the call and stuffed the phone back in his pocket, feeling renewed hope now that all of his friends' friends were involved in helping clear their names.

"Who was that?" asked Michelle.

"An old friend."

"Is he law enforcement? Because I got the distinct impression you're going to be feeding him information."

He gave her the eye, knowing she was baiting him. "Let's put it this way. He's not *our* type of law enforcement, but he has resources far beyond what we have access to, plus none of the restrictions."

She waved a hand in front of her, shaking her head "Okay, okay, I don't want to know. Just don't get me in trouble."

He grinned. "I make no promises I can't keep."

Unknown Location

"Change of plans."

Richter stared at the wall, his heart picking up a few more beats at the buyer's announcement. "What do you mean?"

"I mean just that. I no longer trust you."

He leaned forward in his chair, the phone pressed against his ear as he jabbed at the air in front of him with a finger. "Listen, we had a deal."

"And we still do. However, there was never any mention of over sixty people dying. There is so much attention on this now, that I no longer trust our original plans. There will be *no* handover on European territory."

"Then the price is going to have to go up."

"No, if anything, the price should have to go down. This commodity already had few buyers who could afford it, and now there are even fewer people who are willing to because of how many people died to obtain it. They can't risk being connected to such an event."

His pulse pounded in his ears as things threatened to fall apart. "Those people died for a completely different reason than the theft of the Bible, and you know it."

"I don't care. All that matters is that those people are dead, and the theft of the Bible is associated with it. And who the hell are those two professors? My people tell me that not only are they extremely wealthy, they're very well respected. How did you ever get them involved?"

He smiled slightly at the fact he still knew more than this man. "They're patsies."

There was a pause. "You're telling me that patsies have the Bible I agreed to pay two-hundred-million Euros for, and that you don't even have it secure in your own people's hands?"

He frowned at how quickly that had backfired. "They've already made it out of Spain. They'll be in France shortly. The exchange can still go forward as planned and on schedule."

"As I said, the exchange will no longer take place on European soil. Get it out of Europe, and I don't mean to the United States, I mean someplace where if something goes wrong, the right amount of money will solve any problems we might encounter. Once you can prove that to me, then you'll get your deposit and we'll meet."

His heart skipped a beat and beads of sweat emerged from his forehead. "We'll meet?"

"Yes, you and me."

"I don't meet with people."

"Well, you're going to have to get over your legendary paranoia, because the only way this deal is going to happen is if you and I meet for this exchange."

"But you don't understand, I don't go… anywhere."

"I know. You're always holed up in your little fortress down there. You're either going to have to leave it, or I'm coming to you."

The world closed in around him. "Out of the question."

"Too bad. You call me when you have the Bible secure and then you'll give me the arrangements. Oh, and I want those two professors there to authenticate it." The call ended and his heart hammered, his entire body sweating profusely. He pressed the button summoning Gerhard. The door opened, his man immediately concerned.

"What's wrong, sir?"

"We're going to have company."

Hospital Universitario de Basurto

Bilbao, Spain

Sanchez rapidly took notes as Petra relayed what had happened last night from her perspective. Much of what they knew was from the video the girl had taken, so it was mostly redundant. What hadn't been known was what had happened before she started recording, and after the phone was destroyed.

"And that's the last time you saw the professors?"

Petra nodded. "Yes, when they left with my father to see the Bible."

"And you didn't see them leave."

She shook her head. "I do remember hearing the door alarm, so that must be when they did."

"And that was when?"

She shrugged. "Maybe a couple of minutes before they blew the place up."

"You didn't hear any argument between the professors and your father?"

"No, nothing."

"No tension, no discomfort?"

"No, though Professor Acton seemed eager to see the Bible."

"A little too eager?"

She shrugged. "I don't know. They're all geeks. They get excited about boring things."

Sanchez smiled. "How did your father feel about tonight? Was he happy to be there?"

Petra's eyes brightened. "Oh yeah, he was so excited. So proud." Her face clouded over, her voice becoming that of a frightened little girl. "Are my parents going to die?"

Sanchez couldn't give her an honest answer without devastating her. "I'm going to have to talk to somebody to find out what's going on. All I know is that before I came in here, I heard they were both alive and in surgery. Don't give up hope."

Tears flowed. "If they die, the last things I ever said to them were all in anger because I didn't want to come. I wanted to go to my friend's birthday party. They were right, I barely knew her, but I said I hated them."

Sanchez's heart ached for the young woman. "I have a daughter about your age, and believe me, we fight. That's what parents do with their teenagers, especially teenage daughters. But never doubt that we always love you, no matter how horrible the things you say to us are. They know you love them, and I promise you they love you with all their heart. And if one of them doesn't make it, they would never want you to think that in any way they thought you truly hated them, or that you thought they didn't love you as much as they did the day you were born." She patted Petra on the shoulder. "Listen, stay here. I'll go check on your parents and have somebody let you know what's going on. I might have more questions for you later, okay?"

Petra wiped her tears away with the back of her hand. "Okay. Have you found my brother?"

"No, we're still searching for him. He wasn't where you said he was, and there was very little damage there, so that's a good sign. We think he might just be hiding because he's scared."

Petra stood. "Take me to the museum. If he hears my voice, he'll come out."

Sanchez eyed her. "Are you sure you're up for that?"

Petra squared her shoulders, sniffing hard. "I have to be. He might be all I have left of my family."

Off the coast

La Rochelle, France

"We're here!"

Laura groaned from down below, Acton smiling as he recognized her morning stretch. "Give me a minute."

It had been a long, uneventful night, made easier by the fact they were thieves with impeccable taste. The boat was more than that word implied. It was, in fact, a yacht, a luxury yacht. Fully stocked with food, liquor, toiletries, and clothing of all manner, most of which fit them.

He was already prepared for their trip to the shore, Laura having insisted on taking the first shift on watch last night. She had let him sleep far too long, almost six hours, though their mid-morning arrival had still given her five hours to rest.

His shift had him showered, coifed, and sporting swimwear, the decision to swim ashore forced upon them by the fact they were in a stolen vessel. He had laid out a skimpy two-piece thong outfit he had found as a joke, and every part of him that made him a man took notice when Laura slinked up the stairs in it.

"Umm…holy shit?"

She grinned, did a twirl, then planted a kiss on him that had all the fires stoked. Then she gently slapped him. "Funny guy."

He grinned. "Oh, how I wish I had my phone. There'd be pictures! Sooo many pictures!"

"Over my dead body."

"Drop dead gorgeous body."

She patted his cheek. "Thanks, love, but the show's over." She returned below then emerged a few minutes later in a sensible one-piece, another outfit folded in her arms. "Did you find something to put our clothes in?"

He pointed toward a nearby shelf, his clothes already sealed in a waterproof bag, another containing the Bible. She stuffed her clothes and a pair of sandals in an empty bag, neither of them having found shoes that fit, the owners of the boat evidently blessed or cursed with small feet.

She peered through the window at the shore in the distance. "That's going to be quite the swim."

"We'll take floatation devices. There's no way I can swim with that thing"—he gestured at the Bible—"tied to me."

"Won't it float?"

He shrugged. "It should, but I don't want to be in the water and discover it doesn't, then have to come up with a Plan B."

She nodded. "True." She looked about. "Are we ready?"

"In a minute. First, we eat. God only knows when we'll get another chance."

Guggenheim Bilbao

Bilbao, Spain

"Jean Luc!"

Petra's heart pounded faster and faster with each unanswered call of her brother's name. When they had first arrived, she was convinced the police had searched the wrong hiding spot or had done so unthoroughly, so had sprinted across the crime scene before diving under the stairwell she and her brother had hidden under.

And he hadn't been there.

But there was also no damage where he had been, and no blood.

"Jean Luc, it's me, Petra!"

Still no answer. The police officer with her patted her on the back. "Don't worry, dear, kids that age get scared easily. When the explosion happened, he probably just ran and hid somewhere he can't hear you."

"But what if we don't find him? He could die!"

The woman chuckled. "If there's one thing having a young son has taught me, it's that when they're hungry, they always make an appearance."

Petra smiled slightly. "That's definitely Jean Luc."

"How about we try somewhere else? We'll keep at it—"

Another officer jogged around the corner then whispered in the policewoman's ear, though not quiet enough that Petra couldn't hear.

"We have to get her back to the hospital. There's been a complication with her father. They don't think he's going to make it."

"Daddy!"

Hospital Universitario de Basurto

Bilbao, Spain

Reading strode through the doors of the hospital and presented his Interpol identification to one of the police officers, immediately receiving instructions on where to proceed. After checking into their hotel and getting a bit of the runaround, delaying things interminably, they had finally been given the clearance they thought they already had, and were authorized to interview witnesses.

Though there was only one he was concerned about.

Professor Yves Marchand.

They found his room but the door was closed, the officer guarding it directing them to the doctor in charge. Reading identified himself. "Is he going to make it?"

"Yes. We had a bit of a scare earlier. We thought we were going to lose him, but it turns out we missed something in his initial surgery, so we went back in and were able to stop the bleeding. He's going to be fine, but he's been badly burned. He's facing months if not years of recovery."

Reading peered through the window at Marchand, a young woman he assumed was the professor's daughter by his side. "Judging from the smile on his face, I don't think he's going to care, and neither is she." He turned back to the doctor. "I need to speak with him."

The man frowned. "I don't think he's up for an interrogation."

Reading shook his head. "He's not a suspect, just a witness."

"Oh, okay, then I guess it's fine. Just try to keep it short and calm."

"Understood." Reading knocked on the door then entered, startling the two members of the Marchand family. "Sorry to interrupt. I'm Agent Hugh Reading from Interpol, and this is my partner Agent Michelle Humphrey. I was wondering if you have a few minutes for some questions."

Marchand nodded.

Reading smiled, pulling out his notebook, the more current Michelle her tablet. "First, full disclosure, James Acton and Laura Palmer are two of my best friends. My understanding is you're the one who invited them to the event."

"Yes, I did."

"I also understand that this invitation was extended about a week ago."

"Yes."

"Did you tell anybody that they were coming?"

"Not specifically, no, but their names were on the guestlist I provided to the museum."

"Were they late additions?"

Marchand's eyebrows rose slightly. "Yes, they were, as a matter of fact."

"Then they would have been separately submitted?"

"Yes."

"When would that have been?"

"I would have sent an email the next day."

"Who did you send it to?"

"The event organizer. I can't remember her name, sorry."

Reading smiled. "No problem, we can find that out ourselves."

"Why these questions? What's going on? Jim and Laura are okay, aren't they?"

Reading paused, surprised. "You haven't heard?"

"No, I haven't heard anything, I just woke up a short while ago. Nobody is telling me anything, and frankly, it's pissing me off."

Reading chuckled. "I can respect that. We've been told to keep you calm, but I think you deserve the truth, otherwise you're just going to continue being frustrated."

"Please!"

"Well, right now, Jim and Laura are accused of being behind the bombings."

Marchand's eyes shot wide. "What?" His heart rate monitor ticked faster. "That's insanity! Why would anybody possibly think that?"

"Well, besides the fact somebody went to a great deal of effort to create fake social media accounts suggesting they're animal rights fanatics—which is why I was wondering who knew they were coming in advance—there's footage of them leaving with the Bible only moments before the explosion went off, and getting into a van used to bring the terrorists to the building. And they had the keys."

Marchand's head was shaking with every word. "I don't understand. It can't be them, can it? I mean, I honestly don't know Laura at all, and I don't know Jim much. I met him a couple of times years ago, but we correspond regularly through email. I haven't seen him in years, but I just can't believe he'd be behind this. I don't believe it for a second."

Reading was happy to hear such a staunch defense of his friends. "Like I said, Jim and Laura are my friends. There's no way they're involved in this, and these social media accounts are fake, so they're being set up by someone. We need to figure out who is involved and why they were leaving the building with the Bible."

"All I know is they were animal rights activists pissed off about the fact the Bible was made from vellum."

"Vellum?"

"Calfskin. We estimate that when it was created thirteen-hundred years ago, approximately five-hundred calves were raised and slaughtered to create each of the four Bibles."

"Bloody hell!" exclaimed Michelle. "I can see how that might piss some people off."

Marchand agreed. "Yes. The man who seemed to be in charge—"

"Did you get his name?"

"No, I don't think he ever said it, but I seem to remember him saying their organization was the Animal Protection Brigade."

Reading wrote that down. "We'll check into them. Can you tell us what happened?"

"We were in a secure room, looking at the Bible."

"Who's we?" asked Michelle.

"Myself, Jim, and Laura. We were looking at the Bible, then we heard an alarm go off, just for a few seconds. I thought it was just a fire door being opened by a smoker. I had set it off myself that morning."

"After all this, you better be quitting," admonished his daughter.

He smiled, patting her hand, the movement causing him to wince. "I'm trying, sweetheart."

"Then what happened?" prompted Reading.

"We ignored it, then a few moments later there was some gunfire and shouting. Jim peered out the door and a man, the leader, pressed a gun to his head, so I guess he was waiting at the door."

"It was locked?"

"Yes. He came in, confiscated our phones—oh, I called the police when we heard the gunfire. Actually, Jim told me to. He had Laura look up a map of the museum to see if there was a way to escape, then he opened the door." His eyes popped. "Hey, maybe she found a way to escape, and that's why they went out the way they did."

Reading shook his head. "No, they had the keys, remember?"

Marchand frowned. "Oh, that's right."

"Why didn't you go with them?" asked Michelle.

"Apparently, my daughter was streaming video to the Internet and they figured out who she was. I was brought into the atrium with everyone else, then they threatened to kill us if she didn't come forward. That's the last time I saw Jim and Laura."

"And the Bible?"

"And the Bible. But before I was taken into the atrium, one of their people came into the room and cut open the case the Bible was secured inside."

"Did he take it?"

"No, but I think it was in preparation to take it."

"Did they say what they were going to do with it?"

"The way they were treating it and speaking of it, I had the distinct impression they were going to destroy it." Marchand paused, scrunching his nose. "Now that's strange. If they had keys, then that suggests they were given to them, so that means they didn't steal the Bible, they were *given* the Bible."

"Maybe they took the keys," suggested Petra.

Marchand frowned. "I hadn't thought of that. I guess they could have attacked somebody for them."

Michelle shook her head. "No, that doesn't fit with what happened. If they had escaped with the Bible, they would have immediately turned themselves in to the police."

Reading sighed. "That's the problem. Everything they are doing is making them look guilty. They left moments before the explosion, with the Bible, with the keys to the terrorists' vehicle, and they haven't turned themselves in."

Marchand shrugged, his wince suggesting he regretted the gesture. "You know them better than me, but I just find it hard to believe that the man I met so many years ago, that I corresponded with for so long, would be willing to massacre so many people." He met Reading's gaze. "I don't believe it for a second, which means there must be somebody forcing them into doing what they're doing."

Reading agreed. "I think you and I are on the same page." He checked his notes. "Now, you went into the atrium, leaving Jim and Laura in the secure room with the Bible. What happened next?"

"I'm afraid I'm a little fuzzy on the details. I remember being in the atrium, my daughter coming"—his eyes shot wide—"Oh my God, my son! Have you found my son?"

Reading held out a calming hand. "No. My understanding is they're still searching for him."

Petra put a hand on her father's arm. "I called for him, but he never answered. It was only a few times. They got the call to bring me back here a few minutes after we got there." She turned to Reading and Michelle, choking up. "They said Dad might not make it."

Michelle replied in a calming voice. "I'm sure they're doing everything they can to find him. I understand he wasn't in the main blast area, so it's very likely he's just scared and hiding somewhere. I'm certain they're tearing the place apart to find him."

"The policewoman who was with me said he'd come out when he gets hungry."

Reading laughed. "She has to be a mother! That's exactly what will happen." His jovial response appeared to set both Petra and her father at ease. He continued his questioning. "So, what happened next? Your daughter came into the atrium after they threatened your lives, then what?"

"There was an argument between the leader and one of the other men. I can't really remember—"

"No, Dad, you're forgetting something."

"What?"

"What happened before the argument." She turned to Reading. "When I came into the room, one of them made me log into my Instagram. Then he left, and so did the leader."

"Together?"

"No, separately. It was a few minutes later that we heard the door alarm again, then the leader came back into the room, and that's when he had the argument with the guy who made me log in."

Her father smiled. "Good girl. I forgot all about that." He wagged a finger slowly. "The argument was about some footage. He was holding up a tablet, and he was demanding to know what was going on. Then there was a discussion that I can't really recall too much, but the leader said he was leaving and that anyone who wanted to come with him could. Oh wait, I forgot! The guy he was arguing with had the detonator for the bombs. He shouted at him, raised his hand in the air, and that's when I knew he was going to blow us up, so I pushed my wife and daughter to the floor and tried to cover them as best I could, then the bomb went off. That's all I remember until I woke up here."

Reading finished taking his notes then looked at Michelle. "That seems to suggest that their leader was behind this, and none of his people knew."

Petra turned to her father. "I think he said something about a rich man, Dad, didn't he?"

Marchand's eyes narrowed. "What are you talking about?"

"They said something about a man who had helped them before with money, and I think they were going to sell the Bible so that they would have money to operate."

Her father slowly nodded, his eyes staring into the distance. "That's sounding familiar. Sorry, but I have a wicked headache and my memory is foggy."

Reading decided to let the man rest. "Okay, this is very helpful. If I have any more questions, can I talk to you or your daughter?"

"Of course. My wife might be able to help you too. They tell me she's going to be fine, she's just resting now."

Reading smiled. "Thank you." He followed Michelle out of the room and headed down the hall.

"So, what do you think?"

He regarded Michelle for a moment before answering. "I'm getting the distinct impression that there are a lot of patsies here. I think that this Animal Protection Brigade group took over the museum because of the Bible and what it was made of. Everybody figured they were there for the cause, but the leader had ulterior motives. He arranged for someone to buy the Bible, and nobody else knew until they saw that security footage of Jim and Laura leaving with it. They know something's wrong, they challenge the leader, they argue, he says he wants to sell the Bible, he's leaving, the guy with the detonator is a true believer, doesn't think they should profit off the death of so many animals, so he blows the shit out of the whole place."

Michelle chewed her cheek, her head bobbing. "That all makes sense, but does the timing work?"

Reading stopped, turning to face her. "What do you mean?"

"Well, that security footage was posted *after* the bombs detonated."

His eyes widened. "Bollocks, you're right. Is there other footage out there that we don't know about?"

"Maybe they were tapped into the security cameras."

"Maybe. That has to be it. And it makes sense. They somehow bypassed the rear door security, so it makes sense that they might have access to the security footage."

Michelle shook her head. "I don't think that's what happened."

"What do you mean?"

"Didn't Marchand say he heard an alarm for a moment?"

"That was probably a fire door like he said."

"Exactly. That means they didn't bypass security. Someone let them in from the inside."

Reading cursed. "You're right. Fine, but the bottom line is there is a buyer for that Bible out there somewhere, and I'm willing to bet that whoever is behind this is sitting comfortably in his home, just like these guys usually do, while others do their dirty work. It's probably the rich guy that they referred to, and he's sitting back and telling Jim and Laura where to go so that they can deliver the Bible. So, all we need to do is figure out who this guy is, who the buyer is, and where he's got them going."

Michelle stared at him with a wry grin. "Is that all?"

Trinh/Granger Residence

St. Paul, Maryland

Tommy continued to work at clearing his mentors' good names, his custom-developed software using facial recognition technology to scan image after image pulled from the fake and real accounts associated with the clones of the professors', slowly tracking down those involved.

I should have patented this.

He was disappointed how his idea had been abused, a tech company having announced it had used the same technology to scan and pull the faces from over three billion online photos, then selling access to their facial recognition database to various agencies, not the least of which were law enforcement.

What is this, Communist China?

It disgusted him. He loved the Internet, and he loved social media. What he hated was what it had become—a resource filled with garbage, vitriol, fraud, and hate. Anonymity was the problem, and a lack of

220

consequences. Until anonymity was removed, social media would forever be a useless tool for true discourse and information sharing.

For now, that anonymity was working against him, though his tool was slowly doing its job. He had pulled each terrorist's face from the footage taken by some girl on the inside, and had run them against the professors' profiles, following the breadcrumbs through the fake friends lists, the algorithm digging deeper and deeper until eventually a hit was found for each of them, giving him a direct link to their real accounts.

Many proudly displaying their actual name.

As each came in, he fired them to Leroux, praying his efforts were worth it, because he wasn't sure how much longer he could last.

Mai entered the room, yawning. "Are you still at it?"

He grunted.

"Did you get any sleep?"

"No. As long as I'm making progress, I'm not sleeping. Not until they're safe."

"Is there anything I can do to help?"

He held up an empty can of Red Bull. "Get me more of this?"

Mai shuffled to the fridge and opened the door, bending over to search the shelves. "We're out."

"I know."

She closed the door. "But there were four of them last night. I just bought them yesterday."

"I know."

"Well, I'm not getting you any more. You'll kill yourself. Your heart rate is probably through the roof." She pointed at him. "Look at your hands. They're shaking."

He held them up and frowned. "Huh, I didn't notice that."

She wagged a finger at him. "Okay, no more caffeine or sugar for you. I'm going to make breakfast, low carb, then the first yawn out of you, you get a minimum three hours sleep. You'll do them no good if you're dead."

He checked his phone. "It's five in the morning. It's a little early for breakfast, isn't it?"

"You need something in your system to counteract that garbage you've been drinking."

He sighed. "Fine. But I want ketchup with my eggs. Carbs be damned."

Operations Center 2, CIA Headquarters

Langley, Virginia

"This is an interesting one."

Leroux stepped over to Tong's workstation, having pushed Tommy's intel over to her as it came in. "What?"

"One of these guys is former German Army. He's a demolitions expert."

"Well, that would explain how they were able to make the bombs. What can you tell me about him?"

"According to the profile Tommy found, it looks like he joined them less than a year ago."

"When did he leave the military?"

"According to the file we have, about two months after he joined the Animal Protection Brigade. Their equivalent to a dishonorable discharge."

"What did he do?"

"He punched out a senior officer."

Randy Child, his team's tech wunderkind, offered a suggestion. "Maybe he caught him wearing leather boots."

Tong ignored him. "The peanut gallery aside, around the time of his discharge, there was a report of some missing weapons. It was never solved."

Leroux scratched his chin, several pieces of the puzzle starting to fit. "That probably explains a few things. Start running him down, the usual. Known associates, when he went off the deep end, that sort of thing. I think we might have found out where the weapons went, but we need to figure out where they got the explosives for the attack. I'm guessing we'll find out they were all homemade, cooked up in someone's basement."

"We'll run it down, but you should see this." She pointed at the display at the front of the room. "I've pieced together the footage of all the different terrorists, all seven of them, with the names we've been able to gather. We've been able to link them all to the Animal Protection Brigade. And we think this guy's the leader." A file with a photo was highlighted. "His name is Hugo Peeters. Certified nutbar."

Leroux chuckled. "Okay, send that to Agent Reading. See if he can confirm that he is indeed the leader. Apparently, he's in the hospital undergoing surgery. And start going through everything we can find on him. Go through his social media, find out what emails he has and get into them, everything. We need to find out all we can about him, and see if there's any reference to who their financial backers are."

La Rochelle, France

Acton climbed out of the water, stumbling toward the sandy beach as he struggled to regain his balance with the heavy Bible in one hand and his bag with a far lighter change of clothes in the other. Laura supplied a steadying hand, and they strode from the water, ignoring any onlookers, confidence the key to allaying any suspicions.

It worked.

They rinsed the saltwater off in one of the showers, then dried off with a towel handed to him by Laura, something he hadn't thought to bring. They quickly donned the change of clothes they had brought, then he checked to confirm the Bible had survived their swim.

The phone rang and he grabbed it from one of the bags, putting it on speaker after confirming no one was within earshot. "Hello?"

"Good to see you made it."

He glanced around for prying eyes. "How do you know we did?"

"Because I'm tracking your phone. I know exactly where you are all the time."

Acton frowned at the not unexpected revelation. "Okay, fine, we're in France. When and where are we meeting for the exchange?"

"Oh, I think you misunderstand, Professor. We're not doing the exchange there."

Acton tossed his head back in frustration. "Then why the hell did you have us come here?"

"To get you out of Spain. Nobody is looking for you in France, at least not yet. Right now, you're the two most wanted people in the world, and we need to get you out of Europe as soon as possible."

He tensed, exchanging a nervous glance with Laura. "Out of Europe? How in blazes are we going to manage that?"

"I want you to get yourselves to the La Rochelle Airport. There's a plane waiting for you."

Acton shook his head adamantly. "There's no way we're getting on a plane."

"Professor, if you don't do exactly as I say, more people are going to die. You'll get on that plane, and when you arrive at your destination, you'll be met at the airport. You'll be taken to a secret location where you'll hand over the Bible. And assuming you followed my instructions exactly, you'll be allowed to leave unscathed. Don't follow my instructions, not only will more people die, but so will you."

Laura reached out and took his hand, nodding to him, and he frowned. For she was right. They had no choice, and arguing with the man was pointless. "Fine. Where is this airport?"

"Just a moment…okay, I've activated the GPS on your phone. You'll be able to use the maps function now." The phone vibrated. "I just sent you your destination."

"Just a second." Acton tapped on the link in the message and the map application opened. He brought up the directions from their current location. "That's ten minutes by car. We're on foot."

"Figure it out, Professor Acton. I assume you're an intelligent man if you have that title. I'm sure you and your equally intelligent wife can manage."

The call ended and Acton cursed. "Now what do we do?"

Laura stared at the street running parallel to the beach. "I don't think we have much choice. We're going to have to figure out a faster way than on foot."

"Agreed." He spotted two bicycles lying nearby in the sand and gestured toward them. Laura looked. "What do you think?"

"I think we're not thieves."

"Right now, the world thinks we're mass-murdering terrorists. Besides, we just stole a boat."

She sighed. "But that's different. He's got insurance. Whoever these bikes belong to could be teenagers. Maybe I could leave them a note telling them where we left them."

He gave her a look. "Nooo, because they'll find that note in the next few minutes then tell the police exactly where we're heading."

She sighed. "Sorry, I'm not thinking straight. We have to do something, though."

The stress was getting to both of them, and bad decisions were being made all around. They had to act fast otherwise the bikes might be collected before they made their minds up. "I'll tell you what. When this is all over, if we have to, we'll put ads in the paper to find out who owns them so we can compensate them. Okay?"

She smiled. "Thanks for humoring me."

He gave her a peck then looked around to see if anyone was watching. "Okay, I think we're good." Again with confidence, he walked over and picked up one of the bikes, then carried it up to the street, Laura following suit. He climbed on his and started to peddle, struggling to balance his load.

Somebody shouted behind them.

Operations Center 2, CIA Headquarters

Langley, Virginia

"Michelle and I were discussing the timing of everything, and we need something confirmed. According to Professor Marchand's daughter, the terrorists were arguing over some footage. We were assuming it was the security camera footage we have all seen, but that wasn't posted until after the explosion. We need to know if they tapped the security cameras at the museum."

Leroux looked to Tong for an answer to Reading's question, and she shrugged. "We'll look into it. Why is it important?"

"Well, if they weren't tapped into things, then what footage were they looking at that got one of them mad enough to blow themselves up?"

Leroux's eyebrows shot up. "Is that what happened?"

"Yes. Apparently, the leader, this man we're assuming is Hugo Peeters, was caught on camera letting Jim and Laura go with the Bible. He then admitted to it, saying they were going to sell the Bible to some rich guy so that they could be funded forever, and that anyone who wanted to come with him could. The joker with the detonator was truly touched, didn't agree, and blew them all up rather than have anyone profit off the death of so many animals."

Randy Child spun in his chair, staring at the ceiling. "Truly touched."

Leroux agreed. "Okay, that explains a few things. The detonation was intentional, unplanned for that moment, and none of them knew the leader's plans. The question I have is, why?"

"Why?" asked Reading.

"Yeah. This Peeters guy is nuts. He's clearly committed to the cause. He went there with the intention of killing a lot of people, perhaps even himself, yet he decides to sell the Bible. It doesn't make sense."

"You mean, why would he violate his principles?"

"No, I mean, why use the professors. If your intent all along is to steal the Bible, why not just take it and go? Why stick around for what appears to be about fifteen minutes, then sneak it out the back door with two people you've never met who aren't on your side?"

"You're right. I don't think this was his plan at all. He changed his mind."

Tong rapped her knuckles on her station. "Or was his mind changed for him?"

Leroux smiled. "The rich guy."

"Exactly. Somebody had to bankroll this thing. We've been trying to find any reference to people who funded the organization. These fringe groups quite often have backers with deep pockets who like manipulating things in the background. Maybe someone like that might want the Bible

230

for themselves, or they might recognize its monetary value and have a buyer."

Leroux chewed his cheek. "But again, why not properly plan for it?"

"Maybe Peeters is a true believer as well. He would never agree to going in there if he thought the point was to steal the Bible and profit off the death of those animals."

Leroux jabbed a finger at her. "Now *that* I could see. He goes in with his group with the intent of delivering a message, blowing up some rich people, perhaps even dying for the cause and destroying the Bible in the process, so no one could ever enjoy it or profit from it in the future. But when he actually succeeds in taking the Bible, Daddy Warbucks calls him, change of plans, get the Bible out of there, I'm selling it, and in exchange, I'll fund your organization in perpetuity. Peeters thinks this promise tips the scales in favor of his cause, because he can do more good with the money than by just killing people. He agrees to a plan that by necessity is hastily put together, then he gets caught in the process on camera, his people find out, everything goes south."

"But there's a problem with that," said Reading.

"What?"

"If the moneyman plans on this all along, why doesn't he just have someone waiting at the back door? Peeters just hands the Bible to that person and we're done. Nice and clean."

Leroux paced for a moment, his mind filtering the noise. He stopped. "I can think of only two possibilities. Either this was a last-minute change of plans for the moneyman, or he didn't want to risk having anyone there for the exchange that could be traced back to him. Right now, everything is tied to the Animal Protection Brigade. If the Bible is intercepted, then it is the Brigade and the professors who are being blamed. Nobody has tied anything back to the money."

"Yet," said Child.

Leroux acknowledged his observation. "Yet. And even if we tie it back to him, right now he could just claim he had no idea what they had planned. He thought they were just going to protest the event like they have countless other events. He had no way of knowing what they were planning. But if he were somehow linked to the theft of the Bible by bringing in someone for it to be handed to, then that would prove he knew what they were planning. You don't steal a Bible like that without expecting people to die."

"Which is why they used Jim and Laura," agreed Reading. "But that means someone is guiding them. Someone had to tell them to go to the marina, to steal that boat. Everyone involved at the museum is either dead or seriously wounded. We need to know who's guiding them."

"Maybe they were given those instructions before they left?" suggested Tong."

Child stopped his latest spin. "What, and now they're on a boat floating in the Atlantic, waiting for a call that might never come?"

She shrugged. "Possible."

Leroux exhaled. "If that's the case, that might not be a bad thing. Eventually, they'll give up waiting and turn themselves in."

"Let's hope," said Reading. "Let me know what you find on that security camera footage. I want to just make sure they were reacting to what we think they were reacting to."

"Will do. And check out that file I sent you on Peeters. There's a photo of him in it. See if you can confirm with your witness that he's the ringleader."

"Will do."

La Rochelle, France

Acton continued to struggle, the heavy Bible causing the front tire to swing wildly as he failed to gain enough speed. Laura was well ahead of him, turning back and urging him to hurry.

"It's the terrorists!" yelled someone in French. "Stop them! It's the terrorists!"

His heart sank at the words. If these people thought they were involved, and they recognized them, then that meant the world knew. As did every police officer in Europe. And that meant their lives were in serious risk if they were to encounter any type of law enforcement.

He propped the Bible on the handlebars, then leaned forward, pressing his chest against the massive tome, squeezing it between himself and the bars, finally stabilizing enough to get several good pumps in as their pursuers sprinted after him, the nearest uncomfortably close.

As he continued to pump his legs and pick up speed, the fastest among those offended at their thievery continued to gain until he reached a gentle downslope that allowed him to pick up speed rapidly, his and the Bible's extra weight closing the gap with Laura quickly.

They soon had some serious distance between them and their pursuers, and after several quick turns, they were out of sight and safe for the moment. Laura came to a stop and let him catch up.

"That was close."

He agreed. "Too close."

She held out her hands. "Give me the Bible. I'll put it in my basket."

He frowned as he handed it over. "I wish you had thought of that earlier."

She shrugged as she placed it inside. "Sorry, it's only my second robbery."

Hospital Universitario de Basurto

Bilbao, Spain

Reading's question to one of the nursing staff about their prime suspect was overheard by one of the Spanish officers, who immediately confronted him and Michelle. He took an instant disliking to her, and her facial expression suggested the feeling was mutual.

Yet he had to maintain a professional tone.

"Chief Inspector Sanchez, National Police Corps. Who are you?"

Reading presented his Interpol credentials. "Agent Hugh Reading, Interpol. This is my partner, Agent Michelle Humphrey."

The woman's eyes narrowed. "I wasn't aware Interpol was involved yet."

"I'm familiar with two of the people involved, so head office thought I could be useful."

"Who do you know?"

"James Acton and Laura Palmer."

She visibly bristled. "And how do you know them?"

"We're good friends."

"That's not what I asked."

Reading's cheeks flushed with annoyance. "When I was a DCI at Scotland Yard, they were persons of interest in a case I was working. They saved the life of my partner, and once they were cleared, we found we had a lot in common and became friends over the years."

She grunted. "Quite the company you keep. You said you have a lot in common with them. Are you an animal rights fanatic as well?"

Reading forced a smile. "They're not animal rights fanatics."

"Well, Facebook, Instagram, Twitter, and every other damned thing you can think of that's hip with the youngsters beg to differ."

He held up a calming hand. "If you knew Jim Acton, you'd know that those profiles are all fake. He actually detests social media."

"Or that's what he told you so you wouldn't check him out online."

"Listen, Chief Inspector, you don't know me at all. I couldn't even tell you how to get on Facebook, so there'd be no need to hide anything from me. Besides, I've already confirmed those profiles are fake."

Her eyebrows shot up in mock shock. "Oh? We've barely begun to look into it. In fact, I don't know if anybody *is* looking into it yet. How do *you* know these are fake?"

He bit his tongue. He couldn't tell her how he knew. He couldn't tell her that his source was the CIA. She'd think he was insane, have him arrested and his credentials checked while he stewed in a cell downtown, charged with impersonating a law enforcement official. He had no choice but to backpedal. "I'm sorry, I misspoke. *I'm* convinced. I know they're

237

fake because I know these people. They are not animal rights fanatics. I can't count how many times I've sat down with them and enjoyed a steak or some other animal protein-based meal. They are not vegetarians and definitely not vegan. They don't even own a pet. These people are the best people I know."

She eyed him with disdain. "Well, as far as I'm concerned, they're murdering terrorists until I can prove otherwise. If they're so innocent, they would have turned themselves in by now. The very fact they haven't, tells me they're as guilty as sin."

Another forced smile. "Well then, I'm just going to have to prove you wrong, aren't I?"

"You're free to try, but do *not* interfere with my investigation, or I'll have you arrested. Understood?"

"Understood." He brought up the photo of Peeters on his phone and showed it to her. "Can you at least confirm for me that this is our ringleader?"

She looked at it. "How did you get this?"

"I have my sources."

She frowned at his response. "Yes, though he doesn't look that good anymore. I've just been informed he died in surgery." She pointed a finger at him then Michelle, who had remained wisely quiet. "Remember, don't interfere."

La Rochelle Airport

La Rochelle, France

Acton fished the ringing phone from his pocket, the airport they had been cycling to for almost half an hour visible ahead. He put the call on speaker. "Hello?"

"Listen carefully, Professor Acton, I won't be repeating myself. Go to the private terminal to the right of the main terminal. It's a small airport. You can't miss it. I'm texting you the information. They're expecting you."

Acton spotted the terminal in question. "But we don't have our passports."

"You don't need them. Like I said, they're expecting you."

The call ended and he looked at Laura. "What the hell do you think he meant?"

She frowned. "You know how lax things are at private terminals. I'm guessing he's bribed somebody to let us through."

He stared at the Bible in her basket. "This just keeps getting worse."

"We can always hope we get caught."

"You know what he said if that happens."

"We better get going."

He sighed, then led them to the private terminal where they left their bikes and entered. In record time they were swept through security, the Bible not even looked at before they were then rushed aboard a private jet airborne minutes later.

The entire process took less than ten minutes.

Acton eyed the flight attendant, wondering if she too was on their puppet master's payroll. He tested the waters. "Where are we going?"

She smiled pleasantly at them. "I'm sorry, I haven't been told."

"Can you ask the pilot?"

Another smile. "I'm sorry, he can't be disturbed."

"Who owns this plane?"

This time a genuine smile. "Oh, this is a charter owned by ComfortAir."

Laura took over. "So, this is a private charter?"

"Yes."

"And who chartered it?"

"I'm afraid I don't know."

"So, you can't tell us anything helpful."

"I'm afraid I can't."

Acton eyed her. "Uh-huh. Why do I get the sense you know exactly where we're going, and who's paying for this flight?"

More pearly whites. "I'm sure I don't know." She walked away and Acton turned to Laura. "We're not getting any help from her."

"Agreed. It looks like there's no way we're not going wherever it is he wants us to go."

"Right. And if he can charter a private jet, he obviously has money, and the way we were whisked through security, tells me he's done this before. There's no way he set that up overnight."

Laura gripped his arm. "You realize this probably means no one will ever know we boarded this flight."

He tensed. "Which means Hugh and the others will never find us."

Hotel Ercilla

Bilbao, Spain

"Looks like you're in the wrong country."

Kane glanced at the others then stared at the comm unit, Leroux having called in to update them. "What do you mean?"

"We just got a report that they were sighted in La Rochelle, France," said Leroux.

Niner pulled his phone out, Googling the location. "How the hell did they get there?"

"They must have taken that boat that was stolen," rumbled Atlas.

Dawson cleaned his nails with the tip of his knife. "What were they doing there?"

Leroux chuckled. "Apparently stealing bicycles."

Kane stared at the radio. "You're kidding me."

"Nope, bicycles."

"I guess we should relocate. No point in being here."

"I wouldn't bother yet until we have an actual destination."

Kane glanced at the other four large men in the room, not so sure that was a good idea. "We're getting pretty antsy in this hotel room. Are we making any progress on who's actually behind this?"

"Yes. We've identified all seven terrorists. We're running down their backgrounds now. The ringleader is a guy named Hugo Peeters."

Dawson put his knife away. "There was reference made to a rich guy. Anything on him?"

"We just gained access to Peeters' Hotmail account. We're going through it now, trying to find any reference to people who funded the organization. One of them is probably the buyer for the Bible. If we figure out who that is, we'll know where the professors are going."

Kane agreed. "Well, they always say follow the money. Keep us posted. And hurry. One of us is going to kill someone if we're stuck in here much longer."

"I'm voting for Niner," boomed Atlas.

Leroux chuckled. "We'll do our best."

Operations Center 2, CIA Headquarters

Langley, Virginia

Randy Child spun in his chair, dropping a foot to kill his momentum after the first circuit was complete. "Well, I've been going over the Guggenheim cameras, and I can't find any evidence that they tapped the security system. Every video I've pulled shows they came through the fire door, and we know they kept setting off the alarm. I can't see any way they'd have been able to see the professors leaving with the Bible. The only breach to the system was external, like the Guggenheim reported, and it happened just after the explosion, and a couple of minutes before that security footage was posted."

Leroux turned in his chair to face Tong. "What about social media?"

"The girl's video shows seven of them, with Hugo Peeters in a tuxedo, so we assume he was already inside somehow and opened the fire door letting the other six in. They brought the weapons and explosives with them in the van. They go into the atrium and immediately there's gunfire. Then there's other videos that we've found where people happened to be already live streaming when the attack began. They all show the same seven gunmen entering the room from the same point. We have Marchand's testimony that Hugo Peeters and one, maybe two others went into the secure room where the Bible was stored during the course of events. We have no evidence that anybody went anywhere else in the museum, including the security center where they would be able to monitor the feeds. And all reports are that the security teams fell back as they were trained to do, and tried to get anyone not in immediate danger out of the building. Remember, the gala was in the atrium. All other areas of the museum were still open to the public. All evidence suggests this was just a brute force attack. The only thing out of the ordinary was the fact Hugo Peeters somehow got himself inside to let them in through the fire door. The alarm went off, he let his people in, then the rest is history. No evidence they had access to the security system."

Leroux chewed his cheek. "I think I agree. If they had access, they would have overridden the door security. So, if they didn't have any access to the security system, then what video are they reacting to? They couldn't have seen the video of the professors leaving with the Bible, because it wasn't posted until they were all either dead or loaded with shrapnel. Start going over everything. There has to be another video out there."

"I had a thought."

Leroux turned to Child. "What?"

"The girl said one of the guys made her log into her social media accounts on her tablet so they could delete what she posted."

"So?"

"Well, we don't have access to that. We've only seen what she posted. What if there's something else in her account that they saw but we didn't?"

"But she was already captured, so what could it possibly be?"

Tong's eyes widened. "She was captured, but her brother wasn't. What if he sent her something?"

Leroux's head bobbed at the possibility. "You're right. See if we can get into her accounts and her brother's. Maybe there's something there."

"Does her brother even have an account?"

Child turned to face his station. "At that age, he shouldn't." He attacked his keyboard then frowned. "I can't find anything under his name. Nothing that's linked to his sister's or parents' accounts, anyway."

"They might have good privacy settings created for him, or they might actually be good parents who know an eight-year-old shouldn't have social media accounts."

Leroux clapped his hands together. "Okay, let's get into her accounts and see what we find."

Guggenheim Bilbao

Bilbao, Spain

Reading surveyed the external damage to the Guggenheim with Michelle. The glass at the front was gone, taken out by the blast, and there was evidence of some singeing, however other than that, it appeared remarkably calm.

"I imagine inside is worse."

He grunted. "Much. I'll never cease to be amazed at how inhumane humans can actually be. Imagine thinking doing something like this could actually further any cause, no matter how noble."

"Agents!"

Reading turned to see Sanchez beckoning them to join her at the mobile command center. "I wonder what she wants."

"I don't know, but it can't be you." Michelle flashed him a smile. "I got the distinct impression she didn't like you."

"No idea why. I'm bloody charming."

"Oh, yeah, that's how I always describe you."

"Sarcasm?"

"Ya think?"

He roared with laughter, blessing his lucky stars he and the much younger Michelle had hit it off. They'd never be as close as he and his late partner Martin Chaney had been, but she was more than tolerable.

Sanchez frowned at them as they approached. "I'm glad you can laugh at a time like this."

Reading refused to take the bait. "Good to see you, Chief Inspector. You have something for us?"

She pointed at a monitor. "There's something I want you to see."

They both leaned into the large vehicle and he suppressed a frown at the video showing his friends brazenly stealing a good-sized boat.

"Do you still think they're innocent?"

"Absolutely."

"Even though you're seeing with your own eyes them stealing a boat that's worth God knows how much money?"

"I do. There are all sorts of explanations for what we're seeing."

She stared at him. "Name one."

"They're being told what to do."

"By whom?"

His frustration boiled over at her obstinance. "By whoever is behind this! Haven't you been reading the files on these Animal Protection Brigade people? They're amateurs. There's no way they could put something like this together without help."

"From what we can piece together, it was no more sophisticated than someone opening a fire door."

He shook his head. "Are you being deliberately obtuse? They're based in Belgium, so they needed funding to get here. They needed the knowhow to not only build the bombs, but acquire the supplies. They had to know who to contact to get the weapons and ammo they used, and the most critical thing, they had to somehow get Peeters into an event attended by millionaires and billionaires, where the security was extremely tight. That means he had an invitation or some other means to bypass security. And that last part is critical. We know from Professor Marchand and his daughter's statement that there was a disagreement among the terrorists. There was a reference to a rich guy they were going to sell the Bible to, and it was going to give them enough funding to provide for them forever."

"She didn't tell me that."

He relaxed his tone slightly. "Look, I've been doing this a lot longer than you. I guess I just know the questions to ask. We need to work *with* each other, not against each other."

She regarded him. "You're too close to this."

He understood her reservations, though she was ignoring the obvious. "Yes, but that helps me. You're operating under the false assumption that they are guilty. I know one-hundred-percent that they are not. That allows me to go ahead and ask the questions you refuse to ask, because you're operating under a pretext that is hindering your investigation. Because of that, you don't think to ask the right questions, such as what were the terrorists talking about, why was the device triggered? You think that it was detonated to cover the theft of the Bible by Jim and Laura. They weren't invited until a week ago. They didn't even ask for the private viewing. It was Professor Marchand's idea. These people are innocent, and the sooner you accept that fact, and start investigating the crime from that perspective, the sooner we'll all be able to solve this thing."

Sanchez remained defiant. "That still doesn't explain how they were able to escape with the Bible and the keys."

He suppressed a growl, struggling to remain calm. "They didn't escape. We have to assume that—because they're innocent—we have to assume that they were let go with the Bible and were given the keys with instructions to go somewhere specific. Because that's the only reason they would go the way they did."

"How do you explain them stealing a boat? Why not just turn themselves in?"

He rolled his eyes, losing control. "Oh, I don't know, this is just a guess, but if a museum full of people was just blown up moments after I left, I would realize quite quickly that these people were serious, and that if they told me something along the lines of 'do as we say or more will die,' I would tend to believe that more will die if I don't do what they say! So, when they say steal a boat, I steal a boat, because I don't want more people to die! I'm going to play for time, because I'm assuming the authorities are going to be properly investigating what happened and realize I had nothing to do with it, and will be working to try and save me, as opposed to trying to arrest me."

She stared at him for a moment, her shoulders relaxing slightly. "Agent Reading. Hugh, was it?"

"Yes."

She pursed her lips. "Just a little bit of me wants to believe you, and that's a hell of a lot more than five minutes ago." She held up a hand, ceasing the hostilities. "You're right. Let's cooperate rather than work against each other. Our latest reports have them stealing bicycles in La Rochelle, France."

His tense muscles unclenched. "Yes, I heard that."

Her eyes narrowed. "That's interesting that you should have. It seems you're very well informed somehow. It's my department that feeds Interpol any information they get on this investigation, and I know for a fact that we didn't pass on this piece of intel yet."

"We could have got that just through regular reports."

"Yes, you could have. It's a possibility, however"—she pointed at the computers—"my people have been monitoring for that. I held it back intentionally just to see how well-informed you were. It also appears you were correct that the social media accounts were fake."

He smiled slightly. "Is that sliver of hope widening anymore because of it?"

She didn't return the smile. "It's the only reason we're having this conversation. You said you knew they were fake, and the way you said it told me that it had nothing to do with faith, and everything with you having facts not yet in evidence. So, how are you getting your information?"

"I can't say."

"Uh-huh. Do you think that by not telling me, it's going to make me any more willing to listen to you?"

He chuckled. "No, I suspect it will make you less willing. All I can tell you is that I have sources that I cannot discuss, acquired over years, that I trust implicitly. And when they tell me something, I believe them."

She sighed, clearly not pleased with his explanation. "Very well. Your sources seem to be better than mine, or at least more efficient, which makes me suspect MI6, or worse, CIA. But if they're going to help, then I don't really care where the information comes from." She extended a hand. "Truce?"

Reading smiled, shaking it. "Truce."

Operations Center 2, CIA Headquarters

Langley, Virginia

"I'm in!"

Leroux spun in his chair to look up at Child's workstation in the sloped room. "What are you in?"

"In like flint!"

Tong guffawed. "In like flint? What are you? Eighty? Do you even know what that means?"

Child shrugged proudly. "Not a clue. It's something my grandfather says." He scrunched his nose. "What *does* it mean?"

Leroux leaned back. "Well, you're both wrong." He pointed at Child. "You for saying it wrong"—he rolled his head toward Tong—"and you for not catching that he did."

Tong stared at him. "Huh?"

"It's 'in like Flynn' not 'flint.' It means you've easily accomplished something."

"What's a Flynn?" asked Child.

"Look it up." Leroux pointed at the back of Child's terminal. "You said you're in something?"

"I'm in her accounts."

Leroux stood. "Which ones?"

"All of them. Like a genius, she used the same password for every single account, and her User ID is her Gmail address for all of them, so, once you put two and two together, it's pretty easy to access everything she's got."

"Anything interesting?"

Child smiled. "You're going to love this. It's a direct message from her brother, who *does* have a Facebook account, by the way, just under a fake name to hide it from his parents. It says, 'Please post this to your account and tag me so I can get the followers.'" He pointed at the displays at the front of the room. "Look at this."

Everyone turned to watch a video of the professors, with their hands up, being led toward a door with Hugo Peeters, gun in one hand, Bible in the other, bringing up the rear. There was a brief conversation, the audio muffled, though Leroux was certain they could recover it, before the door was opened. The alarm sounded and the professors left with the Bible. Peeters closed the door and appeared to wait for something when someone else came into frame and the video ended.

Leroux looked at the fully-staffed room. "Well, if that doesn't prove they're innocent, I don't know what does. I think it's safe to assume that nobody out there has seen this. Now we need to decide what we're going to do with it. There's no doubt we have to let the authorities know. It's a critical piece of information that proves their innocence, and with the police operating under the wrong pretext, they need to know. The question is, do we release it publicly so that the world knows the professors are innocent?" He clapped. "Pros and cons."

Tong spoke first. "Pro, if the public knows they're innocent, then they don't blow them away the first time they see them."

Leroux nodded. "Keeping in mind they're in France, not Texas. They're not going to get blown away by a member of the public. No one has a gun over there."

"An overzealous cop could," offered Tong as a defense.

"Yup, that's a valid argument, though hopefully informing law enforcement will deal with that. What else?"

Child raised a hand, still accustomed to school. "Well, if the terrorists have them—because right now we have no clue where they are, but they're going somewhere, and we assume that somewhere is to hand over the Bible—if the terrorists know *we* know they're innocent, could the terrorists kill them?"

"It's a possibility, but the terrorists don't want *them*, they want the Bible, so they are going to do everything they can to get their hands on it. If they kill them because the world knows they're innocent, then they were probably going to kill them regardless. But I think the greatest threat to their survival at the moment is an accidental shooting by a law enforcement officer, or vigilante justice. We can inform law enforcement that they're innocent, but the only way to prevent vigilantism is to make sure the world knows they were forced into this and have done nothing wrong. Anything else?"

Head shakes.

"Good. I can't think of anything that makes me not want to push this out to the public. It also gives a jump-start on trying to mend their reputation. We're less than a day into this. There's still time to prevent this from destroying their futures after we save them."

"Let's do it!" shouted Child, his rallying cry resulting in chuckles and silence. He frowned. "No wonder you guys never have parties."

Leroux laughed then slapped his hands together. "Okay, people, let's do what we do best—influence public opinion."

"Unleash the bots!" cried Child, this time getting genuine laughter in support.

Tong held up a finger. "Umm, shouldn't we inform law enforcement first?"

Leroux paused. "Oh yeah, forgot about that."

Hotel Ercilla

Bilbao, Spain

Dawson's phone vibrated in his hand and as he checked the message, he noticed everyone else's phone had done the same. He smiled at the footage showing the professors being led at gunpoint to the door, then the Bible being handed over. "Well, if that doesn't clear their names, I don't know what will."

Niner pointed at the television. "Turn that up."

Kane, master of the remote, unmuted CNN International, a breaking news alert appearing.

"—breaking news on the terrorist attack last night. CNN has obtained new footage that appears to prove the innocence of Professors James Acton and Laura Palmer. It suggests they were coerced into taking the Bible, and are likely under the direction of the terrorists truly responsible. CNN is—"

Kane muted the television as high fives were exchanged around the room. "Let's hope that spreads far and wide so nobody ends up popping a cap in their asses. Now we just need to figure out where the hell they are."

"Let's hope the boys and girls at Langley can figure it out soon," said Niner. "I'm getting sick of seeing the inside of these walls."

Atlas rolled his eyes. "I'm getting sick of seeing your face."

"You're sick of seeing my face?"

"Yeah, you heard me."

"Then fine!" Niner dropped trou and mooned Atlas. "Is this better?"

"As a matter of fact, it is." Atlas reached over with a meaty palm and smacked Niner on the ass.

Niner cooed. "That was actually kind of nice. Do that again."

Atlas booted him in the ass, sending him flying into the wall, his pants and underwear falling to his ankles, leaving him in a heap of cheeks and crevices. Niner picked himself up and pulled his pants up, the others gripping their stomachs in laughter.

"When we get back to Bragg, I'm filing a report. That's sexual harassment."

Atlas flipped him the bird. "That wasn't sexual harassment. That was sexual abuse. Of me! I shouldn't be forced to look at that narrow little ass of yours."

Niner patted him on the cheek. "You like it and you know it." He headed for the bathroom. "Now I have to see if you've scuffed up my perfect ass-skin."

Spock motioned toward Niner as he exposed his cheek in front of the bathroom mirror. "I don't know if he scuffed it up, but I see a size fourteen imprint on your ass."

Niner tried to get a better view, scurrying in a circle like a dog chasing its tail. "Really? I didn't think it was big enough to fit a fourteen."

Guggenheim Bilbao

Bilbao, Spain

Reading flagged Sanchez down, having just received the exonerating video from Langley. He held up his phone with the footage. "Have you seen this yet?"

"What?" Her eyes widened and she took the phone, watching the video twice. "Where'd you get that?"

"From my contacts, but they've sent it to you as well."

She rushed toward the mobile command center, gesturing for him and Michelle to follow. They picked their way through the wreckage of the atrium, having finally been given an opportunity to see the aftermath of the devastating explosion. All the survivors had been taken to hospital last night, though many of the bodies—and body parts—still remained.

"Ma'am, you have to see this!" shouted one of the technicians from inside the unit, its open rear doors allowing him to spot Sanchez. She climbed in the back and took a seat. "It just came in." She watched it again, several times, the larger screen hopefully confirming to her what Reading already knew.

It was legit.

"Ma'am." The tech pointed at a screen showing CNN International, the same footage playing as he worked his keyboard. "It's all over the Internet. I mean, it's everywhere!"

She turned to Reading. "Who are these contacts of yours?"

He smiled. "Like I said, I can't say, but they're on your side if you're on my side."

Sanchez climbed out of the vehicle, accepting a steadying hand offered by Reading. "Well, it's pretty clear from this video, unless they're putting on a show, that they're innocent."

He frowned. "Please tell me you don't actually think that's what they were doing."

She waved her hands in front of her. "No, don't worry, I don't believe that for a second. You've convinced me, or rather, this footage has convinced me. Now we have to work under the assumption the professors are being forced to do what they're doing, so we have to cast a wider net."

"Why wasn't it cast wide before?"

"Because we froze all their accounts, so we knew they weren't going to be able to go and buy plane tickets or charter airplanes or whatever it is rich people do. They would have to work with whatever cash they had on hand, and judging by the way they were dressed in those photos, I doubt it would have been a whole lot." She bit her lower lip. "So, they stole bicycles when they arrived on the beach. Why would they do that?"

"They had somewhere to go?" suggested Michelle.

"But that seemed a spur of the moment thing. They were spotted easily. Witness reports said they walked out of the water, changed, were seen talking on a cellphone, then took the two nearest bikes in plain sight."

"They're under a time constraint. They had to get somewhere quickly, and walking didn't cut it, and they have no idea how to steal a car without a set of keys."

Sanchez nodded. "Okay, so there's a time constraint component. What is there in the area that a bicycle could get them to?"

Reading thought for a moment. "We have to assume that whoever they're meeting isn't actually there."

Sanchez regarded him. "Why?"

"Because if they were, they'd be getting picked up by a car. They had to bike somewhere not to rendezvous with some person, but to rendezvous with another mode of travel they couldn't be late for."

"Train?" suggested Michelle.

Sanchez tilted her head. "That's a possibility. We'll start running their faces, but it's been a few hours since that sighting, so they've probably reached their destination by now. With all the cameras, we'll find where they got off, assuming they took a train."

"Plane?"

"There is an airport there, but their faces are on every watch list you can think of, so they never would have gotten past security."

Michelle shook her head. "I doubt they'd have their passports on them, and he'd need one even to travel domestically."

"They likely left those at the hotel," said Reading.

"They did. We confirmed that when we searched their room," said Sanchez. "Bus?"

"Possible, though that would be the slowest escape route they could take. What about Uber or something like it?"

Sanchez dismissed the idea. "No, they would have required a smartphone, and we found theirs in a pile of confiscated phones at the blast scene."

Reading sighed in frustration at his own stupidity. "Wait a minute, we're going about this all wrong."

Sanchez eyed him. "What do you mean?"

"Well, we're forgetting that the person behind this has money. Let's assume they're very wealthy. We have to think how a rich person would escape the police. Would you stay in Europe, or do you get the hell out?"

"I would get the hell out," said Michelle. "Every cop on the continent is looking for them and has their faces on their phones or computers."

"Exactly. And can't be bought off if caught. No, they're long gone. If I'm the rich guy, there's no way in hell I'm going to have that Bible, associated with the death of scores of people, handed over to me in Europe. If I'm caught doing that exchange here, I'm finished. No, I'm going to have that exchange in another country beyond the reach of the law, where if I'm caught, I can hand over some cash and get myself out of the situation."

Sanchez frowned. "Well, unfortunately that's about three-quarters of the planet."

"Agreed, but it does mean there are only two modes of travel that can accomplish it, one of which is too slow."

"You mean by sea or by air."

"Exactly, and if I'm rich, I'm not going to do it by sea because it leaves us too much time to figure out what vessel they're on and just intercept them. But if I put them on an airplane, they could be out of European airspace in an hour or two, depending on which direction they're heading. Hell, if they're heading west, they could be out in minutes."

Michelle shook her head. "But we know they don't have their passports, and security would be looking for them, so there's no way they could take a plane."

Reading held up a finger. "Ahh, you're not thinking rich. They would take a private charter. Believe me, I've taken quite a few with them, and it's a different experience than what you and I are used to. Security is extremely lax. The rich don't like to be delayed by ID checks and luggage searches."

Sanchez's head slowly bobbed. "So, there's a chance that it was all arranged, and people were paid to look the other way."

"Exactly. Are there private charters running out of that town?"

Sanchez turned back to her command center and the tech checked his computer. "Yes, La Rochelle Airport has a private charter terminal."

"We need to get there now."

Sanchez agreed and directed her team. "Tell the French I'd like everybody that was working at the La Rochelle Airport this morning held for questioning, or brought back there if they've already left. And I need a list of every single plane that left since they were spotted stealing those bicycles, and what their destinations were. And get me a chopper." She turned back to Reading and Michelle. "You're coming."

"If you're asking, we are."

"I'm not asking, I'm telling. I'm Spanish police, you're Interpol. I'm going to need you on the ground to explain why I'm arriving."

Reading smiled broadly. "So, you do need me after all."

She gave him the stink-eye. "Don't let it go to your head."

Operations Center 2, CIA Headquarters

Langley, Virginia

"Chris."

Leroux jolted awake to find Tong leaning over him at his workstation. "Wh-what?"

"You fell asleep."

He straightened himself out. "Sorry about that, I haven't been getting much sleep lately."

Tong smiled at him sympathetically. "No need to apologize, we all know how you've been burning the candle at both ends with Sherrie's recovery. If you want, I can take over. You go back to her."

He shook the cobwebs from his head, wishing his old Red Bull habit was still out of control. "No, I'll be fine. But once this is over, I'm back on leave and turning off my phone."

Laughter rippled through the room.

"So, was I snoring, or did you find something?"

Child spoke up. "*I* did, but there's no way the low guy on the totem pole wakes the chief."

Leroux chuckled. "What did you find?"

"I found some emails arguing with someone about them not funding their usual protest fee. There's only an initial. It's between Hugo Peeters and this guy O. He's making a request for the customary protest fee for them to attend an animal rights rally in Berlin, and the reply was 'not this time. O.' Then he's asking why not? O says, 'Because you're not effective. I'm no longer going to be funding your group.' Then Peeters asks, 'But what are we supposed to do? Without your help, we can't accomplish our mutual goals.' O says, 'I don't think you're actually contributing to our mutual goals. My money is better spent elsewhere. Please do not contact me again.' So that's the end of that conversation. *Then,* two weeks ago, another email is sent to this O guy, saying 'It's critical we speak about this abomination at the Guggenheim, and their plans to recreate this atrocity.'"

Leroux smiled. "Now that's something. What then?"

"O replies back. 'Agreed, give me a number to call you at.' Peeters gives him a number and then there are no more emails. I guess everything else was done by phone."

"What's the number?"

Child grinned. "It's the number for his parents' house that he lives in the basement of."

Tong gave him a look. "Don't judge. You still live with your folks."

Child shook his head. "Yes, but there's a difference. He moved back in, I never left."

Leroux ended the jousting. "Okay, pull the phone records so we can see who called him around that time."

Tong tapped at her keyboard then gestured to the display as the phone records appeared, highlighting one of them. "Here's a call that came in a few minutes after that email was sent. It looks like it's never called before."

Leroux smiled at their first real clue. "That must be him. Trace it. And run it through Echelon."

"I'm on it."

Leroux checked his messages and was surprised to see Tommy hadn't replied to his last one. He decided the guy deserved a personal call and dialed his number.

"Hello?"

"Hi, is this Mai?"

"Yes."

"Hi Mai, my name is Chris. Can I speak to Tommy?"

"He's sleeping. Can I take a message?"

"Actually, he's been doing some work for me. I just wanted to let him know—"

"Oh, you're *that* Chris! Just a second!" Muffled scratches and a short conversation ended with a sleepy Tommy at the other end of the line.

"Hello?"

"Hi Tommy, it's Chris."

"Oh, hello, umm, what can I do for you?"

The kid sounded exhausted. "Nothing. I just wanted to let you know that thanks to your help, we were able to find footage that proves they're innocent."

"That's great news! Thanks for letting me know. Can you handle this from here?"

Leroux chuckled. "I think we can."

"Good. I'll be asleep until Tuesday."

Marrakesh, Morocco

Acton stared out the window as the plane descended, his eyes widening slightly. He was well aware they were heading south simply by the position of the sun, but their final destination was a surprise.

"Looks like we're in Marrakesh," he whispered.

Laura leaned over for a look. "Morocco? Why the devil would he bring us to Morocco?"

He shrugged. "I don't know, but here we are. I'm guessing he wanted us out of Europe so that he wouldn't have to deal with the authorities there if something went wrong."

She leaned back. "They have authorities here."

"Yeah, but in a country like this, they can be bought for the right amount of money."

Laura squinted with one eye. "But Morocco is stable."

"It's stable, but it has enough problems that the right amount of money buys you anything."

"You're right on that. Do you think we're actually going to meet him?"

"I don't know. I guess we'll find out."

Their flight attendant, who had done her job admirably, attending to their every need except information, approached. "I'll get you to make sure you're buckled in. We'll be landing shortly."

Acton tapped the buckle of his seatbelt. "I rarely take it off." Laura did the same.

"Excellent. When we arrive, you'll be met by a driver. Please get in the car. Everything will be explained to you then." She returned to the back, and as promised, minutes later they were on the ground, a black limousine waiting for them, a chauffeur in the usual accouterments of the trade waiting.

As they disembarked and walked onto the tarmac, the chauffeur opened the rear door and a man stepped out. He smiled broadly at them and bowed. "Professor Acton, Professor Palmer. Please get in."

They complied, no pleasantries exchanged, likely so anyone watching wouldn't have time to get a good look at them. They were followed in by the man, then the door was closed by the chauffeur. "Can you show me the item, please?"

Acton opened the waterproof bag he had been carrying the Bible in since the boat, and let him look inside.

"Thank you." He tapped on the glass separating them from the driver, and it lowered several inches. "Go ahead," he said in Arabic. The glass slid back up and the car gently pulled away from the private jet. He retrieved a cellphone and made a call, switching to German, causing

Acton and Laura to exchange surprised glances. "I've seen it…ninety minutes." He ended the call then smiled at them. "Enjoy the drive, professors." He gestured at the fridge. "Help yourselves. It will be some time before we arrive."

Acton shook his head. "No thanks, I think I'll just enjoy the view."

The man chuckled, puzzling him at first.

Then he noticed the windows were blacked out.

Somebody doesn't want us to know where we're going.

He decided it might be best not to let them know they were already fully aware they were in Marrakesh.

It might just save their lives.

La Rochelle Airport

La Rochelle, France

Reading played diplomat and lead investigator as pleasantries and updates were exchanged with the French National Police representative in charge on the ground. Sanchez was taking the position of second fiddle well, and he made certain not to trivialize her role now that they were on good terms, the ice completely broken on the helicopter ride here.

"Do you mind if we conduct the interrogations?"

Chief Inspector Jacques Bisset shook his head. "Not at all, so long as I sit in on them."

"Absolutely, I wouldn't have it any other way. I used to be Scotland Yard and know how I felt when Interpol would show up as if they owned the place."

Hearty laughter was exchanged. "Then you were once a real cop?"

273

Reading smiled broadly as they were led inside the private terminal. "For over twenty years."

"I think I would miss it too much to leave."

"Sometimes I wonder if I made the right decision." He gestured toward a row of seats occupied by unhappy employees. "Is everybody here that was working this morning?"

"Yes, they had just begun their shifts, so they were all still here."

Reading's expert eye surveyed the suspects. Some were defiant, some were nervous, and some were scared. He pointed at a young woman who appeared petrified, and was purposefully leaning away from the man she was sitting beside, as if she didn't want to be associated with him. "You first."

Her jaw dropped. "Why me?"

He shrugged. "Why not?"

A police officer led her into a room commandeered for the interrogations. She was placed on one side of the lone table. Reading sat across from her, then Sanchez, Michelle, and Bisset occupied three of the corners, the woman sufficiently intimidated.

"Let me start by saying we already know the truth. We just want to confirm it. If you tell us the truth and don't lie to us, then you won't be charged with giving a false statement or, worse, interference in a police investigation. We just need you to tell us what happened in your own words."

She glanced at him for a moment of defiance, her eyes immediately returning to her clenched hands lying in her lap. "If you already know, then why are you talking to me?"

"Standard procedure. We need to confirm what our source already told us, so we know what he told us really did happen."

"I had nothing to do with it."

"Well, that's not matching up with what I was told."

She stared at him, mouth agape. "But I thought you said you knew!"

Reading continued his bluff, the young woman having fallen for it. "Well, if you're saying that you weren't involved, and my source is saying you were, then one of you is lying, so why don't you tell me how it went down as far as you're concerned."

She sighed. "Fine. It's simple. They get a text message with what flight is coming in and what the cargo is, then a thousand euros is deposited into each of their accounts that have been set up for this. They're untraceable. They access them through debit cards. When the package arrives, it's just put through onto the plane. If it's a person, they're just pushed through customs and nothing is checked or recorded."

"What about the cameras?"

"They malfunction for the five minutes it takes to get things done."

Reading hid his shock. "How often does this happen?"

She shrugged. "Usually once or twice a month."

"And is everybody in on it?"

She vehemently shook her head. "No, not everybody. Only the people who need to be. They're usually told ahead of time so the right people can be put on the shift. This one came in at the very last minute. Like I said, I know about it, but I'm not part of it."

"Then why haven't you reported it?"

Tears welled in her eyes. "Because I'm afraid to lose my job, and I'm also afraid they might kill me. These can't be good people, right? But today, because it was last-minute and I was on shift, I was told that I would be cut in on the deal and to keep my mouth shut or else. I told them I'd keep my mouth shut, but I wouldn't take any money."

"Who's the ringleader here?"

She was about to answer when she caught herself. "Don't you know?"

"Like I said, I want to confirm what I was told. I was told you were involved, and you're telling me you're not."

"Nicolas Griveaux."

"He's outside?"

"Yes."

"What flight number was it?"

"I don't remember the number. I can find out for you."

"What was the destination?"

"Marrakesh."

Reading's eyes widened. "Marrakesh?"

"I thought you knew?"

He smiled slightly. "Well, we police say a lot of things that aren't necessarily always true."

Her jaw dropped. "Hey, you lied to me! That's not fair!"

Reading rose. "Young lady, nobody said life was fair, but the law says I can lie."

Hotel Ercilla

Bilbao, Spain

Niner stared at his ass in the mirror, a distinct bruise forming. "You know, you actually can see the tread mark."

"That was the whole idea. You're lucky I didn't hit where I was aiming."

"And where was that?"

"That tight little pucker you've got hidden between those narrow cheeks."

Niner pulled up his pants. "Bullshit, you'd never risk losing—"

The comm gear beeped and Kane grabbed the headset, putting the conversation on speaker. "Go for Whiskers."

"Whiskers, Control. We have a destination for you."

The entire room was all ears.

"Where?"

"They landed in Marrakesh about half an hour ago."

"Marrakesh? What the hell are they doing there?"

"We pulled some video and it looks like they were met at the airport and taken away in a limo. We believe the exchange is happening either in the city or somewhere in Morocco."

Dawson frowned. "Morocco isn't exactly tiny. Can you narrow it down a bit?"

"Not yet, but by the time you get there, we're hoping we'll have a final destination for you. Oh, and Mr. Whiskers?"

The room snickered.

Kane chuckled. "Yeah?"

"You're sanctioned the moment you leave European airspace."

He grinned. "So, can I start killing at twelve miles out or two-hundred? I can never remember."

Leroux wasn't forthcoming. "You'll be on a charter we've arranged, so it will be slim pickings either way. I'd wait until you're on the ground."

Kane smiled at the others. "Ground crew are on the menu. Excellent. They better not scuff my luggage."

Dawson leaned closer to the mike. "Does that mean the CIA is now bankrolling this operation?"

"Delta, you're still on vacation, but we're paying for the plane to Marrakesh and covering everything between your current location and the rest of the op."

Niner eyed the minibar. "Does that include this hotel?"

"If you're in the room Dylan booked, yes."

Niner grinned, rubbing his hands together like Mr. Burns. "Excellent." He began grabbing things from the minibar and tossing them to the others.

"When you arrive, our local contact will equip you. I've sent all the details to your secure email. I've also sent you the file on who we think is behind this. You can read all about it on the plane. Leave all your comms and gear behind. We don't control this charter, so we can't have anyone thinking you're anything but tourists. And you better get a wiggle on. Wheels up in thirty."

"Copy that, Whiskers, out." Kane turned off the equipment and began packing up.

Niner broke the seal on a pack of macadamia nuts. "Let's go kick some ass and eat some snacks."

Atlas snatched the nuts from him. "I think there's been enough ass-kicking in here already, but I'll take your snacks."

La Rochelle Airport

La Rochelle, France

Reading headed for the helicopter waiting to take them back to Bilbao, when his phone rang. He took the call as he turned around and headed back for the terminal and the quiet that lay beyond its doors.

"Hello?"

"Agent Reading, it's Chris Leroux."

"Have you got an update for me? Did that plane actually go to Marrakesh?"

"Yes, sir. We have footage of them arriving in Marrakesh and being met by someone. They got in a limo and left. Kane's team is in the air. They'll be on the ground in less than three hours."

"Bollocks. I was hoping to join them."

"There was no time. I'm afraid you're sitting this one out, sir."

Reading grunted. "Probably for the best. These old bones can't keep up with those young lads anymore. Do we know who's behind this yet?"

"We found a phone number that turned out to be a burner, so it was untraceable, however, using Echelon, we were able to track other calls it made, including several to La Rochelle and Bilbao, all over the past twenty-four hours, all to the same number which was first registered in Antwerp."

"Where Peeters is from."

"Exactly."

"Does that help us?"

"It tells us that Hugo Peeters gave his phone to the professors, and instructions were being fed to them by whoever was on the other end of the burner."

"Were any other calls made from this burner?"

"Yes, as a matter of fact, and you're going to like this. We have one brief phone call made to Richter Telecom in Berlin. Listen to this transcript from Echelon, translated from the original German. I think you'll find it interesting. 'How did you get this number? What do you mean, how did I get this number? Oh, sorry, sir, I didn't realize it was you. Is this a new phone number? Shit! I'll call you right back.'"

Reading smiled as he caught up to what Leroux and his team had already figured out. "So, it sounds like he used the burner phone by mistake, and the person at the other end of the line knew exactly who they were talking to just by the sound of their voice."

"Exactly."

"What's this Richter Telecom? I've heard of them."

"It's a telecommunications company based in Berlin. They're massive. One of the biggest players in the industry."

"Please tell me there's a megalomaniac running it."

"As a matter of fact, their CEO, Oskar Richter, is a well-known supporter of animal rights and various other causes, but get this. He hasn't been seen in years since he went all Howard Hughes and decided the world was out to get him. He's dropped off the face of the Earth."

"And could that particular drop off point be Morocco?"

"Funny you should ask. We actually found him by examining Echelon intercepts of phone calls made from Morocco to Richter Telecom. And we've located him."

Reading's pulse picked up. "Where?"

"Satellite imagery shows that he has a compound about two hours outside of Marrakesh at the base of the Atlas Mountains."

He tensed. "When I hear compound, I'm thinking trouble."

"And you'd be right. It looks like it's walled and fenced in with regular patrols."

He was suddenly concerned for Kane and the Bravo Team. "Are five guys going to be enough?"

"Five normal guys, no, but those five, I think so. If they can confirm they're private security, then they have a green light to take them out. If they're Moroccan troops, it poses a bigger problem because we don't want to be killing soldiers from a country we're not at war with."

"There's no way we can get them more help?"

"No, not in the time we have. Our fear is that as soon as the Bible is handed over, they'll no longer have any use for the professors, and they'll take them out."

He frowned. "That's what I'm afraid of too. Okay, keep me posted. I assume you're passing on this intel through official channels."

"Everything except the intel on where the calls were made from. We don't want to risk a leak that will tip off Richter or his people that we know where he is and are coming for him."

"Understood. Tell the lads, good luck."

"Will do."

Richter's Compound

Morocco

Richter glanced up from his laptop as Gerhard entered. "Are they here?"

"No, sir. They should be here in about thirty minutes. I just wanted to let you know that our dummy social media accounts are being taken down at an extraordinary rate. Somehow, the social media providers have been able to identify almost all of them."

Richter leaned back, overwhelmed by a sinking feeling at the news of years of hard, expensive work wiped away. "How is that possible? They've never been able to do that before."

"They must be getting help."

Richter cursed. "It has to be the CIA. They've always been out to get me."

"It could be."

"How does this affect us?"

"It will hurt our cause until we can recreate the accounts and rebuild everything. These were cultivated over years, so had legitimate-looking history that allowed us to push the causes we wanted more effectively."

Richter pursed his lips, staring at the news playing on the far wall. "Let's wait, but as soon as this is all settled, start recreating them again. We're going to have a huge injection of funds that we can use to further our cause without having to worry about hiding the fact the money has been coming from me. This will allow us to take things to the next level." He switched focus. "Has our buyer landed yet?"

"No. I've been informed he will be at least two hours late due to a delay at his end that was unavoidable."

Richter sighed heavily. "What sort of delay?"

"I didn't ask as I didn't expect the truth would be forthcoming."

Richter chuckled. "You're probably right. Okay, when the professors arrive, bring the Bible to me. I want to see this abomination for myself."

Gerhard stared at the floor, shifting his weight from one foot to the other. "Umm, is that wise, sir?"

Richter eyed him. "Why wouldn't it be?"

"Well, sir, on occasion your…shall we say *passion,* has gotten the better of you. Can we risk that happening again? You might destroy the item in a rage, thus losing the payout of two-hundred-million Euros."

He regarded his butler for a moment, at first angered at the notion. He finally shook his head. "Perhaps you're right. Put it in the viewing room when it arrives, and I'll see it for the first time along with everyone else. And put the professors under guard. I'll want them to authenticate the Bible to the buyer."

"Very well."

"Are our men ready for trouble?"

Gerhard bowed slightly. "They always are, sir. No need to worry, the compound is as secure as it has ever been."

"Are we at full strength again?"

"Yes, sir, that flu bug has run its course. We have all twelve of Mr. Kriel's men healthy. He's put everyone on duty for the duration of this event."

"Good. I want this transaction to go as smoothly and as quickly as possible. The sooner that atrocity is far away from me and the money is in my account, the better. Oh, and make sure the staff are locked down while the buyer is here. I don't want any undue attention drawn to this evening's transaction."

"Yes, sir."

He closed his burning eyes. "I can't wait for this day to be over so I can start to atone for the sin of profiting off the death of so many innocent creatures."

Approaching Richter's Compound

Morocco

"We're here."

Acton tensed as the end of their ordeal was near, and he suspected their lives as well. The car slowly came to a stop then rocked slightly as the chauffeur exited. A moment later, the door opened and he held out a hand for Laura, who took it on instinct. He followed, then their escort. He blinked, this the first light they had seen in hours, and he did a quick turn to take in everything within sight, something his SAS trainer had taught him.

They were in the courtyard of a large walled estate. The main building was directly in front of them, a set of steps leading up to a grand entrance. To either side were support buildings including an impressive multi-car garage to his left with a notorious British sportscar on the lift, its engine torn apart on the floor, a frustrated mechanic pulling at his hair.

He spotted six guard towers, four at the corners, two at the mid-point of the left and right sides, though he couldn't tell if they were manned as their design for some reason left them blind to what was at any sentry's back.

And cameras were everywhere.

"The Bible, please."

Acton reluctantly handed it over to their escort, who disappeared inside the main building, two heavily armed guards stepping through the doors and taking up position at the bottom of the steps, making it clear he and Laura weren't to move.

Mercenaries.

Out of the corner of his eye he spotted the mountains looming large to the east, and the chill in the air suggested they were at a higher altitude than Marrakesh. Not far to the north, he could see the spires of a mosque, indicating a town nearby, then he spotted something unmistakable.

And suppressed a smile.

He turned his back to the guards, lowering his voice to a whisper. "We're in Asni."

She eyed him. "How could you possibly know that?"

"Well, we landed in Marrakesh and traveled for two hours, so that means these are the Atlas Mountains. That looks to be the highest peak, which would make it Mount Toubkal. That narrows down the possible towns in the area, but that hotel down the mountain in that town? That's the Kasbah Tamadot, making this Asni."

She stared at him. "Impressive."

He grinned. "I do aim to please."

"And just how are you so familiar with this area?"

"I'm an impressive guy?"

"Oh, you are that, but even you have your limits."

He chuckled. "Actually, I recognized it from a National Geographic article I read recently."

Her eyes narrowed as she stared at the mountains. "Wait a minute, this area was covered in one of the issues that you were in."

He feigned ignorance. "Oh, was it?"

"Don't sound so innocent. You were rereading your own press, weren't you?"

"I am a vain man."

"A *very* vain man." She lowered her voice further. "You better keep that tidbit to yourself."

"That I'm vain?"

"No, that you know exactly where we are. It could be our death warrant."

He frowned, his genius proving inconvenient. "Good point."

Their escort reemerged. "Bring them!"

The guards stepped forward and shoved them toward the entrance. Acton decided it was best not to protest.

"Come with me," said their escort as he led them deeper into the building.

"What now? You have the Bible. When are you going to let us go?"

"We're not finished with you yet."

"What else could we possibly do now?"

"You will verify the provenance of the Bible to the buyer."

"Why would we possibly do that?"

"Because, Professor Acton, if you don't, you'll die."

He grunted. "You're probably going to kill us anyway."

"No, Professor Acton, we value life. All life."

Acton rolled his eyes. "Yeah, you showed that when you massacred all those people."

The man stopped and turned toward them, his expression suggesting he was genuinely offended. "We had nothing to do with that! We weren't aware that the Brigade had that in mind. We merely capitalized on their plans to take over the museum. We had assumed they were going to make a political statement, draw attention to their cause. My employer values human life, to a fault sometimes. Do as you are told, and you will survive this. Defy us, and you will discover there are horrible ways to die that involve tremendous amounts of pain that can last for days, the most terrible of which is watching it happen to the woman you love while you sit by helpless. Your bodies will be found far from here in the Sahara, near a terrorist training camp, with enough false information planted on the Internet for the world to believe that they were behind the attack at the museum."

"Do you think people will believe that separatist rebels actually committed a terrorist attack over animal rights?"

"No, but they will believe that they funded it, thinking it was for something else. And that those that did execute the attack hijacked the event for their own purposes."

Acton eyed him skeptically. "That's a stretch."

"They'll believe what we tell them to believe. We've been doing it for years, and we'll continue to do it long after we part ways. The Internet is a wonderful thing. It allows any cause to appear legitimate, and with social media, and its anonymity, it can make anything look like it has thousands of fervid followers. As you know, social cred is all that matters to give a cause momentum and legitimacy."

He continued walking, saying nothing further until they stopped in front of a room. He opened the door and held out his hand, indicating they should go inside. Acton went first, finding a simply furnished room, clearly not meant for their captor's honored guests, more likely their staff.

"So, what now?"

"You will wait in here until the buyer arrives. You will then confirm to him that the Bible is indeed the one that was stolen from the Guggenheim. Assuming he is satisfied and transfers the money, you will be taken back to Marrakesh, returned to France, and you will continue on with your lives. Do your part, and you will both be home by this time tomorrow."

The door slammed shut and Acton inspected the room a little closer, spotting a camera in one of the corners. He turned his back to it and indicated its existence to Laura.

Ending any conversation they might have been about to start.

It would be a long wait.

Operations Center 2, CIA Headquarters

Langley, Virginia

"Holy shit!"

Leroux looked up from Tong's workstation. "Language, Mr. Child."

Child blushed. "Sorry, sir."

Leroux chuckled. "I'm just joking. Have you heard the Chief?"

"Now that's a salty tongue!" shouted someone from the back of the room, laughter erupting.

"Shut up!" shouted Child, waving a hand in the air as audio was piped through the speakers.

"*—twenty minutes out. I'll notify you the moment I have the buyer secured.*"

"*Very well. I'll expect your call within thirty minutes.*"

"*Yes, sir.*"

There was a click, signaling the end of the call, the room dead silent except the whirring of fans.

Leroux looked at Child, his hand still in the air, demanding silence. "What did we just listen to?"

"A live call from Richter's burner phone to what I assume is his driver picking up the buyer for the Bible."

"Trace it!"

"Already done." Child gestured toward the front of the room, a map displayed showing a red dot moving along a rural road, rapidly approaching Marrakesh.

Leroux returned to his workstation, grabbing his headset. "Sonya, get me our man in Marrakesh."

"Just a sec." She tapped some keys. "Go ahead."

"Bright Penny, Control, do you read, over."

"Five-by-five, Control."

"We're sending you a target now. It's the vehicle being sent to pick up the buyer. We need it delayed. We can't have him picked up before Delta arrives."

Marrakesh, Morocco

Bright Penny, a.k.a. Rafik Bennani, cursed as he rushed to clear the city limits of his lifelong home of Marrakesh. Langley's orders had come in only minutes ago, leaving him only minutes more to not only get his sniper rifle from its hiding place in his home, but get it into his car without the neighbors discovering he was actually a CIA asset. Not to mention that they needed him to find a position outside of the city to delay a driver without him knowing he had been deliberately delayed.

"He's three minutes from your position."

A colorful Darijan expletive erupted. He spotted a bend in the road ahead with a wide cleared area beside it that would give him a good view of any vehicles approaching. He turned off the road and skidded to a halt. He threw his door open and grabbed his sniper rifle from the back seat, then sprinted toward a large rock that he prayed to Allah would give him the cover from prying eyes he needed.

"Two minutes."

He dropped to his knees and quickly set up his weapon before lying prone, pressing his eye to the scope. "I'm ready. Describe the target."

"Black Mercedes sedan. One minute."

He got a bead on the road and slowly tracked back then smiled. "Got it. Stand by."

He aimed for the rear tire. It would leave the driver with the most control, since the aim wasn't to kill the poor bastard. He inhaled, taking aim at the sidewall of the tire in the hopes the bullet would not only shred any run-flat feature, but pass through the tire and not embed itself in the rim, leaving evidence as to what had happened.

He gently exhaled as he squeezed the trigger.

The car swerved, and for a moment he thought the worst, but after a few tense seconds the driver regained control and brought the car to a halt. Bennani peered through the scope and smiled at the completely disabled rear tire. He rolled to his side and dismantled his weapon, packed it away, then returned to his car. He placed the gun in a hidden compartment in the trunk, then pulled back onto the road.

"Control, Bright Penny. Mission accomplished. Vehicle is disabled, no way to know for how long. On my way to the rendezvous, out."

And next time give me more than ten minutes!

Marrakesh Menara Airport

Marrakesh, Morocco

Dawson frowned at the car that awaited the five of them. Kane shook their contact's hand and he beckoned them to get in, his demeanor that of an agitated local. Dawson wagged a finger at Kane before he could get in the passenger seat.

"Nah-uh. If four of us are getting in the back seat, Atlas is getting up front."

Atlas grinned and kissed a bicep. "It's good to be the king."

"If there's not enough room, I'll sit in his lap," offered Niner.

Atlas gave him an eye as he climbed in. "There's room in the trunk."

"That would look suspicious."

"And sitting on my lap wouldn't?"

"Why should it? I'm just here on a romantic getaway with my lover."

Atlas glanced over his shoulder at the acrobatics in play as the others squeezed into the rear. "I'll get in the trunk before I let him give me a lap dance."

Dawson and Kane were in the corners, an arm each spread across the back, with Spock and Niner wedged between them.

Niner glanced back at Spock. "I feel like your thong."

Spock cocked an eyebrow. "BD, can I get in the trunk?"

Their driver hammered on the gas the moment the last door closed. "I'm sorry for this. Langley sent me on a last-minute assignment. I've got a bigger vehicle for us with all the equipment in it." He glanced in the rearview mirror and smiled. "You don't want to drive into an airport zone loaded with weaponry. It's bad enough I have a sniper rifle in the trunk."

Dawson's eyes narrowed. "Why do you have that?"

"That last-minute assignment. I had to delay the buyer's ride from arriving."

"Did you?" asked Kane.

"Yes, but I don't know for how long. I'll get you guys comms when we get to the secondary vehicle so you can get back in the loop. I understand that charter wasn't secure?"

"That's right." Kane adjusted his position. "Do you think we can reach the pick-up vehicle before he gets back on the road?"

"It all depends on how good he is at changing tires. It's possible. Why?"

"I have an idea."

Outside Marrakesh, Morocco

Bennani pointed ahead at a black Mercedes. "That's him."

Kane activated his comm as he assessed the area, the driver, working on the tire, the only one in sight. "Zero-One, Whiskers. You guys proceed, we're going to say hello."

"Copy that, Whiskers."

Kane smiled at the cuteness Dawson added to his callsign. "Pull over behind him."

"Yes, sir."

Bennani crossed the road and brought their SUV to a halt behind the Mercedes facing in the opposite direction, as the SUV Bravo Team was in continued on. Kane climbed out and walked toward the chauffeur, smiling. "Can we give you a hand?"

The chauffeur glanced over his shoulder as he tightened a lug nut. "No, I'm almost done. Thanks." He returned his attention to the tire as

Kane continued forward. The man noticed, and as Kane leaned in to put him into a sleeper hold, he reacted.

Too late.

Within seconds, the oxygen had been cut off from the man's brain and his struggles weakened as Kane dragged him away from the road and behind a cluster of large boulders. "Finish that tire!" he ordered Bennani.

"Yes, sir."

Kane quickly stripped the driver of his jacket, shirt, and pants, then pulled off his own clothes. He put the driver's on and frowned at how tight they were. And short.

Bennani laughed at him. "I think there's a flaw in your plan."

Marrakesh Menara Airport

Marrakesh, Morocco

Kane positioned the car at an angle then stepped around the front and opened the door, using it to hopefully shield his ill-fitting clothes. The driver, now in the trunk of Bennani's vehicle, had provided them with all the details for the pick-up, and Kane was now smiling at the man they assumed was the buyer as he stepped from the private jet.

Kane bowed slightly. "Sir. I trust your flight was uneventful."

The man nodded. He bent over to climb in the back when he paused, looking at Kane's pants, several inches too short. He said nothing, getting inside, but Kane was certain suspicions had been raised.

He closed the door and climbed in the driver's seat. "We'll be there in about two hours, sir."

The man pointed at the divider. "Some privacy, please."

"Yes, sir." Kane pressed the button to put the partition up, then picked up the earpiece to his comm and pressed it into his ear, allowing him to hear the transmission from the bug he had planted in the rear.

Where his passenger was already making a call.

He glanced at the cellphone jammer he had sitting in the passenger seat. He could stop the man from making calls, though that might raise suspicions if he didn't have any. But they needed to know who the buyer was. He was quite certain that this man was just an intermediary. There was a good chance he was calling his boss, rather than Richter.

"The driver you sent me has ill-fitting clothes. Describe him to me."

Kane cursed and activated the jammer.

"Hello? Hello?" The man growled and Kane smiled, activating his comm.

"Control, I think I've been made. He didn't like the cut of my jib. I jammed his phone, but red flags are going to have been raised."

"Copy that, keep us posted. I'll notify Delta of the situation. They're nearing the compound now."

Richter's Compound

Asni, Morocco

Richter buzzed in Gerhard as he stared at his phone, puzzled. The call had been brief, and odd to say the least, though he wasn't sure if he should be concerned, for it seemed absurd.

"Sir?"

"I just had an unusual phone call from the buyer."

"Sir?"

"He asked me to describe our driver, because the man who picked him up had ill-fitting clothes, then we were cut off."

Gerhard's eyebrows rose. "Ill-fitting clothes? That's ridiculous. All of our staff are meticulously outfitted as per your instructions. Happy staff are loyal staff, and loyal staff are quiet staff."

"Exactly, so if this man had ill-fitting clothes, then he can't be one of ours."

"Have you tried calling him?"

Richter shook his head. "No, I wouldn't recognize his voice if he answered. Would you?"

"I would." Gerhard retrieved his phone and dialed, putting it on speaker. A generic voicemail, not set up because the man had probably never missed a phone call from his employer in his entire career, answered immediately.

"That's odd."

"Not necessarily, sir. You said you were cut off, and we know reception can be spotty at times. Rarely do we talk to our people en route from Marrakesh for just that reason."

"But ill-fitting clothes?"

"That is a puzzle, sir, and does concern me. I'll check the security footage. If his clothes fit when he left, then they should have when he picked up the buyer."

"Let's hope they didn't fit, because if they did, then we have a serious problem."

Gerhard stared at the courtyard camera footage in the security center, peering intently at the chauffeur's sleeves and pant legs. "Do his clothes look like they fit to you?"

The security officer nodded. "Yes, sir. Don't they to you?"

"Yes, they do, I just wanted to make sure no one could be mistaken." He pointed at the screen. "Send that footage to Mr. Richter."

"Yes, sir."

Gerhard headed back to Richter's office, his mind racing. The driver had clearly been replaced. Yet how would anyone know to do it? It made no sense. There was no possible way for someone to know that their driver was heading into Marrakesh to pick up the buyer, unless it was an inside job, and he couldn't see that. The staff was loyal, paid well, and always under surveillance.

He tapped the keypad outside Richter's sanctuary and the door beeped. He opened it and stepped inside. "I'm afraid we have a problem, sir."

Richter frowned. "The clothes fit?"

"The clothes fit."

Richter cursed. "Then something's gone wrong. The question is, what? Our driver is intercepted, the buyer is picked up. How did they know?"

"They would have questioned the chauffeur when they intercepted him."

"Yes, yes, but how would they have known to intercept him? Only we knew he had been sent." Richter's eyes widened. "We have a mole inside the compound!"

Gerhard shook his head. "I find that hard to believe. These are all trusted people who've been with us for years."

"Everyone can be bought. The question is by whom?"

Gerhard decided he had to continue down this train of thought, and only one possibility came to him. "Aren't we forgetting the obvious?"

"What?"

"The authorities. Perhaps they were able to track the professors here."

Richter cursed. "Damn that fool for insisting we meet in person. This is what happens when plans are changed at the last minute. Mistakes are made."

"Sir, this entire operation was last-minute. They had already taken the museum before your plan even began."

Richter regarded him for a moment. "True, but those plans would have been perfect if we had been able to do a handover to someone else. That bastard insisting they be at the meet, and that it be here, caused all of these problems. We could have just put the Bible on the plane and have been done with it."

Gerhard wasn't convinced of his own idea. "But if it were the police, why not just arrest the buyer, and raid the compound? The Moroccans would want to look good on the world stage, especially with so many dead. They could send several hundred troops here and force us to surrender without firing a shot. Instead, they replace our driver? That sounds like an infiltration operation to me."

His boss' head bobbed. "You're right. The Europeans wouldn't send a team here to arrest me without notifying the locals. They're sticklers for procedures, just look at that ISO crap they foisted on everyone. I haven't seen an IT project finish on time or budget since." His eyes widened. "What would you do if I were kidnapped?"

Gerhard's eyebrows shot up. "I would find out where you were and mount a rescue operation."

"And what if you couldn't trust or rely upon the local authorities?"

"I would send Mr. Kriel and his men in."

"Exactly. These professors are rich. My kind of people. They would have their own private security, I'm willing to bet. This could be a rescue op by their people. That would mean limited numbers, so surprise would be a necessity, especially with a compound like this. At most a dozen men, perhaps fewer. If they could get a man on the inside, this substitute chauffeur, they might be hoping to get the upper hand. Just a few minutes of confusion could give them the advantage."

"I'll warn Kriel."

"Do that."

"And the buyer?"

"Let him come. But I want that chauffeur taken down the moment they arrive. Alive. I want to know his plans, how many are with him, everything."

"Very well, sir."

Outside Richter's Compound

Asni, Morocco

"Over there." Dawson pointed toward a large outcropping of rocks that would provide good cover for their vehicle. "We'll hoof it the rest of the way." Atlas pulled them in behind the outcropping and Dawson jerked a thumb over his shoulder. "Niner, check it out."

Niner jumped out and confirmed the vehicle wasn't visible from the road, then gave Atlas a thumbs up before sprinting off toward the compound. Atlas turned off the engine and everyone geared up. After checking each other's equipment, Dawson contacted Langley as they began their hike.

"Control, Zero-One. We're about two klicks from the compound. We'll be going on foot now, over."

"Copy that, Zero-One. Whiskers is twenty-minutes out, over."

Dawson checked his tactical computer for the lay of the land, zooming in on the latest satellite imagery of the compound. He turned to the others. "Still looks like six on the walls, unknown number inside. Control, is there any way in that you guys can see?"

"Negative, Zero-One, and we have no plans for this place, of course. All we can do is give you surface layout. With Whiskers compromised, we've lost our element of surprise, and for all we know, they might cut him to shreds the moment he arrives, over."

"We need to be in position to provide cover, just in case."

"Disco!"

Dawson rolled his eyes. "Thunder. And if I see a dance, there's going to be a friendly fire incident."

Niner emerged from behind a rock, moping. "You're no fun."

"Report."

"I went all around that place. There's no way in that I can see except through the front gate or over the walls. But I've got an idea."

"What?"

"As we already know, there are six on the walls, but here's the good piece of news: none of their positions have a line of sight with each other because of poor design."

Dawson's eyes narrowed. "Explain."

"The guard towers are open to the outside so they can see anything approaching, but are closed behind them so they can't see inside the compound."

Spock cocked an eyebrow. "Why the hell would they do that?"

Leroux replied. "Our profile on him suggests he's paranoid. He might not want them to be able to see anything he's doing within the compound, so had the posts designed so they could protect him from outside aggressors, but maintain his privacy."

Dawson grunted. "Maybe his paranoia is our gain."

Niner continued leading them to the compound. "That's what I was thinking. Here's my idea. They're all uniformed, in black, with cute little berets."

Atlas looked at their own black outfits. "It is a rather fetching color. And slimming."

Niner eyed him. "Stop clenching those glutes so much and you might not need to rely on fashion to slim down that fat ass of yours."

"Vanessa likes my ass, and that's all that matters."

"I—"

Atlas raised a finger. "If you say you like her ass, you're in for a world of hurt."

Niner batted a hand at him. "While it is a spectacular ass, I was going to say I like your ass too."

"Thank you, that's important to me."

Dawson rolled his eyes. "Are you two done?"

"In a moment. You know, my ass is still a little—"

Dawson booted Niner in the ass. "Your plan, sergeant?"

Niner patted Atlas' shoulder. "We'll continue this later." He turned to Dawson. "I think we do the ole switcheroo."

Dawson smiled. "I like it."

Approaching Richter's Compound
Asni, Morocco

Kane checked his watch and knew from his steady speed he was about ten minutes out from the compound. So far, there was no evidence of pursuit, and he hadn't been intercepted. If his cover had been blown, then it appeared they were taking him down at the compound where they could control the situation, rather than do it on a public road and risk an incident with the locals, or the life of the buyer.

It was exactly how he'd do it.

He activated his comm. "Control, Whiskers. I'm about ten minutes out. I'm going to need to know what I'm doing when I get there."

"Copy that, Whiskers. Regretting your callsign choice yet?"

Kane grinned at Leroux's question. The answer was yes. Hell yes. "Not at all. Fang said it was cute. So, what's the procedure?"

"We've been monitoring the compound. A vehicle entered there about fifteen minutes ago. It looks like the procedure is to approach the gate, let it open, then drive through."

"No check?"

"It looks like they rely on recognizing the car. I'm guessing they don't get too many visitors."

"Let's hope there's no secret hand signal. Okay, so I go through the gates, then what?"

"The vehicle we monitored went through then proceeded to the motor pool to the left. However, since you're dropping off a guest, we'll assume you're going to the main entrance. When you come through, you'll be in a courtyard. Go to your right and circle the outer edge then stop at the steps that lead up to the main entrance. Exit the vehicle, then open your passenger's door as a good chauffeur would. If all goes well, you'll get back in the car, then go over to the motor pool, which will be straight ahead of you at that point. Park your vehicle, then the rest is up to you."

"Yeah, but we know that isn't going to happen, don't we?"

"My guess is that their suspicions have been raised, so you'll be surrounded the moment you arrive there, then possibly shot."

"So, what are my options? I'm thinking I can bail on this guy now and save my life, but that means the professors are probably toast. Or I go through with our plan, and I allow myself to be captured without resistance. That distraction might give the boys the opportunity to get inside undetected while all eyes are on me."

"I'll leave it up to you, but they could shoot you the moment you arrive."

Kane shook his head. "No, if I'm a good little terrorist, I'll want to interrogate me, especially if there's no need to kill me immediately." He debated his choices for a moment, coming to a decision that he was confident had the best chance of saving the professors. "I'm going to go for it."

"Are you sure?"

He was certain it was the best choice, though not entirely on whether he'd survive it. "Yeah. But if this ends up being the stupidest decision I ever made, tell Fang I love her, and keep Niner away from her. That horny little bastard will be homing in on her in no time."

Leroux laughed, though he could tell his best friend was fighting to control his emotions. "I'll have Sherrie guard her virtue."

"You do that." His voice cracked. "Thanks, buddy, it's been a blast."

Richter's Compound

Asni, Morocco

"Taking the shot."

Atlas' transmission tensed every muscle in Niner's body as he stared at the sentry on the one-two corner of the compound, left of the gate. The sentry dropped out of sight and Niner bolted from his hiding place, approaching the tower at an angle that took advantage of the blind spots the poor design provided. He reached the stone wall and breathed a sigh of relief at their assessment the stonework would provide plenty of handholds.

He quickly scaled the wall and flipped over the edge, dropping onto the crumpled body of Atlas' handiwork. He confirmed the kill then quickly removed the dead man's hat and jacket. He donned them, picked up the man's weapon, and stood, assuming the sentry duty, praying the faint light and Kane's arrival meant no one had caught him on camera.

He eyed the man's body from his new position and spotted an earpiece. He bent over and removed it, then stuffed it in his free ear. He listened for a moment for any chatter but heard nothing.

Good comms discipline.

He activated his own. "One-two corner secure, over."

Kane gripped the steering wheel then forced his fingers to relax, spreading them out as he eyed the looming gate ahead. "Okay, here goes nothing."

"Good luck."

Two sentries in the corner were visible, and his mind was telling him that he recognized Niner's frame in the tower to the left, though it was hard to tell in the reduced light of the early evening. "I think I see Niner."

"He's in the tower to your left. Don't tell anyone."

Kane chuckled at Leroux's joke. "Thanks for the tip. The gates are opening. No secret hand signal."

He passed through at a speed he assumed normal, then turned slightly to his right, rounding the courtyard, and coming to a stop in front of the steps, no security in sight. "So far, so good. I'm going off comms before I get out of the vehicle. I won't be able to hear you from this point on. Enjoy listening to the boys." He removed his earpiece and stuffed his comms out of sight. "Getting out of the vehicle now."

He opened the door and stepped out. He closed it then reached to open the rear door when shouts and the hammering of boots rushing down the steps confirmed the chauffeur's Oompa Loompa height had betrayed him.

As expected.

"Hands up. Make a move and you're dead," barked a voice with a distinct Afrikaans accent. Kane raised his hands and slowly turned around to face six men with Milkor BXP submachine guns aimed at him. He raised his left arm a little higher. "Left side, shoulder holster."

A battle-scarred brick shithouse, evidently in charge, motioned for one of his men to disarm him. The uniformed man rushed forward, slinging his submachine gun, and relieved Kane of his Glock.

"Any other weapons?"

Kane shook his hands. "Just these."

"Funny. Check his ankle."

Kane frowned. "Fine." He held his foot out and pulled his pant leg up. The man removed his backup weapon.

"Anything else? No self-respecting soldier goes anywhere without a knife."

Kane reached into his pocket and retrieved his blade, handing it over.

"Is that it?"

"Yes."

"Where are your friends?"

He played dumb. "What friends?"

"Your friends that came with you to rescue the professors."

"I work alone."

"I highly doubt that."

"If you knew me, you'd know that nobody ever wants to work with me. I'm too unpredictable and a terrible conversationalist."

"You're telling me that those professors, who are worth hundreds of millions of dollars, have a one-man security team?"

Kane shook his head. "No, because you'd never believe that, and it wouldn't be true. They have a substantial security team, but they use it to protect their students, not themselves, and at the moment, they're halfway across the planet in Peru. I was called in by them to see if there was anything I could do. My contacts found out about your buyer here"—he jerked a thumb toward the car behind him—"so I decided to intercept your driver."

"How did you know they were here?"

"Well, that was easy. That private jet you used, the police already know exactly where it went and that my clients were on it, so my contact inside Europol was able to tell me exactly where you went, and the rest is quite easy for someone with my skills."

The leader approached, glaring at him. "I don't believe for a moment you're here alone. Lock him up. Put a guard on him."

"I would put two on me. I'm really quite good."

The man frowned then turned his back on him as he walked away, apparently done with him. "Put him in with the professors and put another man on the door. There are only twelve of us, and I'll be damned if I'm wasting any more than necessary guarding prisoners."

Kane was quickly grabbed by both arms and hauled inside, suppressing a smile at knowing there would now be two fewer people Dawson's team would have to deal with when they attempted entry. He glanced over at the tower Niner had taken only minutes before he arrived, hoping everything continued to go smoothly for them, despite his day being shot to hell.

Operations Center 2, CIA Headquarters
Langley, Virginia

"Why is everything so muffled?" asked Tong.

Leroux chuckled. "Because we're listening to his boys."

She stared at him, puzzled. "I thought he meant the Delta team."

Child snickered. "No, he meant his balls. Right now, every muffled little sound you hear is the mike rubbing on his scrote."

"Eww, gross!"

Leroux agreed. "Yup, but in a pat-down situation, the number one place one man doesn't want to pat another are the boys, so if you want to get away with hiding something, that's the place to put it." He pointed in the general direction of the speakers overhead. "See if you can clean up that audio so we have a little less sac noise."

Tong scrunched up her nose but turned back to her keyboard. "Just a second." After a few moments, the high-end snaps and pops were reduced and Leroux gave a thumbs up.

"Okay, that's better."

Child cocked an ear. "Wait. Did he just say he only had twelve men?"

Leroux smiled. "Yup, that's exactly what he said. Little does he know he only has eleven." He put on his headset. "Zero-One, Control, we have confirmation that you are dealing with twelve, I repeat twelve, on the security team."

Dawson's voice replied. "Copy that, Control. Everyone, let's keep a headcount. The security team is twelve, repeat twelve, with one already eliminated leaving eleven for those who can't do basic math."

"He's talking to you, One-One," interjected the deep baritone of Atlas.

Leroux chuckled at the insult directed at Niner, the one person who couldn't reply without possibly exposing his position. "Zero-One, the security lead has instructed Kane to be put with the professors and two guards put on the door, over."

"Copy that. Let us know as soon as the security personnel have cleared the courtyard. We'll proceed then, over."

"Roger that, Zero-One, good luck."

Richter's Compound

Asni, Morocco

Gerhard opened the rear door of the limousine and stepped back, bowing. "Sorry to keep you waiting, sir. We had a minor security situation that needed to be taken care of."

The man stepped out and glared at him. "You call that minor? I call that an utter failure. I've never seen such incompetence."

Gerhard bowed once more. "Again, I apologize, however I can assure you that you are safe."

"The situation should never have been allowed to happen in the first place."

"I agree, and we'll be reviewing our security procedures. I can assure you that when you leave here, you will have a full escort."

"I better." The man started up the steps. "Now, take me to your employer. I want to be out of here in fifteen minutes."

"Come with me." Gerhard led him into the main house, the security team following, Kriel ordering one of his men to remain inside at the main entrance, the rest accompanying them to the viewing room.

I think I'll be as happy to see this finished as Richter will be.

Kane was shoved unceremoniously through the door into what appeared to be servant quarters, happy to see the professors still alive. "Sir, ma'am, so good to see you're well."

Acton and Laura caught on immediately, successfully suppressing the urge for any flashy reunion until the door slammed shut. He surveyed the room and spotted a camera out of the corner of his eye.

"Sorry to say my rescue attempt hit a little snag."

"I can see that," said Acton as Kane stepped backward into the corner with the camera and leaned against the wall.

"Your security chief asked me to help since he's in Peru and I was in the area. Unfortunately, the chauffeur they sent to pick up the buyer was a relative of Tattoo from Fantasy Island, and my cover was blown." He twisted the top off his watch and raised it over his head, placing the magnetic transmitter onto the base of the camera. "Just continue to cooperate, and hopefully they'll realize it's not worth killing you two because you don't know where they are."

Acton frowned. "You obviously know."

Kane shrugged as he stepped back into view of the now tapped camera, and hopefully entire security system. "My life is expendable. I knew that coming in. If I die and you two die, then my mission was a bust. If I die and you survive, then it was a success. So, I'm not telling you where we are, you don't know where we are, so they have no reason to kill you." He spun toward the camera. "Because I know you're listening! I'm saying this for your benefit as much as theirs! Because if you kill them, you're in for a world of hurt, because if I can find you, then anybody can find you. Let them go, and there's no reason for anyone to come looking for them." He turned back to the professors, Acton smiling slightly.

"Do you think that will work?"

Kane shrugged. "Doubt it, but you never know."

Gerhard showed the buyer into the viewing room, the Bible in the middle, several bright lights overhead focused on the artifact, one of many seen here over the years. Richter was a history buff who enjoyed purchasing, or borrowing from friends, rare antiquities, and Gerhard had been privileged to see dozens of wonders over the years.

Though this was the first that had been stolen.

"Where is he?"

"I'm here."

Gerhard backed into a corner and out of sight, all light focused on the center of the room, as his employer conducted his meeting remotely, his voice piped in through speakers overhead.

The buyer looked about the room. "Are you kidding me? Sorry, but that wasn't the deal. In person or not at all."

"This is as good as you're going to get."

"Very well." He turned toward Gerhard, squinting into the dark. "Take me back to the airport."

Gerhard didn't respond.

"Fine." A door opened at the rear of the room, hidden in the paneling, and Richter emerged.

"Finally, enough of this nonsense." The buyer extended a hand as Richter approached, his own clasped behind his back.

"Forgive me, but handshaking is a custom that I never understood nor entertained."

The buyer regarded him for a moment. "You're every bit as eccentric as has been described."

Richter smiled slightly. "One of the benefits of being rich. The larger the bank account, the more such things are embraced."

"There aren't many bank accounts larger than yours."

"No, I suppose not. Are you ready?"

"Are we secure?"

"Absolutely. Nobody is getting inside this compound."

"Very well. You have the professors? They are willing to confirm the provenance?"

"I do, and they are, however, this is the end of our face-to-face contact. They cannot see me. They can't know who I am or where they are. I assume that is satisfactory?"

"I don't understand. Why should that matter?"

Richter slowly circled the Bible, and Gerhard realized this was the first time his employer was seeing it.

Stay calm!

"When this is done, I plan on returning them to Europe and releasing them. I'm not a murderer."

"Despite all evidence to the contrary."

Richter spun toward the man, the Bible forgotten. "You and I both know I had nothing to do with what happened at the Guggenheim. I merely took advantage of the situation. Those deaths are *not* on my hands. And as someone who believes that all creatures should be treated equally, I can no more kill an animal than I can kill a human being, without being a hypocrite."

The buyer stared at him for a moment before finally speaking. "Unfortunately, you're going to have to get over your scruples, because my employer insists that the professors be terminated the moment the exchange is complete."

Richter's eyes widened. "Why?"

"Because he is as paranoid as you, evidently, and doesn't want the professors alive to provide any details that might lead the authorities to you, me, or my employer. If they disappear, and the Bible as well, then eventually everyone will give up looking, and we can all continue with our lives. There can be no evidence the Bible was ever sold."

Richter glanced at the corner where Gerhard was standing, as if seeking advice.

He remained hidden.

"Very well, once the exchange is complete, I'll have my men take care of it."

"Excellent. Now, let's conclude our business quickly."

Operations Center 2, CIA Headquarters

Langley, Virginia

Security video from across the compound appeared on the displays at the front of the operations center, causing a smile to spread on Leroux's face.

"He did it." He turned to Tong. "What kind of access do we have?"

Tong examined her terminal. "Full access to the cameras, but no access to the sensors. They seem to be isolated."

Leroux frowned. "We can't override anything?"

"Only the cameras. We have full control, so we can show them whatever we want them to see, jam them, whatever."

"At least that's something."

Tong agreed. "Unfortunately, that means motion sensors, door sensors, anything like that will still be functioning."

"Well, we have to assume those are at a minimum on the inside. See if you can find the professors on one of those cameras."

"Got them." She highlighted the feed.

"At least we know they're still alive." He smiled. "There's Dylan with them." He pointed at another feed showing two guards outside a door in a hallway. "That must be our two guards assigned to them. Show me the courtyard." Tong complied. "Does anybody see anyone?"

A round of no's was the response. He activated his comm. "Zero-One, Control, we can confirm that the courtyard appears empty, over."

Richter's Compound

Asni, Morocco

"Copy that, Control, can you give us a location on Kane?"

"Affirmative, Zero-One. The locator in his watch has him about halfway down the number two side of the main building. Remember, we still don't have any clue about the layout inside until we can use the cameras to map what we're seeing once you get in there and start appearing on them. Kane's locator beacon suggests they went in the door about five meters, then left for five, then right for twenty and then stopped, over."

"Copy that. They said put him with the professors. I assume we have them on camera?"

"Affirmative, they're together on camera, at least for the moment. Don't forget you've got two guards on the door."

"Copy that, we're going to have to act fast. I'm guessing that the buyer won't want to be sticking around too long. Do any of the cameras show the guard posts?"

"No, we're showing no guard posts on any cameras."

"Good. Freeze the external cameras."

"Stand by." Dawson waited, steadying his excited heartbeat, when Leroux finally replied. "Done. You're clear to proceed."

"One-One, you're clear. Do you have a shot at the sentry on the number-two side?"

Niner's voice came in over his comm. "I can barely see him because of this privacy screen or whatever the hell you want to call it. I need him to lean out if I've got any chance at a shot."

"Stand by." Dawson whipped a rock and it hit below the guard post at the center of the wall he was positioned near, hidden behind an outcropping. The sentry leaned out to investigate and Niner fired, his aim true as the body tumbled to the ground.

"Target eliminated."

Dawson smiled. "Zero-Five, take out the two-three position."

"Roger that," replied Spock to Dawson's left. "Two-Three down."

"Number two side secure. Control, any evidence they're aware of anything happening?"

"Negative, Zero-One, no indication from this end they're aware of your presence."

"Zero-Seven, take out three-four."

"Taking the shot," replied Atlas. "Three-Four down."

Dawson rose, no longer concerned with being spotted now that all the sentries on his side of the building were down and the cameras were frozen. "Zero-Five, reposition to provide support to Zero-Seven."

"Roger that," said Spock as Dawson headed for the base of the wall at Niner's position, making certain to stay on the corner concealed from the front, as one sentry position was still manned at the far corner.

"Zero-Five in position. I haven't got a shot, but if he leans out to take a look at that lumbering mass of muscle, I can take him."

Dawson reached the wall. "Zero-Seven, proceed."

"Roger that, stand by." The wait seemed interminable, and Dawson controlled his breathing as he pressed against the wall, knowing his team were pros, and if something went wrong, he'd know instantly.

He prepared for a sprint.

"Taking the shot...target down."

Dawson smiled.

One to go.

Richter Telecom AG

Berlin, Germany

Reading headed for the SUV that had brought them from the airport to Richter Telecom's headquarters in Berlin. Things had moved swiftly once Oskar Richter had been linked to the bombing. The Germans were tearing the place apart, and he, Michelle, and Sanchez had arrived about an hour ago to observe.

Yet none of it concerned him, knowing what was happening right now in Morocco.

"I'm going to go talk to the agent in charge," said Sanchez, breaking off from him and Michelle. "I'll join you in a minute."

"Okay."

Reading and Michelle climbed in the back and the sanctuary the SUV provided, their German assigned driver somewhere else. He fished out his cellphone.

"Do you think they'll find anything of use?"

Reading frowned. "I doubt they'll find anything linking them to the terrorist attack. This had nothing to do with the company and everything to do with the company's founder. But if we could find something that links company funds to the operation, if he somehow got sloppy, then we could file charges against him and the corporation, and he just might lose financial control. If we could make that happen, it might throw the fear of God into others like him that use their wealth to manipulate the masses into believing in their causes, whether just or otherwise."

The phone vibrated in his hand as the call he had been waiting for finally came through. He answered. "Hello?"

"I just wanted you to know that Kane's team has begun the operation. I'll keep you posted."

"Is there any way we can listen in?"

"Is your location secure?"

"Yes."

"Then I don't see why not. I won't be able to communicate with you until it's over. Wait a moment."

Reading put the call on speaker for Michelle's benefit and, at first, heard nothing. A sudden burst of static had them both flinching.

"Target eliminated."

"Zero-Five, take out the two-three position."

The passenger door opened and Sanchez climbed in.

"Roger that. Two-Three down."

"Number two side secure. Control, any evidence they're aware of anything happening?"

Sanchez's jaw dropped. "What are we listening to?"

Reading glanced at Michelle. "Umm, I'm not sure you want to know."

"Negative, Zero-One, no indication from this end they're aware of your presence."

"Zero-Seven, take out three-four."

"Taking the shot. Three-Four down."

Sanchez's eyes were wide. "Oh my God, who are you?"

"I'm a cop, just like you."

She shook her head. "You're not like me. I don't know any cop who has sources like you do."

Richter's Compound

Asni, Morocco

Niner leaned out from his position in the 1-2 tower, peering through his scope at the 1-4 corner opposite him, occupied by the final sentry manning the wall. He placed his finger on the trigger and inhaled slowly, then whistled. The sentry leaned out to see what the fuss was about and Niner squeezed, putting one in the man's head.

"One-Four down."

"This is Control, confirmed all six targets have been eliminated."

"Rapunzel, let down your hair," said Dawson over the comm. Niner tossed a bundle of rope over the side, wrapping one end around his waist and wrist. He felt a tug, and was joined moments later by Dawson. Niner leaned out as he rolled up the rope to see Spock scaling the wall to the opposite sentry position. He reached it unscathed and tossed a line down to Atlas. Niner activated his comm. "I'm glad I'm not you."

"Tell me about it."

Niner chuckled then became all business as Dawson assessed their position.

"Normally, I'd like to leave you here as overseer, but you've got no shot because of this paranoid design." He switched to comms. "Control, can you confirm the courtyard is still empty?"

"Confirmed, Zero-One, all cameras show it empty."

"Copy that. Freeze the image on any camera that has a shot of the courtyard so we can cross to the main entrance of the residence without anyone noticing us."

"Roger that, stand by…okay, you're good to go."

"Copy that." Dawson grabbed the rungs of the access ladder. "Bravo Team, proceed to the main entrance." He slid down the ladder and Niner followed. Dawson confirmed they were still clear and indicated to Spock and Atlas on the other side of the courtyard to proceed. They all sprinted across the cobblestone and mounted the stairs, hugging the entrance.

"Control, status?"

"You're all clear, Zero-One."

Dawson examined the large double-doors they were pressed against. "Anybody on the other side of this thing?"

"If we assume we're looking at the right door, you've got one guard."

"Copy that. Is he moving or stationary?"

"He's standing still with his back facing the door."

"Good, freeze that."

"Stand by…okay, frozen."

Dawson knocked on the door as if he were delivering a pizza, and Niner smiled.

I love this guy.

"Okay, Zero-One, he's turning around, readying his weapon."

"Is he going to open the door or fire?"

"It looks like he's about to open it."

The door opened and Dawson put a bullet in the guard's head. He collapsed in a heap as the four operators swiftly entered, closing the door behind them. Niner grabbed the body with Atlas and hauled it into a closet to the left of the door.

Dawson headed left. "Let's get this done."

The door opened and Acton rose, placing himself between the man now facing them and Laura.

"Professors, it's time."

Kane stepped in front of them both. "Where are you taking them?"

"None of your concern. We got your message that you're prepared to die, therefore you have no need to know anything beyond the fact your wish will be fulfilled."

Kane shrugged. "If I'm going to die anyway, why not humor me?"

Acton placed a hand on Kane's shoulder. "They're just taking us to authenticate the Bible. Basically, confirm to the buyer that this is the one from the Guggenheim and that it wasn't substituted with a fake."

"That sounds interesting, can I come?"

The man at the door chuckled. "Nice try." He stepped back. "Professors."

Acton resisted the urge to show any affection toward his former student, everyone still maintaining the pretense that he was just part of their security team. They followed the man into the hallway and the door was closed. One guard was left on the door, the other accompanying them as they were led down a series of corridors and shown into a dark room with an impressive security door, a bright light shining down on the Bible that sat on a table in the middle of the room. A lone man stood on the opposite side, appearing impatient. The door closed, the guard remaining inside, their escort not joining them.

A voice boomed from a speaker, causing Acton to flinch. "Professor James Acton, Professor Laura Palmer, so nice to finally meet you at last."

Acton recognized the voice and looked about the room for the source of the sound. "We're not exactly meeting, now, are we?"

"If you are to live, then you cannot see my face, now can you?"

"I suppose I should be thanking you for being so thoughtful."

Dawson rounded the corner and squeezed the trigger. The lone guard at the door dropped, and Dawson frowned at the confirmation of what Langley had just relayed.

One guard, not two.

He opened the door and found Kane lying on a bed, his hands clasped behind his back. He smiled as Atlas tossed the dead guard's body into the corner, under the camera. "Control, Zero-One, do you have him looped like that?"

"Affirmative. We're looping the video now. You're clear in that room, over."

Everyone crammed into the room, out of sight of any roaming patrols or staff.

"About time you guys got here."

Dawson shrugged. "It's a beautiful place. We wanted to take in a few of the local sites, catch a show. You know, the usual."

Kane climbed out of the bed, fishing his comm gear out of his junk drawer. "They just took the professors down the hall, maybe thirty seconds before you arrived."

"Control, do you have them?"

"Yes, they went into a room with no eyes. We'll guide you in."

"Copy that." Dawson put a hand on the doorknob. "We've taken out eight hostiles so far, that leaves four more."

Kane smiled as he comm'd up. "I like those odds a lot better. Weapon?" Niner handed him a Glock and a couple of mags. "Control, Whiskers. Do you have eyes on the other four hostiles?"

"Welcome back, Whiskers, we were tired of listening to the boys."

"Huh?" Niner appeared offended.

Kane pointed at his junk and Niner nodded in understanding, winking.

"We have one of them outside the entrance to the room the professors were taken into. The other three we don't have eyes on. We know one went inside with the professors, and the other two might have already been in there."

"Copy that. Let's see if we can take out those two and improve the odds even more."

Gerhard leaned back in his chair, waiting for the call that the business was concluded. He loved his job, admired his employer, and other than the solitariness of his life, he thoroughly enjoyed his position. His salary was significant, and with no expenses, it sat safe in various accounts around the world, waiting for the day he would retire.

And that day would soon be here.

Richter had gone too far this time, and had gone against his advice. As much as he admired and respected the man, the authorities would catch up to him. That much was certain with the arrival of the man who had commandeered the car sent for the buyer.

If he can find us, so can the authorities.

An emergency flash appeared on his screen and he cursed at the communique informing him that their headquarters in Berlin was being searched.

It was over.

Now the question was, did he leave now, or did he wait to inform Richter.

The phone on his desk beeped and he answered it. "This is Gerhard."

"Sir, we've got a problem."

Gerhard tensed as he noted the extension was for the security center. "What is it?"

"None of our sentries are answering their comms."

His heart rate picked up. "None?"

"Yes, sir."

"Is it a comms failure?"

"That's what we thought at first, sir, but then we lost contact with our man on the front entrance, and moments ago, we lost contact with our sentry guarding our infiltrator and the professors."

"Have you notified Mr. Kriel?"

"We can't, sir. He's inside the secure room. There's no communication possible inside there."

"Then contact the guard at the door and tell him something is going on. Then get every man you can to that room and secure it. I'll be there momentarily."

"Yes, sir!"

"Why is it in two pieces?"

"It was like that when it was discovered," explained Acton. "We have no explanation as to why, but the fact it was nearly split at the middle, we assume it was for convenience purposes as opposed to anything spiritual."

The buyer continued to circle the piece, posing his questions, all of which Acton and Laura answered honestly, as there was no possible benefit to lying at this point.

"How can I be certain this is the same one that was at the museum? How can I be certain it isn't a fake?"

"There'd simply be no time. We were on the run the moment it was handed to us."

"Yes, yes, you stole a boat then were put on a plane and brought here. I know *you* had no opportunity, but how do I know the man behind the curtain didn't replace it."

Laura placed a hand on the table beside the Bible. "Because he wouldn't have known what to replace it with."

"What do you mean?"

J. ROBERT KENNEDY

"I mean, only images of a few pages had been released before the beginning of the gala. High-resolution digital images of each page were released publicly yesterday morning. There'd be no time to recreate it. Not on vellum. This isn't like pressing a button and loading vellum into your LaserJet printer."

The buyer's head bobbed as he squeezed a corner of one of the pages between his fingers, as if confirming it was indeed vellum.

An intercom beeped at the door followed by a man's voice. "Sir, we may have a security breach."

A large man in the shadows, armed to the teeth, emerged, and Acton was surprised at how intimidated he felt. "Explain."

"We've lost comms with eight of our men including all six sentries."

"Eight? Comms failure?"

"Negative, sir, comms are working fine, they're just not responding."

"Understood. Don't let anybody get past your position."

"Yes, sir."

The buyer looked at the man. "Should we be leaving?"

"No, sir, this is the safest room in the complex. There is no way anyone is getting in here." He motioned at the other guard who had accompanied them from their room. "Get out there. Nobody gets through."

"Yes, sir."

He then pointed to a dark corner of the room. "You too."

"Yes, sir."

340

Another man emerged from the shadows, scaring the shit out of Acton, who hadn't noticed him the entire time. Both strode out and the door sealed shut with a hiss.

Leaving Acton nervous and hopeful.

Delta is here! But how the hell are they getting in here?

"We've got three, heavily armed, and they're expecting you."

"Copy that, Control." Dawson peered around the corner and was immediately made, one of the men raising his SMG and squeezing the trigger, sending a dozen rounds toward him. He ducked back and dropped to the floor as Atlas tossed a flashbang toward the enemy position.

Dawson heard something odd and cursed. "It's been returned!"

Everyone pressed their hands to their ears, their tactical earphones only doing so much as they squeezed their eyes shut. The grenade exploded just around the corner, somebody obviously on the soccer team in their youth having punted it back.

Yet it still would have them taking cover.

Dawson leaned out, spraying lead at the position, the smoke filling the hallway making it hard to see the enemy. Someone cried out and Dawson kept firing as Niner and Spock swung out low, adding to the wall of lead, Atlas covering their six. They advanced quickly, taking advantage of the confusion, and within moments it was over, the smoke clearing, revealing three dead enemy targets.

And a very secure-looking door.

Dawson pointed at it. "Niner, see what you can do with that."

Niner went to work, placing several charges, then they all stepped back. "Fire in the hole."

The blast was deafening, and it took a while for the dust to clear, only to reveal a slightly damaged door.

Niner shook his head. "We're going to need a tank to get through that."

Gerhard sprinted toward the gunfire, a weapon he barely knew how to use gripped in his hand. What he thought he could do, he didn't know. It was foolish. He was a butler. Yes, he was more than the domestic servant. He helped manage Richter's various philanthropic ventures, his commitment to the cause allowing him to sleep at night guilt-free of the fact they were constantly breaking the law.

Unjust laws should be broken, and any laws that allowed cruelty and enslavement of animals were unjust.

Yet he was still a mere butler, and whoever was attacking the compound had taken out at least eight highly trained mercenaries.

But he couldn't stop himself for some reason.

He came around the final corner and skidded to a halt at the sight of five heavily armed men in front of him. He leaped back as someone shouted, "Gun!"

Gunfire erupted and he stuck his pistol around the corner, firing blindly, his eyes squeezed shut as he trembled with fear.

Atlas tossed another flashbang as they all hit the deck, their opponent firing blindly and wildly, most of his shots hitting the ceiling. The explosion resulted in a cry of agony as the man's senses were overwhelmed.

The gunfire stopped.

They rushed his position, and moments later had him on his stomach, disarmed, his feet and ankles bound. Atlas propped him up against the wall.

"How do we get in that room?" demanded Dawson.

The man shook his head. "You can only get in from the inside."

"Bullshit. That would mean someone would always have to be in there, and you and I both know that's not the truth. How do you open it?"

The man sighed. "You need a code. I don't have it, only my employer does."

"Is he inside that room?"

The man looked away, clenching his jaw.

Dawson kicked him in the gut. "Talk!"

The man gasped for breath. "No. He left a while ago. He's gone. You're too late."

"Sorry, I call bullshit on that too. We've had satellite coverage on this entire area. Nobody has left since we've been monitoring. We know he's still here."

The man's shoulders sagged in defeat. "Fine, it doesn't matter anyway. He's in his saferoom. There's no way you're getting in there."

"I don't care about him. I care about the professors, and that's it. Get us into that room, we get the professors, we leave, end of story. The authorities can deal with your employer. Just get him to open the door to let the professors out, and this can all be over in the next sixty seconds."

"He'll never let you in. It's impossible."

"Why?"

"Because the room the professors are in is part of the saferoom. If you go through that door, then you have access to him. He'll never allow it."

Dawson cursed and stepped away, activating his comm. "Control, we've got a problem. The professors are inside some sort of saferoom, and the only way in is either with a code or for the door to be opened from the inside. Suggestions?"

"Stand by."

Richter's heart pounded with genuine fear, something he couldn't recall feeling in years, if ever. As the attack unfolded on the segregated security cameras outside his saferoom, his panic continued to grow, until he finally thought to act.

He picked up his phone and hit one of the pre-programmed numbers. It was answered on the second ring.

"We have a problem here."

"What?"

"We're under attack. My security team is dead."

"How many hostiles?"

He peered at the cameras, everything a mass of confusion to his overwhelmed emotions. "I can't be sure. At least five, maybe more. They're well-equipped and they took out my team far too easily."

"Where are you now?"

"I'm in my saferoom."

"Very well. We're on our way."

"Send everything you've got. When will you get here?"

"We'll be there in fifteen minutes."

"Hurry!"

Operations Center 2, CIA Headquarters

Langley, Virginia

"Uh oh. We've got another problem."

Leroux didn't like the sound of Tong's voice. "What now?"

"Look at this."

He rose and stepped toward the displays as an image appeared showing a dozen vehicles leaving an army depot. "What am I looking at?"

"A large number of troops just left Ouirgane Barracks, and they're heading in the direction of the compound. If that's their destination, they'll be there in approximately fifteen minutes."

Leroux cursed and activated his headset. "Zero-One, Control. We have satellite imagery showing twelve troop carriers leaving Ouirgane Barracks and heading in your direction. ETA fifteen minutes, over."

"Copy that, Control. I'm assuming we still don't have any external support."

"Confirmed. Recommend you abort the mission and evacuate immediately."

"Copy that, Control, I'll take it under advisement. Out."

Leroux sighed heavily. "How did I know he'd say that?" He turned to the room. "They're not going anywhere until they get the professors, so it's our job to figure out how to get in that room."

Child spun in his chair. "Why don't they just knock?"

Leroux smiled. "That's an excellent idea."

Child stopped his spin. "It is?"

Richter's Compound

Asni, Morocco

Richter stared at the antique analog clock on the wall, its second hand slowly spinning, each time it passed XII indicating another minute passed.

And it had only done so twice since the call had been made.

It would be thirteen minutes until his well-paid-off Moroccan military backup arrived.

No problem.

There was no way anyone was getting in this room. Not in thirteen minutes.

He closed his eyes and drew a slow, deep breath, calming his nerves.

His burner phone rang, startling him, and sending his pulse racing once again. He checked the call display and didn't recognize the number, so he let it ring. It rang again a moment later, this time the call display not showing a number, instead showing a message.

CIA. PICK UP OR ELSE.

His heart slammed into overdrive with visions of Predator drones launching missiles at his compound. He took the call. "Hello?"

"Hello, Mr. Richter. I trust you are secure in your saferoom."

He looked about the room. "How do you know where I am?"

"Mr. Richter, the fact that I'm calling you by your name, should tell you that I know everything about you. I know where you are, I know where your assets are hidden, about your efforts to influence various causes using fake social media accounts. My people are the ones who identified all your fake accounts that are being deleted as we speak. I'm the one with all the evidence that you bankrolled the Brigade, and I'm the one who has the proof that you had no idea what they were planning, and that you had no idea those people were going to die. And let me be clear, I'm the only one with that proof, and unless you let the professors go immediately, that proof will never see the light of day. The authorities are coming for you, you will be arrested, you will be charged with murder and terrorism, and you will go to prison for the rest of your life with cameras watching you twenty-four-seven. All you need to do to avoid all that is release the professors, with the Bible, and then my people will leave."

Richter stared at the security displays, then the clock. He had a decision to make. Wait to be saved, only to be arrested again, or trust a man claiming to be from the CIA, an organization that represented pure evil. "They won't arrest me?"

"You're not my concern. I'm not the police. My concern is for the professors and the item you stole. Open the door, let them out, and you can close the door again to wait for your friends from the Moroccan military to arrive."

"You know about them?"

"I know everything, Mr. Richter. Do we have a deal?"

He again checked the clock.

11 minutes.

He could stall, but rescue was no longer relevant. This man had the proof that could show he had no idea those people were going to be murdered. He had no choice but to cooperate. His shoulders slumped. "Yes, we have an agreement."

"Very good. My people are outside the door. I expect it to be opened within the next sixty seconds."

"Understood." He ended the call and rose. He tapped a code on a panel and a hidden doorway opened, giving him access to the viewing room. Mr. Kriel spun toward him.

"Sir, what's going on?"

Richter held up a calming hand. "I've come to an agreement with the people outside."

"You have?"

"Yes. They're CIA, and they have the evidence that can prove I didn't have anything to do with the murders at the Guggenheim. All I have to do is release the professors with the Bible, and they'll leave. As soon as they're out of here, the evidence will be released, proving my innocence."

"Sir, I assume the contingency is in place?"

Kriel was subtly referring to their Moroccan military failsafe. "It is."

"And they're how many minutes out?"

"Less than ten."

"Then I recommend we just stay here and wait."

"Yes, that might mean we win the battle, but I'll lose the war. The world will think I'm guilty of committing mass murder, and I can't have that stain on my reputation. I believe all life is precious, whether it is an insect, an animal, or a human being. I cannot go to prison with the world thinking I killed over sixty innocent people in cold blood."

The buyer stared at him, his eyes wide, shaking his head.

"Sir, we can protect you," said Kriel, clearly not in agreement with the plan.

"How? All of your men are dead."

"I have more men. We just need to survive the day. I can get you out of here to a secure location where they'll never find you."

Richter nodded. "Yes, that may be, but my reputation will be destroyed, and that's more important to me than my life. I'm supposed to be a force of good in this world, not evil."

Kriel frowned but bowed his head. "Very well, sir, it's your decision to make."

"Unlock the door."

Suddenly the buyer screamed. "No!"

Laura flinched as the buyer reached under his suit jacket, moving it aside enough for her to see he had a shoulder holster.

"Nobody is going anywhere!" he cried as he drew the weapon. The South African reached for his own, but the buyer spun, squeezing off two rounds into the man's chest, sending him collapsing into the corner.

As the weapon swung back toward her and James, she leaped forward and reached out with both hands, smacking his wrist and the top of his hand in opposing directions, causing him to drop his weapon with a scream of agony. She caught it in midair and spun it around, aiming it at him.

"Everybody in the corner, now!" She flicked the weapon toward the moaning guard, gasping for breath, the two rounds to his chest stopped by what appeared to be body armor. The buyer and Richter, their hands up, obeyed. "Now, how do we open this door?"

Richter shrugged. "Just open it. There's no code to get out.

James headed for the door. "Let me try."

Acton pulled down on the handle and pushed against the door, opening it slightly, a hissing sound heard. "Don't shoot, it's Jim Acton! I'm unarmed!"

"Hold your fire!" He recognized Dawson's voice and smiled. He pushed the door open a little more and peered through the sliver of an opening, sighing at the sight of the Bravo Team members that had become friends over the years, as well as his former student Dylan Kane.

"Hiya, Doc," waved Niner.

Suddenly the door was hauled open and Kane reached forward, yanking him into the hallway by the shirt as the others surged through the doorway, shouting for everyone to get down.

"It's secure!" he yelled as he tore away from Kane, concerned for Laura. He rushed into the room as shouts of "Clear!" sounded, no shots thankfully fired. Laura lowered her weapon as Niner and Atlas covered the prisoners.

"You have no idea how glad I am to see you guys," she said, not handing over her weapon, but instead stuffing it in her belt.

"Ditto," agreed Acton.

"What happened here?" asked Kane.

"Like I tried to tell you, it's secure." He wrapped an arm around his wife. "Once again, Laura saved the day."

She shrugged. "I guess we didn't really need you. You guys can go home now."

The team laughed as Dawson walked over to the prisoners. "So, who do we have here?"

Acton made the introductions from left to right. "This is Mr. Richter, this is the buyer for the Bible, though I get the impression he's just a middleman, and this is Mr. Richter's head of security."

Dawson glanced at Laura. "Did you shoot him?"

She shook her head. "No, the buyer did when Mr. Richter said he was going to let us go with the Bible."

Dawson regarded Richter. "And was he going to let you go?"

"Yes, he was."

"Mr. Richter, I've been informed of the deal you made. We'll honor our end of the bargain, however, I need you to call off those troops that are on their way here."

Richter's eyes widened. "I'm afraid I can't do that."

Dawson put a hand on his holstered Glock. "Why not?"

"It's part of the failsafe. Once the call is made, they come here, no matter what, until they confirm in person that I'm secure. All calls, including from me, are ignored."

"Is there a way out of here that we're not aware of that could bypass them?"

"No, there's only one road. The only way to avoid them is to leave by helicopter, and I don't have one here at the moment. I'm afraid you're trapped here."

Dawson cursed, turning for the door. "Okay, people, we've only got five minutes to get the hell out of here."

Acton grabbed the Bible and followed Dawson as they sprinted down several hallways then out the front door, his heart pounding, the concern on the Delta team's faces enough for his relief at seeing them to be forgotten.

Kane burst through the door and into the courtyard, then broke right, toward the motor pool, spotting the Mercedes he had driven earlier. He had already recognized a problem he was sure Dawson was aware of as well, and this was the only solution he could think of.

They had a closed gate, and it would take too long to climb the wall, then descend to the other side. Those troops were only minutes away, and he had no intention of ending up in a Moroccan prison cell.

He climbed in, happy to see the keys still inside. He started it up then put it in reverse and hammered on the gas. The tires chirped and he backed up into the center of the courtyard then cranked the wheel hard to the left, guiding the rear end of the car toward the gate. He had read these cars had a safety feature that would apply the brakes if it detected an obstacle ahead.

He was betting they never assumed you'd intentionally ram something in reverse.

He slammed hard into the gates, the metal and wood doors breaking off the hinges, never designed for an actual assault. The impact cut off the engine, though it no longer mattered. He jumped out and followed the others.

Acton pointed at the car. "Why aren't we taking that?"

"Besides the automatic fuel shutoff?" Kane pointed at the road. "That's the only road out of here, and a mess of Moroccan regulars is about to arrive."

Dawson led them into the rock-strewn landscape when he pointed. "There they are! Everyone down."

Kane hit the ground as a dozen camouflaged army vehicles rushed past and into the compound, the lead vehicle shoving the dead Mercedes out of the way as if it were nothing. Dawson held up a fist, indicating everyone should hold position, then leaped to his feet as the last vehicle disappeared behind the walls of the compound.

"Let's go! Let's go! Let's go!"

Everyone was on their feet, picking their way through the rough landscape, Dawson on point. Acton glanced at Kane.

"Please tell me we're not running all the way back to Marrakesh."

Kane grinned then pointed ahead at an SUV parked behind a rock outcropping. "You're welcome to, but I'll take that."

Acton smiled then came to a halt next to one of the vehicles, sucking in air. "Is it okay to say I'm getting too old for this shit?"

"No, but if you're going to bitch about your age, do it inside the truck."

Acton would have flipped Kane the bird if it weren't for the 75 pound Bible that had his arms feeling like lead.

Dawson leaped in the driver's seat, starting up the vehicle as the others loaded up the rear seats, Atlas taking the passenger seat. He put it in gear and stuttered the tires as he surged them onto the road, checking his rearview mirror to see if anyone had spotted them. "Control, Zero-One. Status report, over."

"Zero-One, Control. The Moroccan units are inside the compound. It looks like they're securing the area with a large number of troops going inside the main building. At the moment, there's no evidence of pursuit, but that's just a radio call away."

"Copy that. Monitor for any units in front of us, and let our man in Marrakesh know that we're going to need an emergency exfil."

"Copy that."

Dawson adjusted his rearview mirror to see the professors. "Are you two okay?"

Acton nodded. "Yeah, we're fine, though I could use a shower. How did you guys find us?"

"We just followed our noses," said Niner, waving a hand in front of his.

Acton gave him a look. "Ha-ha. Seriously, how did you find us?"

Dawson readjusted his mirror to see the road. "It's a long story that involves too much ass-sitting in a hotel in Bilbao with Niner exposing his cheeks all too frequently."

"Niner!" admonished Laura.

He grinned. "It's a nice ass."

Kane finally filled them in. "Let's just say a whole lot of your friends came together to get you out of there."

Laura squeezed Acton's hand. "We're going to thank every one of them personally."

Niner looked at her. "To hell with thanking us, how about paying for our plane tickets?"

Acton's eyes narrowed. "What do you mean? The US Army doesn't fly the friendly skies anymore?"

Dawson chuckled. "We weren't sanctioned until they found out you were in Morocco. This was an entirely volunteer operation."

Laura teared up. "You mean you guys all did this for us? With your own money?"

Niner shrugged. "Well, I've got no woman to spend my money on, so I might as well spend it saving you, darlin'."

Acton hugged Laura. "We appreciate everything you've all done for us, and I promise you'll get every penny of it back."

Dawson grunted. "Well, don't be paying us too soon. We're not out of this yet."

Operations Center 2, CIA Headquarters

Langley, Virginia

"Sir, we've got an incoming call from Mr. Richter's burner to the number we used to call him."

Leroux's eyebrows shot up. "Put him on." Tong nodded and Leroux adjusted his headset. "Yes, Mr. Richter?"

"I just wanted you to know that I've told my Moroccan friends that your people left in a helicopter shortly after I made the initial phone call. They should have no problem getting away."

Leroux gave a pleased look to Tong who returned a thumbs up. "Thank you, sir."

"So, our deal is still in place? You'll release publicly the evidence proving my innocence?"

"Yes, we have a deal."

"Thank you."

The call ended and Leroux switched channels. "Zero-One, Control. We just had confirmation from Mr. Richter that the Moroccans have been told you left in a helicopter, so you should have no problem with them. We'll continue to monitor your route ahead just in case, and we'll coordinate with our local contact for your exfil. We should have you out of there by tomorrow morning."

"Copy that, Control, we're all looking forward to sleeping in our own beds tomorrow night. Zero-One, out."

Hospital Universitario de Basurto

Bilbao, Spain

Acton was exhausted, though no more than Laura, as they walked down the hallway of the hospital. Reading was with them, his partner off dealing with the Spanish police and the extradition of Richter. The Moroccans had arrested him at the request of the Spanish authorities. The Echelon intercepts of the phone calls between Richter and Peeters had been released as promised, revealing that though Richter had bankrolled the attack, he had no idea what the terrorists had planned. The news was reporting that Acton and Laura had been manipulated by him to bring him the Bible, and that they were rescued by private security, though publicly, the fate of the Bible was still unknown.

Their exfiltration from Morocco had proven fairly routine once they had confirmed the authorities weren't after them. The CIA had arranged a charter for them that brought everyone back to Spain, then Delta and Kane back to the United States.

Acton and Laura had remained behind for one last delivery.

"This is it," said Reading, indicating a room just ahead.

Acton stopped at the door and knocked, a smile on his face as he saw Marchand propped up in bed, his wife in a bed beside him, and their two children in chairs along the wall.

"Jim! Laura! Thank God you're all right!"

Acton laughed. "Was there ever any doubt?"

"To be honest, for a while, I wondered if you were terrorists who had stolen my precious Bible."

Acton gave him a look. "What horrible people you must think we are." He held up the Bible. "Should I keep this?"

Marchand reached out with both hands, his eyes and mouth wide with joy. Acton handed him the Bible, sealed in a plastic bag, and Marchand hugged it, closing his eyes. When he opened them, they were filled with tears. "Thank you. I thought it was gone forever."

"It almost was, but fortunately some friends of ours had convenient timing."

"I want to hear all about it, but not today. My son has just been returned to us."

Acton looked at the little boy, sitting in the corner with his sister, who had a protective arm around him. "He wasn't hurt, was he?"

Marchand shook his head. "No, he was just hiding."

Laura smiled. "Where did you find him?"

Petra laughed. "We didn't. He came out looking for food!"

Acton/Palmer Residence

St. Paul, Maryland

Acton entered the code on the keypad to disable the alarm as the home phone rang. He rushed down the hallway and into the kitchen, grabbing the phone on the third ring, his eyes narrowing at the call display. He hit *talk* just before it went to voicemail.

"Hey, Dad, sorry about not calling you sooner. We just got in the door and we lost our cellphones with everything that's been going on. What's up?"

"We lost your mother."

Acton's eyes instantly burned, tears welling as he stumbled backward toward the living room, reaching behind him for his chair. "Wh-what?" He could barely get the words out as his heart went into overdrive. The back of his legs hit the couch and he fell into it as Laura entered the room.

362

"She couldn't get out of bed all day, then she started having trouble breathing. I called an ambulance, but she...she died when I went to let them in. I'm so sorry."

His mind was still struggling to process the words as the tears streamed. Laura rushed to his side, putting an arm over his shoulders, concern on her face as he leaned into her. "What-what happens now?"

His father's words were echoes underwater, something about an autopsy, more details he couldn't process, more apologies.

And that was when he finally realized this was the first time in his life he had heard his father cry.

And it crushed him even more.

He had lost his mother, but his father had just lost his wife, the woman he had loved since he was a teenager, who had been by his side for over fifty years, who had been with him almost every moment of his life since his retirement.

"It's not your fault," he managed. "We're going to leave now. We'll be there as soon as we can be."

"Okay."

"I love you, Dad."

"I love you too."

He hung up the phone and hugged Laura, sobbing, thanking God he lived so close to his parents, and was healthy enough to help his grieving father, who would forever feel the loss of the woman he loved more than anything in the world.

Acton stared through blurred eyes at a photo of his parents sitting on the mantle, and his shoulders shook even harder as he realized he would never again see his mother's smile, hear her laugh, or her caring voice as they spoke.

I love you, Mom.

THE END

ACKNOWLEDGMENTS

This book was extremely difficult to write. My mother died when I was working on this, making it a struggle to finish, yet with a pre-order deadline, I was forced to push through. It helped me take my mind off my grief, though at times it proved too much, leading to countless breakdowns, especially in those early days.

When my best friend Paul Conway died five years ago, I was writing Amazon Burning. To help with my grief, I worked in a character named Pol, whose death was something the indigenous hero of the story was coping with.

I wrote the final scene of this book the day after I received the same news, in much the same manner as Acton did. Every time I read it, it brings back that horrible night that will forever be burned in my memory. By writing about it, I hope it will help me process what has happened as writing about my friend did in Amazon Burning.

As of this writing, it hasn't, but in time, it will, and years from now, the emotions and thoughts of that night will be preserved in a way I'm privileged as a writer to be able to do.

Thank you for your indulgence.

As usual, there are people to thank. My dad for all the research, Fred Newton for some nautical info, Ian Kennedy for some explosives info, Brent Richards for some weapons info, and, as always, my wife, daughter (who helped with some social media info), my late mother who will always be an angel on my shoulder as I write, as well as my friends for their continued support, and my fantastic proofreading team!

To those who have not already done so, please visit my website at www.jrobertkennedy.com, then sign up for the Insider's Club to be notified of new book releases. Your email address will never be shared or sold.

Thank you once again for reading.

Made in the USA
Las Vegas, NV
30 June 2023

74083475R00207